Legend of the Winged Lion

Cheryl Burman

Guardians of the Forest
Prequel

This is a work of fiction. Names, characters, businesses, places, events, locales, and incidents are either the products of the author's imagination or used in a fictitious manner. Any resemblance to actual persons, living or dead, or actual events is purely coincidental.

First published in the UK in 2022 by Holborn House Ltd

Cover Gryphon sculpted by Justin Burman,
Designer at Serpent Forge

https://serpentforge.com

Also by Cheryl Burman

GUARDIANS OF THE FOREST TRILOGY

The Wild Army

Quests

Gryphon Magic

NOVELS

Keepers

SHORT STORIES

Dragon Gift

www.cherylburman.com

Prologue

The common tales, the ones young Sleih and Gryphon are told by their parents and teachers, say this:

The Sleih once dwelt on the high plains. They lived apart from the Madach, practising mild magic and working with metals, gems and woods.

One day, impressed by their artisan skills, the Gryphon flew from their caverns in the High Alps of Asfarlon to persuade the Sleih to venture there. They offered them the chance to learn much more of magic and wizardry, to grow powerful and be content.

In return, the Gryphon benefited from the artistry of these people from the high plains, who translated their poetry and songs into jewellery and beautiful objects.

There is, however, another story. A darker, sadder story carried by the Gryphon line, and held close.

In this story, the Gryphon first dwelled in the Deep Forest of Arneithe. They were guardians of the forest, ensuring the trees grew strong and healthy and the wild creatures likewise.

Now, the Gryphon would dwell there still, except a shapeless dread power came to Arneithe, carried by winds from a distant southern land, far beyond the oceans. What or who made the power is lost in time. What is known is that the power was driven by a fierce consuming desire to vanquish and destroy all good in the world.

It bore within it an evil which infected the birds, the beasts, the trees, manifesting as madness.

The wild creatures fought each other, scratching, spitting, tearing fur and skin. They attacked the trees, ramming the trunks of saplings to bring them crashing to the forest floor. They shredded the bark of those too large to destroy by felling. They clawed and chewed deep into the hearts of even the most venerable trees.

The trees revenged themselves. They bent their boughs to the ground to snatch the creatures up and dash them down. They shook nests from their branches to leave chicks dying in a litter of chewed bark and gnawed leaves.

The gryphons resisted longest. They searched their spells and sorcery, seeking the means to defeat this evil. In the end, they compelled it to manifest itself as a towering cloud of stinking, oily ash. Once it became visible, it might be destroyed, or at least banished.

By then the evil had laid waste to Arneithe. The Forest could no longer be the home of the Gryphon. They fled from the maddened trees and enraged wild creatures. And from the shame of having failed in their guardianship.

One last act they undertook before they fled, in desperate hope it would survive and serve as a protection into the future.

The Gryphon strongest in magic flew to the outermost edge of the Forest, where the oceans stretching east and south begin. There they created a grove in a secret valley shielded by the strongest enchantments.

In the grove they planted one of every kind of tree which had bloomed in Arneithe. They set a mark around this sacred place to ensure it would be known only to Gryphon-kind, or to those whom gryphons deemed true friends. And then they too flew west, to the High Alps.

And the evil? What happened to the evil?

They brought it with them.

Chapter One

A diamond glows

Olban squinted at the diamond. The red glow of the cavern's fire dulled its white light, yet it outshone the crystal cups and precious gems glittering from ledges lining the rock walls. He turned it in his bony fingers, bringing it closer to his green-eyed gaze. The finest of all his jewels. Legend said it had been dug by strong-armed dwarves from dark mines in a far distant country, the name of which had long been lost.

He tucked a strand of black hair behind his ear before taking up a brush to dust a spot of grit. The jewel rewarded his careful effort with a quick shaft of brilliance. Olban started back a step. The glare faded.

He set the diamond, now dormant, on the oak bench next to the dank and brittle book Hestia brought him three days ago. The title, translated from Old Sleih, greatly intrigued him: *The Conjuring of Spirits and Powers.*

'Your long study of the invisible world around us will make the translation easier, I hope,' Hestia had said. She bobbed her eagle head. 'And my Gryphon senses tell me a mystery resides within these pages. A deep mystery, one we should understand.'

When Olban had reached for the book, it seemed to him it flew from where it was tucked beneath Hestia's wing into his eager hands. Excitement sparked in his chest, a feeling he was about to embark on a great journey, one which would, finally, deliver him the knowledge he had craved since his student days, long ago.

Olban's heart beat harder when he read, underneath the title, a warning from the author that the contents should not be read by any novice in the magical arts. They should be pondered exclusively by those with long and successful experience in the use of spells and potions (himself)–and a knowledge of the inherent sorcery of diamonds, according to what Hestia had been able to translate from the faded pages.

'Diamonds?' Hestia had shaken her great feathered wings. 'Diamonds don't play a more special role than other gems in Gryphon magic.'

Olban shrugged. 'Because they're the most valuable of gems? The longest in the making? The rarest?'

Long paragraphs hinted at a mysterious strength which apparently lay deep beneath the caverns. They fascinated Hestia.

'There are,' she said, while the hairs on Olban's neck prickled, 'tales from the Old Ones of a power said to have once dwelled in the deepest depths of the earth.' She moved her eagle head to fix Olban with one dark green eye. 'One of many legends in told tales, never written down. Until now.'

Until this crumbling book, this veiled mention of such a power. The references were obscure. Worse, the pages which might have told what dreadful deeds this power could wreak on those unfortunate or silly enough to waken it, had been ripped out. Or what riches it could bestow on those same individuals.

The mystery entranced Olban. In the deepest depths of the earth? Further below than even the Sleih dare go?

He spent all his time poring over the ragged writing for clues as to how it might work. The unknown crabbed hand had written in an ancient version of Old Sleih, a language near forgotten even by the Sleih seers and the gryphons. It made the covert references more difficult to understand than they might have been.

He could not recall the last time he had been this engaged. He neglected all other duties, often forgetting to eat, studying the text and peering into the diamond, turning it in his hand, thinking, thinking …

Yesterday, Hestia had come to his cavern after he missed another meal. She found him holding the diamond up to the light from a glowstone, the book open on the bench before him.

'I worry about your obsession with this book and with this jewel, old friend,' she said. 'Perhaps it's best left alone.' She tapped a talon on the smudged paper. Olban cringed. 'Whatever power is referred to, I suspect it is not for good.'

Olban stiffened. 'As a seer with long experience of powers magical and spiritual'–he stared at Hestia–'I'm well able to judge such matters for myself.'

She had sighed, folded her midnight-blue wings more closely about her tawny lion body and padded from the cavern.

Olban suspected she wished she hadn't drawn his attention to the book. It had lain in a dark corner of Asfarlon's vast repository of manuscripts, maps, charms and potions until the 'prentice seer, Ilesse, came across it. She and the young Sleih prince, Varane, were searching out a text for Hestia. The prince stubbed his toe on the book as he reached for another. The girl, bright beyond her years and with an unquenchable thirst for learning, had been drawn to its flaking gold title in a language she did not recognise.

Behind Olban, the fire in the pit crackled with a sharp snap.

As if in response, the diamond bloomed with another quick shaft of brilliance, brighter this time, bringing to glistening life the heaps of gems about the walls. The whole cavern glowed with a rainbow of colour–for an instant, before all fell into its normal gloom.

Fire? Olban's pulse jumped. Every sign edged him closer to the mystery.

Why would someone tear out the pages? Assuming they were the ones which explained all. Olban's gut told him they were.

His stomach rumbled and his attention finally wandered to food. He left the room with a last glance at the diamond, dull now as any piece of dirty glass.

Chapter Two

Dreams and visions

'Hestia, are you awake?'

Hestia stirred on her bed of scented meadow hay. She blearily opened one eye.

'Ilesse? What are you doing here?'

She opened both eyes and rolled onto her belly, her neck stretched forward to peer closely at the 'prentice seer. Ilesse's hair fell in tangles about her face, pale and drawn in the night-time shadows. Her eyes were wide and dark as lightless cavern pools. She wore no shawl or cloak over her long nightdress of fine woven grasses despite the cold of the spring night. Her slim feet were bare on the stone floor.

'Is something wrong?'

'No, no, nothing.' Ilesse's breath came in small gasps. 'At least not at this moment.' She shivered, arms at her sides. Her delicate fingers curled into balls.

'Fetch the rug and wrap yourself. Come here to the bed with me.' Hestia pointed a wingtip at the rug lying across a chair by the smouldering fire pit.

Ilesse did as she was bade, sitting cross-legged in the hay between Hestia's outstretched front legs, her back against the gryphon's feathered chest.

'Tell me,' Hestia said, 'what has made you leave your bed on this chilly night?'

'Dreams and visions.'

Ilesse shuddered. Hestia tightened her legs around the girl.

'They've come before.' Ilesse pulled the rug closer about her shaking shoulders. 'Always in the deepest darkness of night. In snatches, nothing which made any sense.'

Hestia broke a long silence. 'And this night is different?'

'Yes.'

'Can you tell me?'

Ilesse drew a breath, held it, slowly exhaled. 'The caverns are full of black smoke, foul-smelling smoke,' she whispered. 'And screams.' The whisper became panicked. 'Gryphon and Sleih shrieking, running through the blackness to their deaths, falling from the high ledges, unable to see the darkness outside against the darkness within.' She dropped her head into her hands. 'It's awful, Hestia, awful.'

Hestia rested her beak gently on the girl's head to comfort her. Her own unease grew. Dreams could be portents, especially those dreamed by a 'prentice seer with the talents Ilesse already showed.

'That's all I saw. At least, tonight it's all I saw.' The girl's voice quavered.

'And other times?'

Another long silence before Ilesse said, 'Sometimes there's a diamond.' She paused. 'Bright light shines from it, blinding me, and I sense a presence, a coldness, a sharp coldness.'

Diamond? Olban's obsession. Hestia stifled an intake of breath.

Another silence. Hestia's thoughts were interrupted by the 'prentice seer asking, 'What does it mean? It worries me, here.' She pushed a hand into her chest.

'What it means, if anything, I cannot tell.' Hestia nuzzled her beak in Ilesse's hair. 'We should tell Lord Tius and King Iaton, however.' She hoped the girl couldn't hear the faster beating of her heart.

'You think it's an omen, a sign of danger to come?'

'Maybe, and maybe it's merely too large a helping of ibex cheese at supper.' Hestia laughed.

Ilesse didn't laugh. 'What will Lord Tius do? What can the king do?'

'Be warned, if warning is needed.'

The silence this time went on so long, Hestia whispered, 'Are you awake, little seer?'

'Yes. I'm thinking.' Ilesse sighed again. She crawled out from between Hestia's legs. 'And I'll return to my own bed, which isn't as scratchy as your straw'–Hestia heard the smile in the girl's voice–'if I may return the rug tomorrow?'

'Of course. Come after first meal and we'll go together to the king and Lord Tius.'

Hestia slept no more that night. As dawn approached, she padded to the ledge outside her cavern and faced southwards, as she had done in the afternoon when listening to the young prince, Varane, struggle with his Challit oath. Bright in all other ways, Varane could not get past the first sentence of the oath he needed to soon recite at his coming-of-age ceremony. She heaved a soft sigh at the memory of Ilesse, who had mastered the oath after two readings, encouraging him in her gentle way.

In the dawning light, Hestia's eagle eyes picked out the thin line of green which marked the high plains below the Alps. Stretching away from them were the grasslands where the Madach lived in their scattered villages. Hestia had never seen the grasslands, for gryphons rarely flew above those peaceful fields. And the Sleih never ventured there from their home in the High Alps, not since Aseera.

Why did she think of Aseera? Her troubled heart grew heavier at the memory of the young woman, lost in an avalanche many years ago. Her frozen body lay under the snow, somewhere. Old history.

The tips of the Alps emerged from the grey pre-dawn, pink and gold in the sun's first light. The promise of a fine day did not lighten her heart.

***

With Ilesse at her side, Hestia walked across the red-streaked rock floor of the Eternal Chamber, past the fire pit where embers glowed, towards the two rulers of the High Alps of Asfarlon. The fire's warmth fell gently on her feathers and burnished Ilesse's leather leggings to a warm sheen.

Hestia had been many times to this chamber–as a member of the Council, as petitioner and advisor–yet it still awed her.

Unlike the lavishly furnished caverns where the Gryphon and Sleih had their dwellings, this chamber called for serious discussion, not the reading of poetry or admiration of art and craft. In addition to the chair and rug, a long plain table was placed in front of one of four tall-windowed walls. Three-legged stools lined one side for the Sleih seers and a runner of thin hide covered the floor on the other for the gryphons. Neither were comfortable for long.

What the chamber lacked in comfort, it made up for with wide views. Set at the peak of the tallest of the High Alps, its windows–the transparent panes blended through magic and chemistry–looked over the white-tipped mountains, range upon range to merge finally into the skies. Hestia imagined the chamber hanging like a glass bubble in the sparkling mountain air, suspended from nothing.

'You asked to see us, Hestia?'

Tius Lord Gryphon rested on his tawny lion haunches. His yellow eagle beak arched proudly from between heavy white brows. Its long sharp tip curled in towards the delicate white feathers which he wore like a beard. He held his black-feathered wings close against his body, their tips merging into the thick pelt beneath him. His tail, with its heavy brush of dark hair at the end, stretched behind him.

Iaton, King of the Sleih, sat beside him on a jewel-decorated stone chair. His light golden skin and long, straight dark hair matched Tius's colouring perfectly, as did his calm, strong nature.

They were friends as well as rulers. Hestia remembered the two in their much younger days. 'Inseparable,' some had said, always gladly, given they would govern the High Alps of Asfarlon for many years.

Iaton held his silver-clad arms wide. 'We welcome you, and you also, Ilesse, 'prentice seer.'

Hestia bowed her feathered head and ruffled her wings in a return greeting. Ilesse bobbed a curtsey and kept her gaze on the floor. Perspiration gleamed on her forehead.

'Thank you, Sire.' Hestia lifted a wing. 'Ilesse, our most gifted 'prentice seer and a sensible young person in every way, has something she is impelled to convey to you.'

Both Tius and Iaton turned their emerald-green gazes on Ilesse.

'What is it you wish us to know, 'prentice seer?' Iaton said.

Ilesse lifted her head and pushed a shiny black braid over her shoulder. 'Dreams, visions, nightmares, my lords,' she whispered. Her fists clenched and unclenched.

Tius and Iaton exchanged glances.

'Yes?' Iaton said. 'Tell us.'

Ilesse stared past the rulers to the view of the High Alps beyond. She raised her hands to her chest, her fingers pressed tight into the wool of her tunic.

'The caverns are alight.' She paused, drew in a shuddering breath. 'There is fire and black smoke, acrid smoke which makes eyes weep and throats burn.'

Iaton's eyes widened briefly. Tius tilted his head to one side.

Ilesse drew another ragged breath. 'Gryphons fly from the caverns, falling to their deaths with torched wings, feathers and fur alight.' Her quavering voice grew louder. 'We, the Sleih, cannot escape. We have nowhere to go, for upwards is fire, and down, into the mountain depths, is deathly smoke.'

The girl's eyes stared. Hestia believed she no longer saw the Eternal Chamber, or the rulers. She saw flames and death.

'Oh!' Ilesse cried. She reached out her arms like a blind person, swayed, and would have fallen except Iaton jumped from his chair and held her upright.

'Here.' Tius moved from his rug. 'Place her here.'

The king laid the fainting girl gently on the rug. Hestia padded to the door, calling for wine and water. She returned to peer into Ilesse's pale face, to lay her beak against her wet forehead.

Ilesse's eyelids fluttered. 'Did I faint?' she asked.

'Yes,' Iaton said softly.

'Did I tell you my dreams?'

'Yes, you told of fire, smoke and death.' Lord Tius hooded his eyes.

Ilesse pushed herself up to lean on one elbow. She took the proffered wine, sipped at it. Her face slowly recovered its normal golden glow.

'Can you tell about the diamond, too?' Hestia said. 'If you have the strength?'

Iaton frowned. 'There is more to this vision?'

Hestia nodded.

'Sometimes,' Ilesse said, 'I dream of a diamond, which flashes. It's nothing like a normal glittering shine–the flashes blind me. I cannot see, but I can feel.' She took another sip of wine, placed the stone cup on the floor and pushed herself up. She trembled. Hestia reached out a wing to steady her.

'What do you feel?' Tius gazed closely into Ilesse's half-shut eyes.

'A coldness. A stabbing coldness. It hurts, like a knife wound.'

Silence hung, until Ilesse said, 'I'm sure there's more, although when I wake I cannot remember all the dream.'

Iaton patted her shoulder. 'Terrible to be troubled like this, Ilesse. I am sorry you have such dreams.'

'Are they an omen, Sire?'

'Who can tell? We must hope not. No-one else has told of such. Perhaps it's simply a nightmare you have.'

The gravity in his voice told Hestia he sought more to comfort the girl than to dismiss her visions as merely bad dreams.

Tius lifted his beak high. 'Whatever this may or may not portend, you have told us, 'prentice seer, and you will tell us if more comes to you.'

'And my lords are warned,' Hestia said, 'should there be a need for warning.'

She tapped Ilesse's arm with a wing. 'If you are recovered well enough, find Varane please, and both of you wait for me in my rooms.' She laughed. 'We have our prince's lessons to deal with and we need clear heads for those.'

Iaton frowned. 'Varane is not learning his lessons?'

'No need for concern. His mind is not one of a scholar, although it could be if he chose. He much prefers action over academic study, which I think is not a bad attribute in a prince and an heir, don't you, Sire?'

Iaton sighed, apparently reluctant to agree.

Hestia didn't wish to discuss Varane's scholarly abilities. She peered into Ilesse's eyes, pleased to see their normal bright intelligence shining through.

'Go along,' she said. 'I will see you shortly. There's a matter I wish to discuss with Lord Tius and King Iaton.'

'Of course.' Ilesse bowed her head to the king and gryphons, walked past the fire pit to the arch which led from the Eternal Chamber, and down the wide staircase.

Hestia watched her leave before turning to the two rulers, who were once more seated on their rug and chair respectively, waiting for her to speak.

***

'Is what you wish to discuss linked with the 'prentice seer's dreams?' Lord Tius said.

Ilesse jolted to a stop where the stairway curved out of sight of the arch.

Shouldn't listen, she told herself, not moving.

Hestia's voice came clearly through the opening. 'I know not, Tius.' A pause. 'Ilesse is a constant student, hungry for knowledge. She takes in everything and wants more. Her gifts for empathy and for hearing the thoughts of others are apparent already. One day, she will be a powerful seer and for this reason I must consider her dreams, especially such as these.'

Ilesse's cheeks blazed at the compliments. She wanted very much to hear what was said next.

'I have other reasons for concern,' Hestia said. 'Recently I gave Seer Olban an ancient text from the repository which speaks of a power hidden deep below us. While the text does not appear to say so directly, my reading and my intuition tell me this power should not be disturbed.'

A shiver tingled along Ilesse's spine. She stayed glued to the step.

'And why does giving Seer Olban this text concern you?' the king said.

'He has become obsessed with the mystery, spending all his time staring into a diamond.'

Ilesse's stomach jumped.

'Why?' Lord Tius asked.

'My lord, the text appears to claim a diamond's glow is needed to release this hidden power.'

'Diamond?' Lord Tius' sharp tone suggested he knew something of diamonds and powers.

The king exclaimed, 'As in the 'prentice seer's dreams?'

'Yes, and also–'

Ilesse flinched as Varane came in sight at the bend in the stairs below her. He stared up. She held a finger to her lips and hurried down to her friend.

'Shh,' she whispered. 'We must leave and'–she leaned close to Varane, wide eyes gazing into his face–'you never saw me here.'

'Why, what is it? Is something exciting happening?'

'I hope not,' Ilesse said. She ran past him, down the stairs. 'We must go to Hestia's and wait for her. You can practise your Challit oath.' She grinned over her shoulder. 'You should know it by now. I mean, it's not overly long or difficult to remember.'

Varane scratched at the jewelled band keeping his shoulder-length dark hair from his face. He puffed out his cheeks and descended the steps in a reluctant plod. 'It's all right for you. You're clever.'

Ilesse frowned. 'And you're not? Hestia disagrees.'

Her frown transformed to giggles as she walked along the wide tunnel, hearing Varane mutter behind her: 'I, Varane, prince of the Sleih, heir to the King of the Caverns of the High Alps of Asfarlon, where the Sleih and the Gryphon abide, do promise … umm …'

'… as one bound to the noble charter,' Ilesse called.

'Yes, of course … noble charter which our forefathers in their great and infinite wisdom … oh, it's boring.' Varane ran to catch her up. 'Why can't I read it?'

'Read it? Be the first heir to the Sleih to read their Challit oath?' Ilesse laughed. 'I don't think so.'

Chapter Three

Into the depths

The image of the diamond, dulled by the gloom of the cave as it lay by the broken text, filled Olban's restless mind.

He squirmed on his bed, throwing out a skinny arm to shrug off the heavy furs. Despite the coolness of the night, his skin burned. In his uneasy sleep, the diamond threw out bright shafts, glittering, inviting him.

He opened his eyes, pushed himself up and left the rumpled bed to stride barefoot through the stone arch into his work room. His eyes quickly found the gem amid the shadowed light coming from the dying embers of the fire pit. He nodded as if greeting it, lit a lamp, drew up a stool and bent over the faded text of the old book. It drew him like a moth to a flame–enticing, dangerous.

A fever of excitement descended on him as he scoured the pages with frowning eyes, tracing the long-lost words with a slim finger. His hair fell to the yellowed parchment and he brushed it behind his ear in an impatient gesture.

The diamond sat on the bench, its radiance no brighter than the lamp by which Olban worked.

The power beneath, he translated aloud, *is lit by diamonds.*

He said it again, this time in Old Sleih. A brief shimmer of light erupted from the gem and immediately died. Olban eyed it, brows raised.

The power? There was another meaning of the Old Sleih

word. Treasure. The word could also mean 'treasure.'

He puffed out a short breath.

Of course!

How had he missed it? In his mind's eye he saw the runes carved above an iron-barred doorway at the top of a long flight of steps far below the dwelling caverns.

The treasure beneath, the runes had always been translated as saying. The dwellers of the High Alps assumed the treasure referred to had once glowed within the stony walls of a shallow cavern at the bottom of these steps. The old texts were silent about this treasure, however, and no-one knew what happened to it, for the cavern was empty. Treasure held now was secured in a nearer cave, guarded with Gryphon magic.

Treasure or power? Had they been wrong all these years?

He heard Hestia's voice preaching at him about letting the power lie. He shuddered, and while he wanted to blame the cold, he couldn't banish the thought that Hestia was right.

He sighed and carefully closed the text. Picking up the diamond, he carried it with him to his bedchamber, pulled the heavy furs over himself and the gem and soon fell asleep within their warmth.

Not for long.

The stab of cold hard edges digging into his side woke him, hot and restless.

He lay awake, watching the soft glow from the fire pit shaping crooked shadows on the rocky walls. His mind spun.

He was a powerful Sleih Seer.

He could control anything which might happen.

Nothing would happen anyway.

The cavern of the treasure was not the cavern of the power.

If there was a power.

It was all so long ago, if it was true at all.

He breathed out noisily, scolding himself. Was he a child to be afraid to solve this puzzle?

He threw off the furs, slipped his feet into sandals, tossed a woollen shawl over his shoulders and lit a glowstone from the fire. He lifted the diamond, holding it close to his body as he crept from the bedchamber.

***

Ilesse too, tossed in her bed, her dreams vivid.

'No!'

She woke so suddenly her head swum. The darkness gave her nothing on which to fix her staring gaze. The dream's dread images of smoke and fire and screams, of gryphons and Sleih tumbling to their deaths, feathers and hair alight, danced their macabre dance around her.

Her skin burned like a fever. Her breath came in gasps.

It seemed a long time she lay on the sweat-dampened bed. A long time before the garish dream faded, before her head stopped spinning and her breath came normally.

Hestia. She should go to Hestia.

She slowly sat up, letting her eyes take time to adjust to the blackness. When she could more or less see, she swung her legs from the tangled covers and onto the icy floor, snatching up Hestia's rug (unreturned) to keep the cold at bay.

The fire in the pit had shrunk to grey ashes, throwing neither light nor heat. Ilesse picked a glowstone from the shelf at the head of her bed and walked towards the fire to light it. As she approached, the grey embers abruptly flared, sending out a shaft of white light.

She started. Like the diamond's light in her dreams.

She bit her lip, recalling Hestia telling King Iaton and Lord Tius about Olban and his new passion for glittering white gemstones. And saying how talented she, Ilesse, was and how she would be a powerful seer one day.

Frowning, she lit her glowstone before walking to the curtained opening. She pushed the curtain aside and moved swiftly and quietly down the passageway–away from Hestia's comfort, towards Olban's dwelling. The lateness of the hour didn't dissuade her. She needed to learn more. It could not wait until morning.

***

The diamond grew warm in Olban's grasp, giving out a soft glow. It shone in the dim passageways as he stepped purposefully past the drawn curtains of the sleeping caves and the black openings of sitting and eating rooms.

The white light led him on, down wide staircases he had used a dozen times a day, down long hallways with stony floors trodden smooth over the years by countless feet and claws and pads, to narrower stairs and rougher floors. Down into the depths of the caverns he walked, where the musty odour of rock and damp earth filled his nostrils, unimpeded by scents from fragrant oil lamps, warm people and rich feathers.

Deeper and deeper the white light took him.

Somewhere along the journey, Olban discarded the glowstone, along with his doubts about the wisdom of this expedition.

The diamond shone more brightly in the darker depths.

***

Ilesse's glowstone dimmed to a pale yellow. It didn't concern her, because the same bright light which guided Olban guided her. She had reached a curve in the passage leading to the seer's rooms at the same time he pushed aside his curtain and strode off, away from her.

She hadn't called out, knowing he would send her to her bed.

She followed him, silent in her slippered feet, curious about the purpose of this late-night journey.

Down past the hunters' caverns with their faint perpetual smell of wet fur and blood; down past the familiar halls and caverns of the artisans, where her parents lay asleep; down to where she had never ventured before, for there had never been any reason. The air grew musty, colder. She pulled Hestia's rug closer about her shoulders and walked on.

Olban hesitated at a gaping opening. He held up his light to shine it on runes carved into the stone lintel.

Ilesse's heart thumped. The light he carried was a diamond. Large and bright.

She squinted at the runes, recognising them as Old Sleih. Otherwise, she had no idea what they signified.

Olban nodded sharply, as if confirming an earlier notion. He stepped through the opening where an iron-barred gate hung from one hinge. The gate was almost entirely rust, pitted and broken, testament to its great age. Certainly no longer a barrier to whatever it once guarded.

Unease swelled in Ilesse's mind at the sight of the diamond. She should go back. No good could come of this evidence of her dreams. She half-turned, into blackness. She could never find her way, not in the dark.

Clutching her fading glowstone, she quelled her fear and hurried after Olban and the guiding light, into another staircase.

Olban scurried downwards and Ilesse had to scamper like a mouse over the uneven steps. Deep craters in their centres bore testimony to the thousands of footfalls they must once have seen. She pressed a cold palm to the rough wall, balancing herself in the constricted, winding space for fear she might tumble down onto the hurrying seer. The darkness beyond the diamond's light was absolute. Her glowstone offered no more brightness than a glow worm on a summer night. The only sounds were her beating heart and stifled breathing. She worried Olban would hear her, for he had stopped. Ilesse stopped too.

***

Olban lurched to a halt. The long flight of stairs had ended. He teetered at the brink of a wide gap in the earth floor.

Placing one foot behind him to steady himself, he lowered the gem to judge the depth of the void.

Pure blackness.

He remembered now. The void was believed to have been an extra defence, a means of making it difficult for robbers to leave the cavern with their arms full of treasure. He should have remembered earlier, for there had been another clue in the fragile text: mention of a stone crossing–the translation roughly meant something like a barrier bridged by rock.

He grinned, jubilant. He had guessed correctly.

The 'treasure' was the power, and he, Olban, Seer of the Sleih, had solved the puzzle of where this power, if it existed, likely abided.

Hestia would be thoroughly put out. He gloated on the thought.

He eyed the stone crossing. It seemed solid.

He should cross over, see where it led. Hestia would be more upset when he reported such an act of daring.

He lifted one sandalled foot and brought it down experimentally on the stone. Solid. He lifted his other foot. One foot after the other, slow and firm, arms outstretched, he moved cautiously forward.

The diamond grew hot in his hand, too hot to hold. He couldn't set it down so he brought his arms forward and tossed it from one palm to the other like a burning coal. The action unbalanced him and for the first time he felt fear.

He should return to his bed. Bring others down tomorrow.

He took a step backwards, wobbling on the bridge. And gasped.

A sharp white brilliance burst from the void like a climbing lightning strike.

Up it soared before his dazzled eyes, searing through the roof of the cavern, through layers of earth and rock, seeking starlit sky.

A flash of white, harsh light struck his hand. Olban dropped the gem as if scalded. It bounced on the stone bridge, once, then silence. It had fallen into the depths.

Blinded, trembling, his hand burning, he wished he had heeded Hestia's advice.

The brilliant whiteness vanished. Olban rubbed his eyes as abrupt darkness pressed on his head and shoulders like a physical weight.

Fast, panicked panting which matched his own thudding heart sounded behind him.

Someone else was here?

He opened his mouth to cry out. He coughed. Oily, viscous air, thick as smoke, choked his breath. It wound around his eyes and ears. It filled his mouth.

He spluttered, grew dizzy. He sunk to his knees on the bridge, clinging to the uneven surface. His breath rasped. He willed himself to stay conscious, willed himself not to fall.

Terror sent his gut to water.

A deeper blackness tugged at his arms and legs, a sharp physical dragging.

Olban screamed. He tumbled into the void.

***

Ilesse's eyes shut tight against the brilliant white light. The terrifying thought she had been blinded made her hesitate to open them. She fluttered her eyelids and breathed a loud breath of gratitude. The glowstone's faint yellow light gave comfort in the enveloping blackness.

She sniffed. An acrid stink rose up the steps, and with it, the seer's screams.

'Olban!'

She stumbled forward. The foul air smothered her with its heavy thickness. She was forced back, up the steps. Mouth closed against the gagging smoke, taking shallow breaths through her nose, she pressed one trembling hand against the wall to steady herself. In her other hand she kept tight hold of the glowstone, its dim radiance a reminder of brighter places elsewhere.

Up and up, past the broken hinges of the rusting gate, and now she ran. She tripped over rough stones in the floor, clutching her light. The smoke thinned. Her stifled breathing eased. She raced along the halls, up staircases, always up.

Hestia.

She must reach Hestia. Her thick head and muzzy thoughts slowed her. It became harder and harder to run, or to walk. Her eyes were heavy, the lids puffed and sore. She came at last, somehow, to her own room, stumbled through the curtain and onto her bed, shaking and icy.

Hestia.

She could not lift herself from the bed. Could not walk another step. Her aching eyes closed.

The glowstone fell from her hand onto the floor and died.

Chapter Four

Drudgery in Darnel

Gweyr scowled into the greasy water, withdrew her reddened hands and picked up the sloshing tub. She marched it through the open door of the inn's scullery and tossed the grey contents onto a lavender bush. With a sigh, she marched inside, plonked the tub on the workbench and stamped into the stone-floored kitchen to fetch the kettle simmering on the big iron stove.

'Not finished those pots, luv?'

Gweyr's father–known to his regulars as Barnaby and by the sign above the front door of the Boar's Head as Edward Barnaby, Innkeeper–stood at the wooden table which filled much of the room. If he shuffled sideways, he could squeeze between the table and the crammed dressers and overflowing cupboards along the whitewashed walls. At this moment, he had his considerable belly pressed against the edge of the table while he reduced a pile of potatoes, carrots and onions to rough chunks with skilled flourishes of his knife. Beside the pile of chunks, a large pot held a chicken carcass and dried beans.

Gweyr summoned a wry smile. 'Chicken soup, again?'

If Mam was here, it would have been carrot soup today. A too familiar lump rose in her throat.

Da raised an eyebrow and tilted his head in the direction of the scullery.

'Nearly done.' Gweyr huffed. She wrapped a thick cloth

about her hand and picked up the kettle.

'Make sure you top it up, won't you, luv?'

'Sure, Da.' Gweyr squeezed between the table and a dresser, mumbling, 'And sweep the bar and the tap room and dust Mam's chaos of old horseshoes and bells,' as she went back to the pots.

Hardly light on this late spring day and she had been up since before the cockerel's first crow. When all was finally ready for the day's business she might have time to wash herself and do something with her hair to look a little tidy for Da's customers.

Mam had always coo-ed over Gweyr's long, bouncy dark curls, inherited from Da given Mam's hair hung long and straight and black as a raven's wing. It was her most precious memory of her mother. Right up until the illness took its last solid hold on her, Mam lovingly brushed Gweyr's hair each night while telling her wonderful stories of ancient times. Da had once joked that at fifteen, his daughter could brush her own hair. That was before the illness. Afterwards he never said anything, even when Gweyr turned sixteen.

Just as the clutter of horseshoes in the bar hadn't been culled to make things easier, Gweyr didn't have the heart to do the practical thing and have her hair shorn off. But neither was she diligent about the nightly brushing, which meant the dark curls waved about her thin face like a smoky halo.

As she scrubbed the pots, Gweyr played bits of Mam's stories in her head in her mother's lilting voice. Wonderful stories of heroes and heroines, of flying beasts which talked, and wise beings who tended the beasts and rode them into battles against spine-tingling evils.

These wise beings weren't Madach like Gweyr's people. Sleih was what Mam called them, with a touch of wistfulness suggesting their loss from the world–if they ever existed in it at all–touched her in a special, personal way. In any case, these wonderful beings and their talking beasts always won against evil.

Gweyr swished the last pot through the hot suds, set it on a towel on the workbench to dry and wiped her hands on a cloth. She fingered the silver chain around her neck–the one Mam used to wear and gave to Gweyr on her fourteenth birthday—closed her eyes and imagined herself a beautiful princess riding her magnificent winged beast into battle.

Da poked his head through the opening. 'Don't leave it too late to fetch the bread, will you, luv? I hear Whittion is travelling, which means those young apprentices will be baking pies and naught will be left if you don't go early.'

Gweyr pulled her lips in, grimacing.

'Sorry, luv.' Da reached out a huge hand to rest it gently on her shoulder. 'You know how much I depend on you, how grateful I am,' he said. 'You're learning quickly and I'm proud of you. You'll be a great innkeeper when I'm gone.'

An awkward silence added itself to the end of this sentence, with Gweyr filling in the missing 'too'. Da shrugged, shamefaced, and slipped out the doorway.

Mam hadn't suffered the illness for long. Gweyr tried to find consolation in the thought, but the too strong memory of her mother's once lightly tanned face faded to white, pain lines etched deep, drove away the consolation. She kicked the workbench's leg and threw the sudsy cloth down with a vicious thwack. Some days were worse than others. Today was looking to be one of them. She squeezed her damp eyes, picked up a basket from the floor and went into the garden, down to the silent cockerel and his harem of hens, to collect the eggs.

***

Knees bent under the weight of the bag of grainy flour over his shoulder, Allsop staggered from the dark, chilly store room into the pre-dawn greyness of the bakery kitchen. He dropped the bag with a thud to the stone floor. He winced, glad it hadn't split. Mess, money and time, Master Whittion would have moaned if he'd been there to see it.

He frowned. The master should have returned from his trip to Flaxburgh by now. Not like him to be late.

His fellow apprentice, Conall, grabbed the bag, slit the top and heaved the contents into the wide maw of the mixing vat in one effortless movement of his muscled arms.

Allsop shook his own skinny arms, wishing the daily exercise of lugging bags of flour would one day put muscle on them too.

'Still no master?' Conall flicked a length of auburn hair from his freckled forehead.

'No,' Allsop said abruptly. He folded his arms across his apron. 'And we're very low on flour. We might have to buy from our own miller.' He rolled his eyes. 'Zach Beddle would more than like the custom–he'd cherish the chance to say I told you so.'

He took up the measured pots of yeast and salt from the workbench, tipped them into the vat and added a pitcher of water. 'Can never fathom why Master Whittion insists on travelling all the way to Flaxburgh to buy flour which is no different from our own miller's flour.'

Conall fetched a long wooden paddle and stirred the mixture. 'He only does it from time to time.' He stopped stirring and sighed gustily. 'Master Whittion must like a bit of adventure occasionally. I'd go, if it was me. More often too.'

Allsop arched his eyebrows at this variation of Conall's ongoing litany of how dull life was, and bent to the big oven. He struck the tinder and set alight the twigs piled high inside, thrusting more bundles into the rapidly warming space. He squinted at the leaping, crackling flames. He should give this job to Conall, see if avoiding being scorched was excitement enough for him.

By the time the fire was well alight, Conall had tipped the dough onto the floured table. He divided it into large sections and Allsop took his place at one end, Conall at the other. The slapping of the dough and the snap of the fire were all that broke the silence.

The niggle of worry gnawed at Allsop. Where could Master Whittion be?

'Do you think we should send someone to look?' he said.

'Look?' Conall's brow furrowed. 'Oh, you mean for the master?' He shrugged. 'No, it's only been a couple of days. He's probably having a grand adventure which he'll tell us about when he gets here and I can wish I was there too.' He wiped his hands on his apron with the slow exaggerated movement of one who did not wish to be unadventurously baking bread. 'Why don't you make another batch of your famous pies?' He grinned. 'The more pies baked, the quicker the master'll come racing home.'

Worry dampened Allsop's own grin. 'True. To catch me in the act of wasting flour and butter.'

He hoped Conall's prediction would prove to be true.

***

By late afternoon, two loaves remained on the shelves in the shop. All pies had sold, either fruit or meat, family size or dainty single bites.

The master had not returned. Allsop's disquiet had simmered all day. With the slowing of the bakery's busyness, it blossomed into full anxiety. Had the master suffered an accident? Or had old Chester broken a leg, leaving horse, wagon and master stranded on a lonely stretch of road?

He peered through the doorway to the kitchen where Conall scrubbed the long table. 'I think we'll shut up shop for the day.'

The shop bell rang and Allsop swung about to greet this last customer.

It wasn't a customer. A harried-looking master, wringing his hat in his hands, stepped through the door.

'Master Whittion.' Relief the master had come home, apparently safe, beat against a nagging wonder at the flustered face and the hat-wringing. And why had he chosen to come in through the shop? Didn't he have a wagon of flour out back, waiting to be unloaded?

Master Whittion closed the door behind him, took a deep breath, scanned the empty shelves with his sharp black eyes. His expression relaxed.

'Here, at last,' he said.

His dire tone did nothing to allay Allsop's fretting.

Dark stubble roughened the master's normally clean-shaven face. His uncombed dark hair sprang up in curling tufts. His clothes were awry, his trousers mud-stained and stuck with bits of straw. A button was missing from his travelling jacket.

Conall appeared from the kitchen. He stared. 'Did something go wrong?'

Allsop joined in with a questioning stare of his own.

Master Whittion gave his hat another twist. 'Yes, indeed it did. Terribly wrong. Me and Chester are more than grateful to be home, and alive.' He straightened out the crumpled hat and replaced it on his head. 'I'll tell you both all about it, after we've unloaded the wagon and tended the horse. Poor Chester went lame not a mile from here. Not surprised, after what we've been through.' He ran a hand through his tousled hair. 'It's why I stopped outside, didn't want to make him limp one more step than he needed to with a wagon of flour.'

'I'll fetch the farrier,' Allsop said.

'Yes, do.' The master nodded. 'I'll unhitch Chester and take him to the stable. We'll have to bring the bags through here.' He puffed out his cheeks at this further inconvenience. 'Come along then, let's to work and afterwards I'll buy you both an ale and you can see what you make of mine and Chester's adventures.'

Chapter Five

Whoom!

The balmy spring evening drew the villagers out of their homes into the stony lanes, pulled by an invisible force to the Boar's Head where the cosy bar heaved with relaxed customers. Allsop sat with Conall and Master Whittion at a table by a deep-ledged window overlooking the village's one road. The chat was noisy, the laughter cheerful and the pipe smoke thick. Barnaby wiped his brow and counted his coins. His daughter drew the frothy ale and weaved with practised confidence through the mob with loaded trays.

The master tilted back his head to savour his drink, set it down on the ring-marked table and ran a finger around the tankard's edge. He sighed heavily.

Conall and Allsop glanced at each other. Secretly, Allsop doubted if the story would live up to these carefully nurtured expectations.

'Getting there was easy.' Master Whittion finally began, his gaze on the low beams above their heads as if the words he needed were written there. 'It was getting home proved difficult.'

'What was difficult?' Conall said.

'Lightning and storms. Though they were the least of it.' The master sat back and crossed his arms over his chest.

Allsop's mind wandered to home, to his quiet kitchen and comfortable chair where a book awaited him. He had found the book–a favourite collection of fairytales from his childhood–tucked in a drawer in a chest. The chest had come with him to Darnel at the insistence of his mother, who had reluctantly conceded he could not possibly remain at home in their hamlet of Atias, no matter how early he rose each day, and learn his baking trade. Allsop looked forward to renewing his acquaintance with the adventures of the mythical Sleih and their allies, the Gryphon. Legend had it these magical beings once lived among the Madach. A long, long, timc ago.

He smiled. If ever.

'Wasn't no laughing matter, young Allsop Kaine.' The master pouted and Allsop explained he understood this. He apologised.

Master Whittion grunted and picked up his ale. 'Good.' He took a sip, set the drink down. 'Where was I?'

'At the beginning.' Allsop swallowed a sigh.

'Yes, of course.' The master placed his elbows on the table. 'As I said, the journey to Flaxburgh was easy enough. The first night we spent at Dorton, the inn there being most comfortable.'

He waved his hand to emphasise the comfort of the inn.

'We came to Flaxburgh too late the next day to do our business. Straight to the Lion and Eagle we went, for tasty food and a soft bed for both me and Chester.'

He took a sip of his drink. Allsop wriggled in his seat.

'Ah, good stuff.' The master peered into the tankard. 'We ate, and afterwards, the night being warm, I took an ale into the garden. As the miller was there I gave him notice of my order, which I considered useful as I was doing it and then of course it proved to be more useful later when–I'm getting ahead of myself.' He took another gulp and set the ale down once more, plump fingers curled around the fancy handle. 'Now, where was I?'

'Sitting outside,' Conall prompted.

'Oh yes, of course.' The master tapped his chin. 'We sat outside, talking. The night grew late and I began to think we would all be sent to our beds shortly. I was peering at the inn door looking out for the landlord when–whoom!'

***

Gweyr waited for Da to pour more drinks for her to carry to the customers. She fiddled with her silver chain and watched the baker and his apprentices. Master Whittion seemed to be telling Conall and Allsop a long-winded tale, likely about his travel to Flaxburgh. She wished she could escape serving drinks to listen in. Doubtless it wasn't much of an exciting tale, but anything to do with the world beyond Darnel fascinated her.

Da had met Mam in Flaxburgh, although Mam didn't come from there. Her family hailed from one of the hamlets strewn like tossed gravel over the high plains. She had come to Flaxburgh with a friend for Gahain Day, when the northern peoples feasted, danced and sang to celebrate the passing of the harsh winter. Da had been buying hops and, as he told the story, had come home talking of nothing and no one except the beautiful, dancing, black-haired girl he would marry.

'You with us, luv? Can't let ale go flat or folks thirsty.' Da waved his hand over the full tray.

'Sorry, Da.' Gweyr collected her thoughts and the tray.

'And on your way back'–Da hooked a thumb at the tables of dirty glasses and plates–'could you collect the empties too, luv?'

Gweyr nodded. She could collect empties, with a short delay. She hastily delivered the drinks, and with ears deaf to further demands took her empty tray to the bakers' table.

She arrived in time to hear Master Whittion say, 'Whoom!'

***

'Whoom?' Conall repeated in a wondering tone.

Allsop glanced up at the hovering Gweyr. One hand held a

tray, the other fiddled with a silver chain at her neck. He tilted his head towards Master Whittion. 'Come to hear the rest of the tale?'

She bit her lower lip and banged the tray silently against her apron. Allsop slid along the bench. He patted the empty space. 'Your da won't mind, I'm sure,' he whispered.

Gweyr briefly raised her eyebrows, set the tray against the wall and sat down.

The master acknowledged his new listener with a quick nod and carried on.

'Whoom!' He stretched out his arms. 'The tables where we sat look north, to the Alps. Beautiful view, although being night we couldn't enjoy the view right then. Not until those Alps were all lit up by, whoom! White light, like lightning, but'–the master leaned in close, gazing from face to face–'this lightning went up, like it exploded from the mountains. It went up. And'–he wriggled closer–'there was no thunder, no clouds. A perfect starry night it was. One bolt, one whoom!' He threw up his hands, raised his eyes to the ceiling. 'And then, and then, it made a great arc in the sky and flashed down, way, way to the east.'

The east? The Deep Forest of Arneithe sat way, way to the east. Allsop's spine tingled. Few dared to enter Arneithe, with its dark shadowed secrets and, the stories said, wicked trees which walked in the night or snaked out their roots to trap unwary travellers.

The master sat back, a faint smile on his lips above the unshaved stubble. 'Everyone talked at once. What was that? and Where did it come from? and What does it mean? and Will there be another one? and so on. All questions to which, of course, no-one had an answer.'

'Does anyone have an answer now?' Gweyr's eyes shone, seemingly spellbound by the tale.

'No lass, they don't.'

Allsop's impatience at being kept from his book softened at the sight of Gweyr's shining eyes. His lips twitched before he remembered this was no laughing matter.

'That's not all the tale, is it?' Conall prodded. 'You said you and Chester had a tough time coming home.'

The master drew a deep breath. 'Yes, we did indeed. Extremely bad.' He gave his empty tankard a gentle shake. Allsop jumped up and hurried to the bar.

'Gweyr's not annoying you is she?' Barnaby asked with a frown. 'She's supposed to be fetching in empties.'

'No, no, Mr Barnaby.' Allsop counted out his coins. 'The master's telling us about strange happenings on his trip to Flaxburgh. I'm sure he enjoys a bigger audience than me and Conall.'

Barnaby grimaced and turned to serve another customer. 'Do us a favour, please, and send her off to her chores soon as he's finished, will you?'

Allsop returned to the table, his interest in the story piqued. He gave the master his fresh drink and his full attention. 'And then?'

The master took the hint. 'And then I went to check on Chester, worried the sudden light might have upset him. I needn't have been. He was perfectly cosy on his bed of straw. I hurried to my own bed and tried to sleep.' He blew out a dramatic breath. 'No use at all. That lightning set me to worrying, it was so strange. I tossed and turned and eventually I must have slept for I woke, late, and worrying not about lightning but about my business with Flaxburgh's miller. I rushed through breakfast, collected a refreshed Chester and off we trotted to the mill.'

Master Whittion gave his listeners a grim smile.

'Yes?' Gweyr raised her hands, palms up. 'Don't stop, please.'

***

The lightning flashed again, this time in Gweyr's head. And

with it came the memory of her dream. The one she used to have when she was small. Since Mam's passing it had returned, coming to her most nights. A bright light, a girl in a hooded cloak, a dark gap in the earth. It was all she could remember, the rest slipping away on waking.

Was it lightning she dreamed of? She was being fanciful. What would her vague dreams have to do with Master Whittion's whoom?

Besides, other questions crowded her mind. Had the miller vanished, in a strange aftermath of the whoom of lightning? No, the miller was there, ready with the bags of flour. All very ordinary. The miller's son helped with the loading, payment was made. Off the master went, clicking the reins at Chester who was less than enthusiastic about the heavy load he had to cart along the tracks and lanes.

'And all was fine. In the beginning.' Master Whittion paused, his lips set in a tight line. 'But we hadn't reached the first village out of Flaxburgh when it started.'

'What started?' Gweyr hunched further over the table. She caught a glimpse of Allsop's twinkling brown eyes, secretly mocking her. She sniffed and gave her attention to the story teller.

'Storms and wolves. The master closed his eyes and shuddered.

'Wolves?' Conall's voice pitched high with excitement.

Gweyr sucked in a breath. Allsop's eyes widened. The wolves had shocked him out of his silent amusement.

'Wolves, howling, all around us, and thunder rumbling, though the rain held off which was something.' Master Whittion took a quick sip of his drink. 'There shouldn't be wolves on the grasslands at all, let alone in the middle of the morning.'

Gweyr tried to imagine it. Once, Mam had taken her to Flaxburgh to visit a dying friend. She had ridden pillion on the family's black mare, Millie, and they had stayed in other people's inns, comparing them, unfavourably, with the Boar's Head. It was all farmland and occasional villages between Darnel and the faraway Flaxburgh, with a handful of coppices scattered along the way. Not wolf country.

She stretched further over the table. 'Did you see the wolves?'

'Yes, yes, indeed we did. First though, we saw the wolves' trail.' Master Whittion pursed his lips. He patted Gweyr's arm. 'My dear, you had best close your ears at this part.'

'No, no, please go on.'

The master raised his eyes to the smoky ceiling. 'Dreadful sights. Lambs and sheep, slain in the fields. Mother ewes lamenting their lost ones, babies nuzzling pitifully at teats which give succour no more.'

Gweyr's stomach turned queasy.

'Where were the farmers and shepherds?' Conall said.

'Oh, they were there, silently cleaning up, herding the survivors to the winter barns. Their dogs' noses were stuck to the ground, and such a yowling and yelping they put up as I've never heard from farm dogs before. All too keen they seemed, to hurry those poor sheep out of those fields. And themselves and their masters too.'

'I heard the same story from my wife's cousin yesterday.'

The speaker was one of a silent crowd which had gathered around the table. Gweyr looked up. Da had come from behind the bar, a glass in one hand, a tea towel in the other.

'South though, the other way.' The man waved. 'Nearer the Deep Forest. Bad business, bad business. Sheep and cows, even horses slain and the farm dogs crazy with anger, or fear.'

'Down south?'

'Yes, he'd come from there, and right pretty hastily too, after seeing the slaughter.'

The master pointed at the speaker. 'Had he seen wolves?'

'Didn't say he had. Reckon he'd eyes only for the road and saw nowt what wasn't between his horse's ears.'

A few customers chuckled. The master glared to silence them. 'I saw the wolves,' he said. 'A great pack of them, in the fields alongside the road, heading north.'

A shiver trickled down Gweyr's spine.

'Wish I'd been there.' Conall's eager voice suggested to Gweyr the apprentice baker truly did wish he'd been there. She gave him an appraising glance and was rewarded with a cheeky grin which made her blush. Allsop, on the other hand, pursed his lips and settled his skinny frame against the wall. Cowardly, Gweyr decided.

The master grunted. 'No, you don't, young Conall. Don't wish for such horrors, in case they happen. I tell you, me and Chester took to our heels, Chester needing no whip to encourage him. I thought about dumping the flour.' He threw out his hands. 'That would've meant stopping and making us a sure target. We galloped on as fast as the old horse could go.'

'Poor Chester,' Gweyr murmured. She would visit him tomorrow, with an apple and a carrot. They understood each other, Chester and Gweyr.

'We drove into the next farmhouse we came to,' the master said, 'where the good farmer and his family were busy locking up their stock, and locking up their house in case wolves could open doors. They took us in and I slept in the cart in the barn, with one eye on the barn door and Chester next to me, shaking all through the night.'

Gweyr wasn't sure if it was the master or Chester who shook. She didn't like to ask, thinking it may have been both.

'Did you hear the wolves in the night?' It was the miller, Zach Beddle, who asked, with a slight smirk.

Gweyr eyed him with disapproval. His disbelief of the tale radiated from him, clashing with his unpleasant glee that Master Whittion was well-rewarded for his disloyalty in buying flour from those northern folks.

'No. All quiet. We headed out early and begged lodging in another barn long before dark. The farmer knew of the horrors and was bringing his stock in.' He tut-tutted his remembered sympathy. 'Poor Chester made such a whinnying when I left him with the sheep and cows I felt obliged to sleep a second night in a barn.' He brushed a piece of straw from his jacket and huffed. 'Anywise, here we are, all in one piece and not dinner for wolves.'

'You think the wolves'll come here?' The farmer who asked the question squirmed on his stool.

Gweyr wanted to know too.

'I trust not. I think–and this is just my opinion–I think those wolves came from the Deep Forest and were racing to the High Alps.' Master Whittion gestured vaguely northwards. 'I think, and this is my opinion as before, it had to do with the lightning, the lightning which went up and not down.' He inspected his barely touched, flat ale.

'Maybe, maybe not.' The farmer nodded and shook his head by turns. 'In any case, I'm off home to set my dogs to guarding.' He wagged a finger at the gathered company. 'And if I was you, I'd be off home too, lock your doors and windows. Strange times, strange times.'

He strode to the door, collected his hat and coat from a peg, and walked outside with no farewell.

Gweyr watched him go, her mind full of wolves and slaughtered lambs. And lightning, the bright light of lightning.

Her dream tickled her mind again. A bright light, and a girl. Herself? She blew out a breath. The wolves were no dream, nor was the suffering of the farmers. A coldness settled in her gut.

'It's late and I'm off too.' Allsop stood up. 'Bakers must rise early.'

His words stirred the listeners into action. Gweyr jumped

up, pushed back her hair, grabbed her tray and began collecting glasses. Da hurried to the bar, one step ahead of those needing fresh drinks to help them chew over Master Whittion's story. Most customers, however, collected coats and hats and departed in groups of two or three, whispering to each other, shaking their heads and glancing at the baker as they left the inn.

Chapter Six

Fever

'Ilesse, what are you doing? We're late for Hestia. And you're missing all the excitement.'

Varane's call stabbed like a blade through Ilesse's aching head. She opened her eyes, shutting them quickly at the light, dulled as it was, flowing from the passageway into her room.

'Why are you in bed? Are you ill?'

'Ill?' Ilesse didn't know if she was ill. She did know every muscle was tender and any movement painful. Her head throbbed. Her throat was raw, like she had swallowed broken glass.

Varane tugged at the curtain. 'Yes. Are you ill? It's late and we should be with Hestia already.'

Hestia.

Ilesse needed to tell Hestia about … about … Hazy images swam before her painful eyes. Oily smoke. Screams. A blinding light.

What was it?

She couldn't think.

Varane came into the room, dropping the curtain. The dimness soothed Ilesse's aching eyes.

'You look strange,' Varane said. 'Your eyes are too bright and your skin is all, kind of, damp looking.' He stretched out a hand and lightly touched her forehead. 'Hot.'

'My head aches.' Her voice rasped and she gulped with the

pain of speaking. 'My whole body aches.'

'I'll fetch Hestia.' He was gone, allowing the light to momentarily re-enter as he pushed aside the curtain.

Ilesse closed her eyes, shivering under the furs on her bed. Her hot skin stretched taut and dry like she had been baked in an oven.

She must have dozed for she had no idea how long it was before Hestia padded into the chamber and bent over her. The gryphon tut tutted, resting her beak briefly against Ilesse's burning brow.

'I've sent Varane for a Healer,' she murmured.

The Healer who came was the elegant Queen Ceantha, Varane's mother, wife to King Iaton and a Seer of the Sleih. Queen Ceantha looked into Ilesse's too bright eyes, touched her cool fingers to her dry skin and peered into her mouth. She declared it to be a fever and the 'prentice seer would recover in a day or two. She prescribed rest, a potion of gentian root to calm the fever and arnica for the aches.

Hestia shooed Varane from the room. 'It might be contagious, and with your Challit soon upon us, my prince, it would be no good at all if you were taken sick.'

Varane grumbled but left, halting at the cavern opening to call to Ilesse, 'Get well soon. I hope these avalanches don't disturb you.'

'Avalanches?' Ilesse croaked.

'Yes,' Queen Ceantha said. 'They began late in the night and do not appear to be ceasing.'

'To be expected this time of year.' Hestia's tone was brusque. 'What with the spring melts and summer soon upon us.'

Queen Ceantha pursed her full, deep red lips and tugged the furs closer to Ilesse's chin. 'So many though?'

Hestia raised her wings in a gryphon shrug. 'Yes, there do seem to be more than usual.'

'And the rumblings from deep within the caverns? Which

started at the same time? Are they to be expected also, Hestia?'

Rumblings? Ilesse, sweating but too overawed at being tended by the queen to protest at the closeness of the furs, drew in a breath at a sudden coldness piercing her mind.

Hestia didn't respond, saying instead, 'We should leave the girl to rest, Ceantha. I have asked Myar to come and tend her daughter for a day or two if she can be spared.'

Mother would be here?

The rustle of the curtain pulled aside and let fall told Ilesse the gryphon and queen had left. Alone, a surge of long-past homesickness swept over her, despite her fogged mind telling her it had been two years since she left her family's rooms among the artisans.

Two years she had dwelled in the higher caverns, studying magic, and more, with Sleih and Gryphon teachers–a sacrifice families made, with sad pride, if their child showed promise to become a seer. As she fell into a restless sleep, Ilesse imagined Myar's delicate silversmith's fingers stroking her forehead. How comforting it would be to have her here.

The potions took effect. She slept without dreams.

***

The councillors murmured to each other as they waited for the meeting to begin. Hestia noted that one stool on the Sleih side of the table remained empty. Olban had not yet joined them.

She took a place near to the king.

'Welcome.' Iaton smiled. 'I hear our 'prentice seer suffers a fever. How does she fare?'

Hestia lifted her wings. 'She recovers, slowly. Although whether it is a fever, I am uncertain.' She lowered her voice. 'I suspect these dreams, which do not abate, are the cause of her illness. You saw for yourself the stress they bring to her young mind.'

'Hmm. I have been thinking on those dreams and I worry

about them.' Iaton stroked his beard. 'But first let us deal with what is happening in reality.'

Turning away from Hestia, he called the councillors to attention.

'Welcome,' he said. 'Today we must decide what action to take in the face of the abnormal number of avalanches and the great rumblings heard beneath us.'

'Avalanches and rumblings which are over,' a dismissive voice said loudly, 'from what I see and hear.'

Olban entered the chamber. He strode purposefully to the vacant stool, his shoulders back and his lightly bearded chin lifted high.

Hestia bobbed her head. Such a confident stance was not normal to the seer. He tended more to an academic stoop, gained from long years of poring over mouldy texts.

The councillors muttered at this unapologised for, late, and abrupt, entry. Iaton's forehead creased. Tius flicked his tail.

Olban didn't sit. He leaned over the table with his fingers splayed on its smooth surface.

'Do nothing. That's my advice.' He faced the king in an unblinking challenge.

What had happened to his myopic squint? Hestia's unease grew.

'The avalanches have eased and the noises and tremblings in the deep caverns are indeed quiet, for now,' Iaton said. 'But we do not know what damage has been caused and what danger that represents.'

Olban huffed. 'Do you plan to send people out onto the mountainsides or into the depths to measure this damage?'

Tius lifted a wing. 'Seer Olban, please remember your manners.'

'Manners?' Olban arched his eyebrows. 'My apologies,' he said, with not quite enough contempt to be called out for rudeness. 'I simply see no reason to risk lives in ridiculous explorations.'

'Yet,' Tius said, 'we cannot risk all our lives by remaining in ignorance.' He shifted to address a middle-aged seer halfway down the table. 'Rahin, have you found a willing guide?'

Hestia looked at Rahin. With his long and deep studies of the magical properties of gems, he was well acquainted with the Sleih miners who worked the deep tunnels.

'Yes, my lord,' he said. 'One Thrak, whose grandfather mined the long-abandoned tunnels where these rumblings are centred. He is curious, and willing to guide us to find out what has happened.'

'What foolishness, to risk lives in a fall of rock.' Olban snorted.

Hestia shook out her wings. She had never known the seer to be rude.

'You have just said,' Rahin pointed out, 'there is nothing happening which is of concern, meaning it should be safe to descend.'

Olban sniffed. 'It's no matter to me. I won't be going.'

Chapter Seven

Wolves and bears

Wrapped in layers of woollen shawls, Ilesse curled in a chair by the fire pit reading a text she had begged her mother to fetch from the repository. It was about the magical properties of gems and Ilesse had scoured the section on diamonds to learn what she could. According to the text, diamonds were of no more significance than other gems. She rifled through the last pages, hoping for more. There was nothing.

'Here is Varane to visit you.' Myar moved aside from the opening of the room to allow the prince to stride in.

Ilesse closed the useless book with a snap and looked up, smiling.

'Are you better?' Varane squinted in the dim light. 'Because I can't, I just can't, learn my silly Challit oath without your help. Hestia only frowns and says, "Try harder, my prince."'

'Yes, I have recovered.' Ilesse laughed. 'Hestia might allow me to return to my lessons tomorrow. Whatever was wrong, I'm better, and ready to help with your oath.'

'It's not just the oath.' Varane flopped to a fur near Ilesse's chair. 'There's all kinds of things going on. Hasn't Hestia or your mother told you?'

'My prince.' Myar shot a warning glance from where she was folding clothes into a bag ready for leaving. 'Our patient needs rest, not tales of strange happenings.'

'Strange happenings, Mother?' Ilesse frowned. 'You have to

tell me. You can't hint and then let it go. Please!' She looked down into Varane's shining green eyes.

He didn't wait for permission.

'Wolves and bears,' he said, waving his arms, 'and strange rumblings deep below the caverns.'

An icy band squeezed Ilesse's heart. She pressed her hand against her chest, gasping at the pain.

'What's wrong?' Varane demanded.

Myar twisted around and hurried over. 'What is it?'

'Nothing, nothing.' The band loosened, fell away.

Myar peered into Ilesse's eyes. 'You're sure?'

'Yes, Mother, I'm sure. Can we let Varane tell his story, please? I want to know about these wolves and bears.'

Varane slumped onto the fur. Myar went on with her packing, glancing over her shoulder from time to time at Ilesse and the prince.

'Ashta and her hunters have seen them,' Varane said. 'From high up in the Alps, they've seen wolves and bears, in packs, marauding across the snows and glaciers, then disappearing like they'd fallen into crevasses.'

'Disappearing?' Something, like … glee … how, why? … spiced Ilesse's curiosity.

'Uh huh. Their tracks stop, as if they've taken to the air. Ashta believes they've come from Arneithe, across the grasslands and high plains.' He blew out a breath. 'The poor Madach. Imagine what horrors those packs must do rampaging through their farms and villages.'

Grisly images sent their tendrils through Ilesse's mind as if expecting to be welcome there. She recoiled in horror.

'Poor Madach, indeed,' she whispered.

'Ashta's taken her hunters east, to the Forest, see if they can trace where they come from.'

'Ah.' Ilesse imagined Ashta flying above the plains to the Deep Forest of Arneithe. By gryphon standards, she was young, with feathers whose colours changed, faded and brightened depending on where she happened to be. Her lion body might be as tawny as any other gryphon, but when she wrapped her wings about herself she could disappear in a cavern, or a forest, or on a snowy mountain slope.

She won't find them.

The thought, in a voice not her own, startled Ilesse. She brushed her hand across her forehead. Warm and damp.

'And these avalanches,' Varane prattled on. 'Many many more than there should be for spring. The lower caverns vibrate too, like there's earthquakes or a great monster stirs down there.'

The icy band clamped itself around Ilesse's heart. This time she didn't cry out. She caught her breath softly, not wanting to trouble her mother.

'And the rumblings?' She spoke quickly, hoping to ignore the pain into disappearing.

'They are to be explored.' Hestia pushed through the curtain in time to hear Ilesse's question.

'Hestia!' Varane jumped up to stand by Ilesse's chair.

Ilesse smiled a greeting. 'Tell me, please, everything.'

Hestia placed her beak against Ilesse's forehead, blinked but said nothing. She stepped away.

'Difficult conversations, that's what's been happening,' she said. 'Wolves and bears, avalanches, shakings and boomings, which, thankfully, grow quieter and less frequent day by day, although the seers will delve into the depths to find their cause, if possible.'

Ilesse wriggled in her chair. A weight descended on her shoulders. The cold band around her chest tightened further. She drew a shallow breath.

News of avalanches and rumblings and this awful tightness. Did they have something to do with each other?

'Seer Olban, on the other hand,' Hestia said, 'is determined nothing is amiss and we should go on as normal. That in itself is not unusual for Olban. He hates being distracted from his studies.' Hestia lifted her wings. 'It's his behaviour! It borders on the arrogant, mocking our desire to seek answers, saying winter boredom is making us see portents and evils where there are none.' She sighed. 'Some of the seers agree with him.'

'Olban?' The band squeezed tighter. Ilesse pressed her fisted hand to her chest.

'Yes, Olban.' Hestia fixed an eagle eye on Ilesse. 'What about him?'

Steps, endless flights of steps. Screams. Viscous smoke wrapping itself around her head, smothering her. Fleeing through black passageways, her only light the fading glowstone ...

'Olban.' Ilesse's voice fell to a whisper. She grasped her layers of shawls closer to her suddenly chilled body. The stabbing in her chest worsened. She found it hard to breathe. 'The night'–she gulped a painful breath–'I fell ill. I remember. I followed Olban.'

Varane lifted his chin. 'Why?'

Myar abandoned her packing and walked to Ilesse, laying a hand on her shoulder.

Hestia's eyes on Ilesse were as green and hard as any emerald. 'Indeed. Why?'

'I'm not sure I know.' Ilesse struggled for the reason as she fought to keep her voice calm. She drew another short breath and let the words tumble out. 'It was what you said, Hestia, to King Iaton and Lord Tius, the day we told them about my dreams. After you told me to leave.'

The white membrane closed and opened over Hestia's eyes, as it did when she was annoyed or upset. 'You eavesdropped?'

Varane's mouth fell open. Myar blushed, sending guilt pangs through Ilesse's heart.

'Yes, briefly.' The knife-like soreness in her throat was back.

'Because I heard you talk about me. You told them about Olban and the diamond, like in my dreams …' She lifted a flushed face to Hestia. 'I went to Olban's caverns and he was leaving, his hand lit by a bright light. I followed. The light was a diamond.' She dropped her head, gulping air. The pain in her chest rose through her throat, gagging her next words. 'I shouldn't have. I'm sorry.'

'Where did Olban go?' Varane danced from one leg to the other. 'Where did the diamond take him?'

'Down,' Ilesse rasped. She pushed both hands against her chest, willing the tightness away. 'I don't know where, I don't think I could find it again.' She winced at the pain in her throat.

'Down, and then what?' Varane stopped hopping and bent forward to peer into Ilesse's face. 'Did he go somewhere special? Was he looking for something?'

Hestia laid a wing on Ilesse's head. 'No more questions,' she said. 'Can you not see she is unwell?'

Ilesse could not grow warm. She gripped her shawls with icy fingers to pull them tighter. A chill like death seeped through her whole body. The effort of her long explanation had sucked away her regained strength. She looked at Hestia, answering Varane's question.

'He fell, from the bridge.' It was all she could manage.

The terror of the darkness after the brilliant light, the sound of the seer screaming as he plummeted into the chasm–the scene played in her mind, fragmented. Her brain span in wild circles.

'Daughter, drink this.' Myar held out a stone mug.

Ilesse took the mug in a trembling hand. The scent of honey sweetened the bitterness of gentian root and she sipped, grateful for the soothing effect on her throat. The tightness in her chest eased, leaving her utterly weary, sapped by the memories of that night.

Hestia, Myar and Varane watched her with careful, curious

faces. She pressed the warm mug between her cold palms and forced herself to finish her story.

'There was a light.' She swallowed, took another sip. 'It came up from the chasm. Olban screamed, for a long time.' Her shaking hand sent liquid sloshing over the mug's edge before Myar gently removed it from her grip.

'How did he get out?' Varane said.

'And why has he not mentioned this?' Hestia asked softly, as if to herself. She touched her beak to Ilesse's head. 'Are you sure this is not part of your dreams, my Ilesse?'

'Oh, a dream.' Varane fell to the fur with a loud humph.

'No, Hestia, not a dream.' Ilesse frowned. 'You say Olban is here?' Her certainty faded. 'And he has said nothing?'

'Nothing of night time wanderings or lights or stone bridges over chasms.' The gryphon hesitated as she spoke about bridges and chasms. Ilesse would have asked why, had she not been so sleepy. She desperately needed to go to her bed and close her eyes.

'My daughter needs more rest,' Myar said firmly. 'The oath will have to wait, Varane.' She helped an unsteady Ilesse from the chair and guided her to the bed.

Ilesse dropped onto the furs and closed her eyes, hearing her mother say, 'I will stay another day at the least. Something ails her.'

***

Hestia sat on the ledge of her cavern, her eagle eyes searching the meadow below. Soon the grasses would become a jewelled tapestry of wildflowers, a rich source for healers. Young Sleih would be instructed which of the purple, white and blue flowers to harvest and where to dig for roots. The healers would replenish their stores of powders and potions to use against bruises, fevers and the aches and pains of ageing Gryphon and Sleih. The meadow also inspired Sleih goldsmiths, silversmiths and artists who would wander under the summer sun taking heed of shapes and colours to inspire their artistry. And those gryphons of poetic leanings would bask with folded wings and hooded eyes, listening to birdsong, watching the rise and dip of butterflies and contemplating rhymes and stories to entertain the young ones on winter nights.

Today nothing stirred on the meadow, or on the glacier or the mountain slopes beyond. Or in the sky. Where were the birds, the wild creatures?

Hestia's heart lay heavy in her chest, recalling the recent council meeting when Iaton had given permission for Ashta to take her best hunters east. He had advised her to be wary of being seen by the Madach, not wishing to cause them further alarm.

Olban had interjected. 'I would expect,' he said in a tone which suggested he had no sympathy for the Madach, 'seeing Gryphon in their skies would be more frightening to the ignorant peasants of the grasslands than a handful of wolves wreaking havoc in their fields.' He arched his dark brows. 'If they insist in their stupidity on living as exposed on those plains as they do, they must be used to death and destruction.' His lips curled in a sneer.

Tius had glared at Olban with lidded eyes. 'Olban, your views do you no credit. Please desist from sharing them.'

The seer's glare had sent a shiver along Hestia's spine.

There on the ledge, with the late spring sun warm on her feathers, she shivered again. Chaos and death, like in the 'prentice seer's dreams, hovered at the edges of her Gryphon foresight, knocking to be allowed in. She tucked her tail tight against her haunches, her heart thudding.

***

'Olban, a word before you rush off, please?' Hestia stretched out a wing to the seer's arm as he made his way out of his cavern.

'In a hurry, Hestia.' He didn't spare her a glance, strode down the passageway.

She paced beside him. 'It's important.'

'What then?' he grumbled.

'Did you venture into the deep caverns several nights past? Guided by a diamond's brilliance?'

Olban peered sideways at her, his green eyes slitted. 'What has made you ask such a nonsense question?'

She was about to say, 'Ilesse followed you.' She didn't, made reluctant by a stab of fear. 'I overheard a conversation in the hallways. Somebody–I no longer remember who–mentioned they had seen you, crossing the end of a passageway. They'd wondered at the brilliant whiteness of the light from your hand, not knowing what it was.'

Olban stopped, stared at Hestia. 'I have undertaken no night wanderings of late, with or without white lights coming from my hand. Now, may I go on?'

'Of course. I'm sorry to have detained you, old friend.'

Olban's back stiffened. 'I apologise for my brusqueness. There is much on my mind.'

'Is it the ancient text I brought you?' Hestia curled her tail. 'The book on conjuring powers and spirits? How goes the translation?'

Olban barked a short laugh. 'Not at all. The translation goes not at all. I heeded your advice and took the book to the repository, to a place where I trust no prince or 'prentice seer will stumble across it.'

'Very wise, I suspect, very wise indeed.'

Olban gave a curt nod and hurried away. Hestia watched until he disappeared from her view, her mind and heart in turmoil.

Her strong powers of the mind told her Olban lied to her.

It frightened her he would know this, yet seemed not to care.

Chapter Eight

A miner and five seers

Olban held his shining glowstone high. His other hand caressed the diamond deep in the pocket of his coat. He gazed around the low cavern, barely lit by a lantern fixed above the opening where he stood.

Yes, there. His eyes rested on a wooden door, cracked with age and crossed with iron bands. A rust-spotted hook straddled an iron ring deep in the wall to hold the door open.

'Olban!' The seer Rahin peered up at him. 'I understood you wanted no part of this exploration. Are you here to wish us well in any case?'

Us? Olban took in the gathered seers.

Sheema. Of course. Doubtless she viewed this trek as an opportunity to prove her worthiness to rise to councillor.

Hiasin, young and curious. He constantly bombarded the senior seers with questions about the properties of gems and which ones offered more scope for magic than others and how did you tell and so on. Another obvious volunteer.

And Zadir. Solitary Zadir, shutting himself in his caverns with his texts and tools and orbs and globes over the long winters. He would have a more educated idea of what they might find below. Yet still he came.

Olban's lips gave a brief upward twitch. They would do. Especially Zadir.

He moved to the doorway, and stopped. Something there–

the hook and iron ring?–discomfited him. He crowded against Rahin, out of their way.

'I do wish you well,' he said.

He held the glowstone over the edge of the opening. Fissured and uneven steps descended steeply between rough rock walls. The drip of water carried from far below. He turned so suddenly Rahin had to grab the edge of the opening to stop from tumbling down.

'I wish you well,' Olban said, 'because I will join you.'

'Good news.' Sheema pursed her mouth. 'I for one will appreciate an experienced councillor accompanying us.'

Rahin raised his eyebrows at the snub. Hiasin covered his mouth with his hand to mute a giggle. Olban smirked. Zadir appeared not to have heard, bearing the look of one who knows he has to endure the vapid ramblings of others before the real adventure can begin.

'Are we ready?'

Olban swung around at the thunderous question. It came from Thrak, a giant of a Sleih with his neck rising like a tree trunk above his hide tunic. The miner would guide the seers through the tunnels. Olban's smirk returned. Let Thrak see how much his strength endured in what was to come.

Sheema scowled. 'There's no need to shout.'

Thrak scowled too, waving an arm thick with muscles. 'You'll be grateful enough for my big voice, Lady Sheema, when we're in those lightless caverns.'

'Why?' Sheema taunted. 'Will it help us see better?'

'Thrak, Sheema, please, this is not a time for squabbling.' Rahin held his hands out in a plea.

Thrak crossed his massive arms and Sheema fiddled with the leather bag hanging from her shoulder.

'Now'–Rahin looked at each of his companions, except Olban–'as Thrak has asked, is everyone ready? Glowstones? Water? Strikers?'

The seers nodded.

'I know you're all familiar with the mining tunnels,' Thrak boomed. 'This is different. There'll be no marked ways, no lights beyond what we carry, and we don't know what falls, rifts and other obstacles we'll come across.' He stared at each of them, including Olban. 'So, my lords and Lady Sheema, I need your promise you'll do exactly as I say, at all times.'

Sheema opened her mouth, caught Rahin's glare, and shut it. They all, except Olban, obediently murmured, 'Yes, yes, naturally.'

Olban approved their obedient natures.

He signalled for Thrak to enter the staircase. He stepped in after the miner. Sheema, Rahin, Hiasin and Zadir came behind, each bearing a lit glowstone.

***

'Well done, my prince.' Hestia's beak opened in a beam of approval.

Ilesse and Varane perched cross-legged on the ledge outside the gryphon's cavern, their backs to the unfolding mountains. Varane's face glowed from more than the bright mid-morning sun. He had recited the whole of his Challit oath without hesitation. Ilesse grinned with him.

The prince's success did not fully distract Hestia's thoughts from what might be happening right then in the caverns' depths.

She had sought out Olban before first meal, anxious about the changes she saw in him, needing to talk more about the night Ilesse said she followed the seer. She found him leaving his rooms, his heavy cloak thrown over his gown, his normally sandalled feet encased in soft leather boots. In one hand he carried a glowstone. The other was deep in his pocket, playing with something lying there.

'You go with the others into the depths?' Hestia asked, reading his intention.

'What I do is none of your concern.' Olban had sniffed and passed by without a further word.

Hestia sighed and drew her attention back to the sunny ledge.

She curled her tail, bobbed her head. 'Excellent, my prince. And again, please.'

'Again?' Varane's self satisfied grin upended into horror.

Ilesse laughed. 'You need to be able to recite it in your sleep. You know you do.'

'Oh!' Hestia murmured. 'There is a sight we have not seen in many an age.'

Ilesse and Varane twisted around.

'Ashta and her hunters.' Varane pointed at the gathering of flying gryphons, many carrying a Sleih rider. 'Flying to Arneithe. Why today, with all this cloud below?'

While they basked in sunshine, white clouds filled the valleys, hiding the meadows and forests where the hunters' prey, whether deer or wolves and bears, might be found.

Hestia's eagle gaze sought out Ashta leading the group. 'The cloud will hide them from any Madach eyes as they cross the high plains,' she said.

'Of course.' Varane's hand shaded his eyes as he followed the hunters on their swift flight. 'They'll cross the grasslands and the Madach villages too.'

'Too late.'

Hestia started at Ilesse's strangled voice.

The 'prentice seer stood, squinting into the sun at the receding hunters. She put splayed fingers to her mouth. 'They are too late. It has begun.'

Hestia blinked rapidly at her strained high giggle.

The giggle stopped, abruptly. Ilesse's eyelids closed. She sank down to sit against the rock, her hands in her lap.

Varane frowned at Hestia, who touched her blue wing tip to the 'prentice seer's shoulder.

'What is wrong? What's happening?' she asked.

Ilesse gave a great shudder and opened her eyes. 'Have you finished your oath already, Varane?'

***

Down. At last, down.

Impatience pushed at Olban's mind. Thrak moved too cautiously.

He stepped close to the miner's heels and earned himself a grumbled, 'Don't crowd me, Seer Olban, else we'll both end up falling down these endless stairs.'

'Do you know what lies at the bottom, Thrak?' Rahin said.

Olban's lips curled. Thrak didn't know. And Olban wasn't telling.

'Grandfather tells me there's a chamber at the bottom with many tunnels off,' the miner said. 'We go left from these stairs, counting five tunnels to our left and four to our right. We take the fourth to reach the chamber.' He waited, apparently giving them time to understand.

Olban's curled lips turned into a quiet snicker.

'From there,' Thrak said, 'he could give no advice beyond warning to take care. We must decide what to do when we reach this chamber.'

Olban explored the chamber in his mind. He knew what he would do.

Ahead, Thrak's heavily booted feet clumped on the stone stairs. Behind Olban, the lighter leather-shod feet of the seers pitter-pattered like whispering mice. The glowstones threw wavering shadows on the cracked steps, making it hard to judge where each uneven edge began and ended.

Olban walked confidently, sniggering softly at the hesitant footfalls behind him.

'How much further?' Sheema's tone was peevish.

Thrak shrugged. Olban glanced over his shoulder and arched his eyebrows. Sheema glared.

Down.

Olban's impatience eased with the descent. Eagerness took its place. He lifted his chin and inhaled deeply. A sharp, subtle scent of wet ashes and old smoke hung in the musty air.

Could the others smell it?

No one said anything. Maybe they were distracted because the stairway at last ended and Thrak led them along a tight, low tunnel. The miner splashed through the dank puddles. Olban also made no attempt to avoid the water, not caring about the dampness seeping into the hem of his gown and soaking into his soft boots. Excitement fluttered against his rib cage. He took in another lungful of air, savouring the distinct aroma.

Immediately ahead a sudden rumbling boomed through the tunnels.

Thrak pivoted to face the group. 'Get down!' he shouted. He crouched against the wall, arms over his head.

The seers threw themselves to the wall, pressing into it.

Olban remained standing, staring forward.

'Olban!'

A deafening crack drowned Sheema's cry.

Rocks cascaded from the roof. They bounced towards the seers in a clashing ringing of stone against stone. Dust and shrieks filled the air.

It didn't last long. Coughing, mingled with the scattered patter of clods of earth, broke the silence which followed.

'Is everyone all right?' Thrak pushed himself from the wall to survey his charges.

Olban twisted about, watching. Three of the glowstones had gone out, adding to the thick gloom.

Sheema brushed splinters of stone from her shoulders with shaking hands. Hiasin ran a hand through his hair. Zadir shook himself like a wet dog and Rahin busied himself relighting his glowstone.

'Do we go on?' Sheema said. Her voice quavered.

‘That is up to you.’ Thrak waved at the fall which blocked the width of the tunnel. ‘We can clamber over it if we wish to carry on.’

Rahin lifted his light to better see the fall. ‘I say we go back and–’

‘We will go on.’ Olban held Rahin’s gaze.

His frowning face relaxed. ‘Yes,’ he said, flatly. ‘We have come this far.’

Olban’s gaze took in each of the others. Thrak first, then Hiasin, Sheema and finally Zadir. None argued.

Chapter Nine

'Be still'

Olban came last in the group as Thrak led the awkward clamber over teetering rocks. Hiasin slipped when a large stone lost its unsteady balance. Spots of blood showed on his gown where it pressed against his grazed knees.

Past the rockfall, Thrak hurried them on. Creaking, straining noises rumbled through the tunnel. They sounded at a distance. Olban ignored them.

'Will we be able to get out?' Hiasin said. 'What if there's another, bigger fall?'

Rahin humphed. 'I said we should have–'

'All will be well,' Olban cut in softly.

'How do you know?' Sheema's voice rose.

'Lady Sheema, please, no shouting,' Thrak pleaded. He glanced up at the packed dirt and rock roof, shaking his head.

'You are safe with me, Sheema,' Olban said.

Sheema opened her mouth, shut it, and walked on.

Thrak counted off the tunnels to the left and to the right.

'Four,' he said.

'No, I make it three,' Sheema countered.

'Four,' Rahin said firmly and Sheema humphed.

Thrak had already moved into the tunnel. Olban knew the miner and Rahin had counted correctly. He followed Thrak.

This tunnel sloped steeply down, slippery with glistening wetness. The biggest rocks which had fallen from the roof had rolled to rest at wherever the bottom might be, leaving a scattering of smaller ones to skitter under any walker's feet. The seers, ahead of Olban, jerked their glowstones as they scrambled to stay upright, causing their shadows to jump like puppets on strings.

Olban's own light held steady, as did Thrak's.

'I wish I had never agreed to this.' Hiasin's fright showed in his trembling voice.

'All will be well,' Olban murmured. It was an automatic response, for his mind had flown ahead to where he wanted, needed, to be.

Down, down. His keen impatience grew.

The grey walls shimmered with damp. Licks of green slime gleamed like poison where the glowstones' pale lights reached them. The air was icy.

Olban's skin warmed as if he basked in sunshine. He took another long, satisfying breath. The scent on the air strengthened. Surely the others must smell it.

'Bitterly cold down here,' Rahin complained. 'Colder than the mining tunnels normally are.'

Thrak kept walking. 'It's not far to the chamber, if Granddad remembers it right.'

He made it sound like the chamber would be warmer than the tunnel. Olban grinned, unseen.

'There's a strange smell too.' Hiasin sniffed and coughed. 'Can you smell it?'

'Damp and stale air,' Rahin said, in a less than confident tone.

Thrak stopped, stooped low and held his glowstone forward. He hesitated a moment before crouching under a low arch. Olban followed, and behind him Rahin, Sheema, Hiasin and Zadir.

The arch led to a large and bare chamber. The cracked floor dipped and rose, a miniature mountain range buckled by an earthquake. Puddles of brown water gleamed in the light from the glowstones. More rocks lay tumbled here and there.

They each lifted a light and peered upwards. Blackness.

The glacial air soothed Olban's skin like scented oils after a bath. He sucked it in, relishing the fragrance.

Hiasin cleared his throat. 'The smell's stronger here.'

Rahin nodded.

More low arches were spread around the chamber's round wall. Nothing distinguished one from the other, yet Olban's eyes went straight to the furthest passageway. He strode towards it, eagerness welling in his chest.

'Come,' he commanded.

'Pardon?' Sheema. Still reluctant to obey.

Olban kept his annoyance from showing in his face. This close, he could stand no more delay.

'My dear Sheema,' he said quietly. 'I believe this is where we will find the source of the rumblings, groanings and shakings we have endured these past several days. Isn't that why we're here?'

Zadir moved swiftly to the passage indicated by Olban. He stopped beside the arch, his glowstone pale against the darkness beyond. The others all talked at once.

'How can you know that, Olban?'

'Shouldn't we explore each tunnel in turn?'

'Shouldn't we split up? Be faster.' Hiasin, over his fright and keen to move on.

Olban snorted. 'No. We should all stay together.'

'However we do it,' Thrak said, 'someone needs to stay here to raise any alarm.' He folded his arms and glowered.

'You stay, Thrak.' Olban bent his head as if offering a gift. 'After all, you have guided us as far as you can.'

Sheema's eyes widened.

Thrak's glower deepened. 'I can't let you go off without me. You're in my care.'

'I doubt if wild creatures lie in wait for us,' Olban said, restraining his wolfish grin.

'More likely things which it takes the power of seers to understand.' They were the first words Zadir had spoken since the beginning of the exploration. He faced the tunnel which Olban wished to pursue, waiting.

Thrak took a step forward. 'I'm your guide, Seer Olban. I can't stay here while you take yourselves into possible danger.'

Olban shrugged. 'You will be in the way. You are not coming with us.'

Thrak scowled and opened his mouth to protest further. Olban cast him a piercing glance. The miner closed his mouth, stood motionless.

His eyes on Thrak, Olban beckoned the others to enter the tunnel. 'This way, come along.'

Zadir had gone ahead, marching stolidly forward. Olban ushered the others to follow. Hiasin scuttled through.

'What have you done to Thrak, Olban?' Rahin remained where he was.

Sheema also hesitated, glancing between the silent Thrak and Olban.

'Don't you see?' Olban said gently. 'Now is the time for seers, not for miners. Thrak will be our watchman.' He summoned them once more with a slow wave of his hand. He looked intently from one to the other.

They forgot their hesitation, walking rapidly to the arch and into the passage.

Olban's gaze rested steadily on Thrak's face.

His eyes unfocused, the miner's arms hung limply at his sides. Olban curled his lips in a soft sneer. He walked into the tunnel, beyond Thrak's vacant view.

Down, down.

He pushed his way to the front, seemingly to lead the party. In truth, he had lost interest in his companions as they trod their cautious way along this new tunnel.

Hurry, hurry.

The air became oilier and the odour stronger.

Sheema muttered, 'What is that stench?'

Olban glanced around at her muffled voice. She had lifted her cloak to cover her nose and mouth. Deep frown lines marked her forehead. He faced forward before drawing a slow, relished breath.

The roof grew lower. Olban ducked his head, kept up his swift pace. The gap between himself and the others widened.

Rahin called out. 'How far are we going, Olban?'

'I see nothing unusual here,' Sheema said, 'and I'm worried about this awful stink.'

'This stink might lead us to the cause of all the disruption,' Hiasin said.

'It will lead us.'

Zadir's certainty brought a sharply accusing response from Sheema. 'Do you know something of what we might find, Zadir? Because if you do, you might have told us before we came down here.'

Zadir didn't break his stride. 'I suggest I have studied more tomes and manuscripts in my lifetime than you have done.'

'And?' Rahin prompted.

'Wait,' Zadir said, no inflection in his voice.

Yes, wait. Olban crouched forward. The tunnel narrowed as well as becoming lower.

'If we go much further, we'll have to back out,' Rahin said.

'This awful stench, it's getting worse.' Sheema gagged behind her lifted cloak.

'Olban, your light. It's dimming,' Hiasin called. 'And yours too, Rahin.'

'All our lights,' Rahin muttered.

'It's the air. It's thickening, and greasy.' Sheema's voice rose in panic. 'We have to get out of here.'

There were cries of assent, the shuffling of feet and the rustle of clothing as the seers tried to turn around.

The glowstones faded, and died.

'No!' Sheema cried out.

Absolute darkness.

Olban, unmoving, listened to the frightened cries, the yelps as toes were trodden on and elbows found contact with ribs and hips. The air filled with acrid smoke. Its heaviness caressed his face, creeping into his eyes, his ears, his nose.

'I cannot breathe!'

Olban smiled at Rahin's strangled cry.

He drew the smoke deep into his lungs.

The seers wheezed, choked. Their breathing came in panicked gasps, each shallower than the last.

'Help us.' Hiasin, desperately trying to draw in air. 'Please, somebody, help us.'.

Help?

Olban shrugged.

'Be still,' he commanded.

The seers were still.

Chapter Ten

A stranger visits

Cooling water streamed over Allsop's head. He shook wet hair from his eyes, dipped his mug again. This time he gulped the water down his parched throat.

'Ahh, good.' The heat of the bakery kitchen had dried out his whole body.

He took a third dip, plumped onto the stone bench and sipped, slowly this time. He stretched out his legs and closed his eyes, letting the busy hum of bees soothe his tired mind. He sighed. Best go back to work before the master hunted him down.

He heaved himself from the bench and wended his way towards the kitchen. He stopped. A grave voice he didn't recognise spoke from inside.

'… strange lights and rumblings from the far Alps, Whittion. Rumours of the mountains moving, or–'

'Yes, yes,' the master said. 'I witnessed the lights myself, Rebar, or at least one extremely strong, vivid light. Like lightning, except it went up, not down. And then–'

'You saw it yourself, here in Darnel?' Worry tainted the stranger's voice.

'No, no. In Flaxburgh, when you missed our meeting.' The master's reproach was muted.

Allsop expected the stranger to apologise, although perhaps this part of the conversation had already happened. In any case, the master did not wait for a reply.

'And then my journey home–' he said.

'You saw this in Flaxburgh? Ah, much nearer the High Alps there.'

'And then my journey home,' the master persisted, 'proved fraught indeed. Wolves, Rebar, wolves.'

'I've heard, and seen their destruction, although I'm grateful not to have sighted these packs myself.'

Allsop took a step forward, thinking he should make his presence known. The stranger, Rebar, spoke.

'Zoledore has summoned the wizards to conclave, Whittion, to think on this.'

Allsop halted mid-step, mouth agape. Wizards?

'He fears the high plains and the grasslands are in danger from whatever is happening in the High Alps of Asfarlon?'

The master didn't sound like the fussy, self-important baker whom Allsop knew. Was it the master who spoke? The stranger, Rebar, had plainly said Whittion. Who else by that name would be in the bakery kitchen?

'... insistent we cannot afford to assume not. For there is something else you should know.' Rebar paused.

Allsop quietly placed his raised foot to the ground and twisted his head to hear more clearly.

'There have been rumours of great-winged beasts flying over the high plains. Bigger than horses, with tawny bodies and wings of many hues, moving eastward, to the Deep Forest.'

The master snorted a laugh as Allsop tried, and failed, to picture these great-winged tawny beasts bigger than horses.

'Gryphons? Flying above the high plains? Flying to Arneithe?'

'If the accounts are true and not the vivid imaginings of lonely shepherds, then perhaps they could be gryphons.' The solemn tone told Allsop Rebar and the master knew of these flying creatures. 'Zoledore chooses to believe, as he always has.'

Gryphons? Allsop had assumed the Gryphons in the old tales were people, like the Sleih. Now he wondered what nature of bird or animal they might be, or were supposed to be, outside of the vivid imaginings of lonely shepherds. If the shepherds were right, did the Sleih also exist? And maybe they weren't people either. His head reeled with possibilities.

'A legend, Rebar, a legend. Despite what our most senior wizard believes.' The master snorted. 'Next you will tell me there are rumours of gold-skinned people with green eyes and hair as black as a raven's wing coming out of holes high in the Alps.'

'The Sleih?' Rebar paused. 'As Gryphon and Sleih are always linked in the ancient tales, doubtless we will hear such rumours, true or not.'

Allsop's brain worked hard to take this in. The Sleih were people after all. Or once were people. Sort of.

There was another silence. Allsop eased his tense body. Should he go inside and confess to overhearing this unreal conversation?

He should. He took a firm step forward.

'None should know of the wizards' conclave, Whittion. The villagers and the farmers will be fearful soon enough once these rumours spread. We should not heighten their fear by letting them know they have wizards in their midst.'

'Baking their bread for them.' The master chuckled, a sound more familiar to Allsop. 'Which reminds me, I should see to my loaves. Is this conclave to be in Flaxburgh as usual? Tell me when it is, while I rescue whatever it is I smell burning.'

The master's voice grew fainter as he moved to the ovens. Not faint enough that Allsop didn't hear him mutter, 'Where are those dratted apprentices?'

He couldn't go in through the bakery kitchen. With his head full of white lightning, flying beasts with huge wings, gold-skinned people and wizards in tall hats waving magical staffs, he stumbled along the gravel path to the gate in the wall which would take him to the stables and store rooms.

Chester whickered at his approach, resting his neck on his stable door and begging with pleading brown eyes for a carrot. Allsop mumbled an apology for his lack of carrots, went out to the lane leading to the road and thus into the front of the bakery.

'Where have you been, young man?' The master poked at a pair of darkened, unsellable loaves with a pudgy forefinger. 'And where's Conall?'

'Sorry, Master, I, I …'

'Oh, never mind, come and help me with this next batch.' The master humphed and glared, his hands on his hips. 'You and young Conall both need to learn the meaning of responsibility, and soon I suspect.'

Allsop hardly heard him. He looked about for the stranger, Rebar. He had gone.

Chapter Eleven

Whispers

Ilesse held her hand to her forehead to shade her aching eyes from the sun's glare reflecting off the glacier. It flowed, a blue and white scar, down the mountain and past the meadow where Varane's Challit would take place Her gown of blue and silver–her favourite colours–rippled with her movement, fanning a cooling hint of breeze against her legs.

She tossed back her hair, adorned today with ribbons to match the gown. Her gaze fell on Seer Olban, pacing towards her. Glittering lines of magical runes rose from the hem of his deep green councillor's robe, curling in vertical waves as he walked. The diamond-shaped ends of the chain around his waist swung like a pendulum in time to his firm stride. The seers Hiasin, Zadir and Sheema clustered behind him. Their eyes never left his back.

Ever since the disastrous venture into the cavern depths, they were always with the seer. Rahin, and the miner Thrak, remained in the tunnels. They died from the smoke, Olban said. King Iaton forbade any search for their bodies while the source of this fatal smoke remained unknown.

Olban fixed his gaze on Ilesse.

'Do you find the sun too bright, 'prentice seer?'

Ilesse squirmed. 'I am not fully recovered from my illness, Seer Olban.'

'Yes, your illness.' Olban's sardonic smile remained fixed.

His eyes glinted with a malevolent darkness which drew Ilesse's unwilling gaze. 'Wandering in the caverns in the chilly night air is not conducive to apprentice seers' good health, I should think.'

She clutched her gown with damp hands. Did he know she had followed him?

Olban's stare poked at her thoughts like the tip of a hunting knife, searching … for what?

'Ah.' He nodded, as if he read confirmation in her thoughts. He took a step closer, his eyes mocking.

Ilesse stared too, a rabbit caught in a hunter's trap.

No need for fear, 'prentice seer.

Her eyes twitched as the unexpected whisper rose in her mind.

You desire knowledge, wisdom. All such seekers must take risks to achieve the desires of their heart.

Yes. They were the desires of her heart. To know all, to be wise, to cast magic as the best of the seers and gryphons cast magic. The murmuring continued, assuring, welcoming, telling how her desires would be fulfilled, all wisdom granted, if she heeded the seer's beckoning.

Her breath came in excited rasps. Her mind opened–

'Olban.'

Hestia's sharp voice whipped Ilesse's dreamy mind into reality. What had happened? She took a step backward, distancing herself from the seer.

He lifted his mocking gaze to the gryphon.

Her eagle eyes glared at him, but her words were for Ilesse. 'Varane needs you. To go over his oath.'

Ilesse couldn't help a prickle of irritation. 'Can't he leave me in peace for one minute?' she snapped, and immediately felt ashamed.

Olban tittered. His dark gaze swung unhurriedly from Hestia to Ilesse. The tingling in her body, as exhilarating as the first dive into an alpine lake, beat against her stronger need to escape those prying eyes.

Hestia twitched her tail. 'It's his Challit. You're his dearest friend. He's nervous. Of course he wishes you to be with him.'

Ilesse bit her lip. 'I know, Hestia. I'm sorry.' She lifted the hem of her gown and walked to the green and silver royal pavilion. 'It's the heat,' she called over her shoulder. She slid her hand under her hair to lift it from her neck. 'So hot today.'

***

'What did you say to Ilesse?' Hestia fixed an emerald eye on Olban's gloating face.

'Merely sympathising with her on the glare of the sun.' He chuckled and strode off. His three attendants trailed after him.

Hestia watched them go, both curious and anxious at the mute devotion of the seers. Not like them at all, especially Sheema. She also wondered, with the same anxiety, at the arrogant stride Olban had adopted. She lifted her beak sharply, noticing for the first time the new sprinkling of white in his black hair. Had heavy burdens recently been placed on his thin shoulders?

She puffed out her neck feathers. Olban didn't appear worried by anything. In fact, he seemed less worried now than in all the time Hestia had known him.

***

'I, Varane, having reached fourteen years and therefore being of age …'

Varane paced the pavilion, splendid in deep green trousers of finely woven grasses and a shimmering white silk shirt streaked with silver. A silver circlet of green emeralds gleamed on his golden brow. Ilesse, perched on a cushion, pretended to listen. Her mind kept drifting to Olban.

How was he alive?

Dreams, Hestia had assured her. Her journey that night,

Olban's fall into the chasm, were the wanderings of Ilesse's fevered mind, a symptom of her illness.

She wanted to think it was a dream. Her head and her heart refused to let her.

Varane chanted on, eyes squeezed in concentration.

Ilesse recalled Olban's stare. Goosebumps crawled on her bare arms. Chilling. Yet … her heart beat faster at the memory, excitement pulsing in her blood as if being presented with an unexpected gift. A yearning welled inside her–for knowledge, wisdom, to hasten the day when she would cast her own magic with a grace and ease surpassing the most gifted of the seers.

'How did I do? It was perfect, wasn't it?'

Varane's anxious voice broke into her dreaming. She stifled a frown.

'Yes, perfect.' She checked the testiness in her voice, hoping he didn't hear it.

He knew her too well.

'What's wrong?' He threw out his hands. 'You're all out of sorts, but it's me who should be nervous. You only have to watch.'

'I'm nervous for you, my prince.'

Ilesse smiled and Varane humphed, and grinned. Thoughts of Olban fled. She tugged at the blue and silver ribbons tangling with her hair. She really was nervous for her friend.

'Come on.' She clambered up from the cushion. 'Time for the grand event. You're ready.'

'He is indeed.' Hestia padded into the pavilion. 'Your father and Tius, Lord Gryphon are in place. The Council is assembled and Sleih and Gryphon of every level in the caverns await your presence.'

Varane pulled in his stomach, pushed back his shoulders and glanced down to pat the gleaming, jewelled hilt of the sword hanging at his side. 'We're ready,' he said.

The glow of jewels on the hilt of the blade, named Celeste,

came from the form of a flying gryphon engraved there. The sword had passed through the royal Sleih line for generations. Once, the old tales proclaimed, it served its masters well in battles. Now only ever needed for Challit ceremonies and pageants, woe betide any heir who failed to keep the sword clean and honed.

Hestia lifted a wing. 'Ilesse and I will take our places. You can follow right behind.'

Ilesse kissed Varane softly on his cheek, whispered, 'Make us proud,' and followed the gryphon from the tent.

The pavilion had its back to the glacier. In front, facing the meadow, a low dais had been placed, garlanded with wildflowers. At each corner, ribbons of real silver interwoven with brilliant green emeralds had been imbued with Gryphon magic to float in the breeze like the gossamer threads of spiders..King Iaton, Queen Ceantha and Lord Tius waited for the prince, talking to each other.

'We do love an occasion to dress up,' Ilesse whispered to Hestia. They stood alongside the dais, watching the gathering.

Bright-hued silks and laces adorned every Sleih man, woman and child. The Sleih councillors stood out, with their deep green gowns embroidered with silver thread. They put Ilesse in mind of trees shimmering in sunshine after rain. The gryphons glittered with exquisite, jewelled gold and silver chains displayed around necks, ankles and tails. Their feathers–blue as the sky, grey as clouds, black as night or green as the meadow grasses–gleamed richly in the sunshine.

Ashta and her hunters had returned from their fruitless searching in the Deep Forest of Arneithe and paraded on the grassy slope. Sleih and Gryphon alike glowed, their wooden spears and bows bright with green and silver streamers. Ashta's feathers were rainbowed today to blend with the colourful crowd.

Ilesse's heart swelled with pride when Varane stepped onto

the dais. He bowed to his parents and Lord Tius.

'Welcome, Prince Varane.' Lord Tius' strong voice carried across the crowd.

'Welcome, my son.' King Iaton bent his head and smiled. 'Today is your Challit, and the day on which you swear fealty to the Sleih and Gryphon of the High Alps of Asfarlon. This is the first stage of your journey towards your inheritance, for one day you will sit here as king.'

Varane gave a slight shake of his dark head, denying there would ever be a time when his father did not sit as King of the Sleih of the High Alps.

King Iaton chuckled. 'We hope it is a long way off, my prince, yet it will come.'

A murmuring arose in the crowd, which Ilesse took to be a good-humoured reaction to the king's words.

The murmuring grew, bubbling into anxiety.

A scream cut the hot air. Shouts rose.

Ilesse peered among the crowd. Varane swung around to find the source of the noise.

Hestia lifted her head and searched also.

Cries arose. People pointed and waved at the space behind the platform.

'What is it? What comes over the glacier?'

Over the glacier? Ilesse ran around the pavilion to peer across the sun-brightened ice.

A heaving mass of white creatures raced silently across the glacier, heedless of its jagged ridges, heedless of its cracks and crevasses, as sure-footed as if they ran through a grassy field.

A stab of excitement, of triumphant glee, pricked Ilesse's heart.

Chapter Twelve

Refugees

In the week after the stranger's visit, Allsop couldn't stop thinking about Master Whittion being a wizard. No matter how many sideways glances he gave the master, he detected no wizardly behaviour. Although, what did wizardly behaviour look like? He would sit in the courtyard with a mug of water and recall the odd overheard conversation. His mind filled with images of wolves, vaguely shaped flying beasts and green-eyed people until he remembered the loaves in the oven and had to run to the kitchen to rescue them.

'Think the dough's had enough kneading.' Conall grinned from the other end of the table where he shaped rolls, laying them in rows on a tray for proving.

Allsop stared at the dough like he had no idea how it came to be on the table. 'Guess it has.' He let out a quick breath. 'How's the oven going?'

'It'll be roaring by the time this lot's ready.' Conall waved his hand over the covered rolls.

'I'll tend shop then,' Allsop said. 'Give the master a break.' He rubbed his hands clean with a wet cloth, dried them on a towel, and walked through to the shop.

Empty.

But beyond the wide bakery window with its shelves of fresh bread, a crowd of villagers gathered. The attraction was two ordinary carts pulled by oxen. The drivers and passengers had left the carts and filled the road. They talked to the villagers, frowning, shaking their heads and throwing out their arms in great agitation. The villagers shook their own heads and clasped their hands in sympathy with the newcomers' distress. Master Whittion's plump face crumpled in concentration as he questioned a tall man with muscled bare arms. Barnaby stood close by with his daughter, Gweyr, who cradled in her arms an unknown and sleeping toddler.

'What's going on?' Conall peered through the window, brushing his floury hands against his apron.

Allsop shrugged and hurried outside, Conall close behind.

'... white wolves, red-eyed and fanged, and bears, white too, with teeth hanging to their chests, all heading south,' the muscled man told Master Whittion. 'They rampaged through the village in the middle of the night. Not a piglet or a chicken or a cat or a dog not locked inside ever found ...'

Allsop winced at Gweyr's ashen face. She drew the toddler closer to her as if afraid white wolves would snatch it from her arms there and then.

Rebar had talked about wolves. Master Whittion saw them for himself. Neither had mentioned the wolves were white, and nothing had been said about bears. Could this be a new, different threat?

'Only wolves and bears? Nothing else?' The master peered into the man's frowning face.

He gave a sharp nod. 'Isn't it enough, Master Baker?' he snapped.

'Yes, yes, quite enough, quite enough.'

No flying beasts, such as Rebar had jested about. A pity. Allsop snorted quietly. As if they could ever be real!

A frowning Gweyr relinquished the toddler into the arms of a crying woman who was led away by a farmer's wife.

Allsop stepped to Gweyr's side. 'What is it?' he said. 'Who're these people? What's happened?'

She bit her top lip. 'Refugees, from the far north, a hamlet on the high plains beyond Flaxburgh attacked by white wolves and bears from the Alps.' She gazed after the farmer's wife and her guests. 'They've been fleeing for days. Other families have stayed in villages further north. These–well, you saw that woman's distress. I think she'd travel south until the oceans stopped her, and even then …'

'The wolves Master Whittion talked about when he went to Flaxburgh weren't white, were they?' Conall said.

'Those wolves came from the south, going to the Alps. These white ones come from the north.' Allsop could make no sense of it.

'Allsop, Conall, come with me.'

The master's quietly serious voice sounded unlike his normal tone. He strode into the bakery, expecting his apprentices to follow. Allsop had heard the master talk in such a voice once before–when Rebar addressed him as Whittion the Wizard and not Whittion the Baker.

He glanced at Conall, who raised an eyebrow and went after the master. Allsop followed. As he walked through the shop doorway the patter of soft footsteps behind made him glance over his shoulder. Hard on his heels, her mouth set in a determined line, came Gweyr.

'Where are you going?' Allsop said.

She stuck out her chin and strode past him with a swing of her arms, declaring, 'I want to help.'

He shrugged. The master could throw her out if he didn't want her there.

Because something was up, for sure.

The master paced the kitchen, sighing and shaking his head. Allsop's suspicion about something being up hardened into almost-fact.

'Gweyr?' The master ceased pacing to raise an eyebrow.

'I'm sorry, Master Whittion,' she said, not sounding sorry at all. 'It seemed you wanted Allsop and Conall for some reason to do with those poor people and the wolves and bears, and, well, and ... I thought I could help, somehow.' She breathed this last out in a rush, fiddling with the chain around her neck.

Master Whittion pursed his lips and creased his brow. He squinted into Gweyr's blushing face. 'Astute of you, young lady.' And to Allsop's astonishment, added, 'Please stay.' He rubbed his chin. 'These troubles in the north are getting worse.'

He gazed at the three young people lined up along the table, weighing them up like flour for loaves.

Weighing them up for what? Allsop kept his eyes on the master's face, trying to show his worthiness for whatever he needed to be worthy of. Gweyr straightened beside him. Conall lifted his chin to the ceiling in a soldier-like stand to attention.

'I must travel,' the master said, 'near to the Deep Forest.' He lowered his voice, although who was there to hear? 'I will meet with people who should know more of what is happening, and seek advice and counsel.'

If Allsop hadn't overheard the conversation about the wizards' conclave, it might have been him and not Conall who said, 'Travel? I thought you and old Chester had enough of trouble when you went to Flaxburgh.'

Gweyr tugged at her chain. 'It'll be dangerous, Master Whittion, like we know from these northern folk.'

Master Whittion set his gaze on Allsop. 'You also have an objection to this?'

Allsop's face burned with more than the heat of the kitchen. 'Ah, umm,' he stuttered. Then in a rush, 'It's the wizards' conclave you go to, Master? Someone called Zoledore has summoned you all.'

The master flicked his eyes to the door into the shop. He put his finger to his lips.

Conall's eyes widened. 'Wizards' what?'

'Hush,' Master Whittion implored.

Gweyr wriggled her shoulders. 'What wizards?' she whispered, leaning close to the master. 'Who's Zoledore?'

He lowered his finger to wag it at Allsop. 'Spying on your elders and betters, hey?'

'Not deliberately, Master, not at all.' Allsop ran a hand through his hair. 'I was in the courtyard when I overheard you and Master Rebar talking, and at first I didn't want to interrupt and then I thought I should let you know I was there, except when Master Rebar said about'–he dropped his voice to a murmur–'flying beasts and wizards and conclaves, well'–he gulped–'I thought he, and you, might be angry with me, so I, so I ...' His long and hurried explanation tailed off in the face of the master's grinning enjoyment of his discomfort.

Gweyr and Conall gaped, although Gweyr did murmur 'flying beasts' in a wondering tone.

'Ah yes.' The master smirked. 'The flying beasts. Rumours based on fairy stories from long ago.' He dismissed the flying beasts with a flick of his wrist. 'You heard me ask if anything other than wolves and bears had been seen, and the man's answer, No.' He humphed. 'Whatever our wizard leader Zoledore believes, I think we must rely on ourselves to deal with this threat, not wait about for heroes from ancient legends to come to our aid. Wolves and bears–physical creatures which arrived from somewhere and can therefore be driven back to whence they came.'

He stroked his beard. 'How, I have no idea, which is why I must attend the conclave.'

The ringing of the shop bell startled Allsop. Master Whittion stared through the doorway like someone who has forgotten he has a bakery to run.

'Tut,' he said. 'We'll talk about this later. There's bread to bake and sell first. A half day will make no difference.'

Chapter Thirteen

A wizard in their midst

While Conall and Allsop baked loaves and rolls, Gweyr helped the master deal with a stream of customers. Everyone had to buy their daily loaf immediately–and at the same time gossip about the poor folk fleeing wolves and bears.

'Doesn't your father need you?' Master Whittion asked Gweyr.

She went on serving. 'We have a new kitchen girl and she's a good worker,' she said. 'Da can do without me for a bit.'

He gave her a sideways look. Determined not to miss any possible excitement, Gweyr pretended not to notice.

'What can I get for you, Mrs J?' She smiled at the next customer.

Over the day, she learned there were northern folk who had not fled, reluctant to abandon their homes to rampaging wolves and bears. These were farmers who herded their surviving livestock into barns and sheds–and themselves and their families with them–praying the attacks would stop.

'Their stores of feed are low after the winter, of course,' a farmer's wife said. She had taken in a family of refugees and needed to visit the bakery to supplement her own homemade bread. She huffed heavily as she stuffed loaves into her basket. 'Those cows and sheep should be out in the fields grazing this time of year, not bundled up in sheds eating their winter feed.'

The stories not only stirred Gweyr's sympathies. All through the day snatches of her old dream, the one she'd started having again, slipped into her head. The girl, the bright light, a blackness ahead like a hole in the earth. Why?

At last the bakery shelves were bare, floors and benchtops scrubbed, the oven fire laid for the next day. Gweyr hung the 'Closed' sign on the shop door and walked into the kitchen to join the master, Allsop and Conall seated on stools pulled up to the table.

'Wizards?' Conall wiped his hand across his sweaty brow as he took in the morning's revelations.

Gweyr settled in, eager for adventure.

The master poured light ale from a clay jug into four glasses and passed them around.

'Yes, wizards.' He let out a loud sigh. 'In olden days there were many wizards, acknowledged in their communities, respected, and their advice on all manner of things heeded.'

'What happened?' Gweyr's disappointment was intense. Why hadn't she lived in ancient days when wizards abounded in every village?

'Folks decided they knew better than the wizards, didn't need them anymore.' Master Whittion took a sip of his ale.

'Why go into hiding?' Allsop asked.

'Ah, that's come about since people began blaming us for all kinds of mishaps. We went from respected and sought out, to being blamed for every farmer's two-headed calf and every housewife's butter which wouldn't churn.'

'How unfair.' Gweyr scorned her fellow villagers' stupidity.

'Indeed, yes. Life can be unfair, sad to say.' The master took a long draught from his glass. 'A full wizards' conclave,' he said, 'is a rare event.' He glanced at Allsop. 'It will not be the usual simple journey to Flaxburgh to meet with a handful of my fellows under Rebar's guidance. This time, Zoledore summons us all to the edge of the Deep Forest, to Ledrith, a place once famed as a source of powerful wizardry.'

Gweyr had an immediate and deep desire to visit Ledrith.

'We're to meet a week hence,' the master said, 'at the full moon of this first summer month.' He grimaced. 'I don't know how the full moon helps, but Zoledore insisted.'

'Where is this Ledrith?' Gweyr had never heard of it. One of many places she'd never heard of, she acknowledged with a touch of bitterness.

'North and east of here. A mere hamlet, mostly huts belonging to woodcutters, tree felling being the sole business of Ledrith these days. Apart from the rare wizards' conclave.' He huffed. 'The local people know nothing of those. The cavern entrance where they take place is well hidden and guarded by secret spells known only to us wizards.'

The master held himself taller on the bench.

Eyes wide like a begging dog's, Gweyr said, 'Secret spells? Can you tell us, Master Whittion?'

He gave her a sharp glance. 'I cannot, for then they would no longer be secret, would they?'

Gweyr's eyes narrowed briefly before she laughed. 'No, they wouldn't.'

'What do you want us to do, Master?' Allsop unfolded his arms to rest them on the table.

Gweyr wondered, with a sniff, if he was keen to steer the conversation from uncomfortable things like secret spells and hidden caverns.

'I had wished,' the master said, 'for you and Conall to mind the bakery, as usual. However …' He ran a finger absently around the rim of his glass. 'Given the stories these people have brought with them today, I might face more on the journey than I, riding on stolid Chester, would wish for. Therefore I'm asking one of you to accompany me. On good, fast horses.' He looked up from his glass to mutter, 'Where we'll get those in a hurry, I've no idea, not around these parts.'

'I'll gladly accompany you.' Conall jumped up, knocking

over his stool. 'I'm strong, quick on my feet, good with my fists too.' He punched the air to show how good he could be.

Gweyr wriggled. Her hand went to her chain. 'Me,' she blurted. 'It has to be me.'

The master peered at her, a tiny smile playing on his lips.

Gweyr wriggled harder, struggling to find a way to tell him it wasn't all about escaping the dreary routine of the Boar's Head. 'I have to be there, Master Whittion, I know it.' A soft voice in her head drove her. The dream, the bright light, the girl …

The master laid a plump hand on her arm. 'No, no, my dear. Apart from anything else, how could I risk the eternal wrath of your father?' His rueful grimace explained he wasn't prepared to do this. 'No, it has to be Conall or Allsop.'

'Me,' Conall insisted. 'Allsop's the better baker. He should stay behind.'

Allsop didn't argue. Gweyr wondered how much of a boring coward he really was. She couldn't care about Allsop. She clasped her hands before her face.

'It's important. I know it–'

'Your desire for adventure is strong, young lady, but my answer remains No.' The master wagged his finger at her. 'Think of your poor father and what he's been through already.'

Gweyr's desperation muted. The master was right. Possibly. 'I'm sorry,' she mumbled.

'Conall, you will come with me,' the master said, 'as my bodyguard and helper. We'll leave the baking business in Allsop's hands and Gweyr to help her father.'

Conall grinned. Allsop managed to look disappointed.

The decision did nothing to ease the need welling inside Gweyr. 'I guess I can't let Da worry,' she said, half-heartedly, 'or leave him to do everything by himself. Although having the new girl makes it easier.' She stared into the air above the master's head. 'Yes, she's a hard worker,' she said softly.

***

Mid-morning two days later, Gweyr leaned on the sill of an open upstairs window of the Boar's Head. She chewed her lip and watched the villagers bid Master Whittion and Conall good luck on their journey. For of course everyone knew of this brave (and most considered foolhardy) excursion to learn more about the dangers in the north.

Gweyr had listened to the miller, Beddle, mutter over his beer the previous night. 'What's it got to do with us? Those northern folk fleeing from a few bears, panicking over nothing no doubt. Why go looking for trouble?'

'Whittion says he knows people who can help us if we need help,' Da said, a glass and a tea towel in his hands as always.

'Going in search of heroes, eh?' Beddle snorted. 'Next thing you know, he'll be arriving here with those fairytale lot, the … the … you know, hair as black as a raven's wing, eyes the colour of emeralds?'

'The Sleih,' Da reminded him.

Gweyr's spine tingled. Yes, the Sleih! A bright light, a girl … the Sleih… oh, why could she never remember that one dream? Maybe because there was nothing else to it. A girl carrying a light. Not important.

'Yes, Sleih.' Beddle had slid his empty glass across the bar. 'Another please, Barnaby.'

This morning, the miller wasn't among those waving the adventurers off. Da stood outside the inn, brandishing his tea towel like an ancient sword.

When the adventurers had disappeared and the villagers returned to their homes and chores, Gweyr moved from the window, with an effort. If anyone had been there to see, they might have noticed a deep longing in her green gaze.

She sighed, and hurried downstairs at Da's bellowed, 'Gweyr, where have you gotten to, girl? Work won't get done by itself.'

Chapter Fourteen

The white horde

The distance between the rippling horde and the green and silver pavilion swiftly closed. The creatures' white fur shone as brightly as the glacier itself. Wolves, and bears too, but bigger than any wolves or bears should be. And malformed, with twisted tails, oddly bent legs and great lumps protruding from backs. Even from this distance, Ilesse sensed their terrible, ruthless menace.

Her breath caught in her throat.

My beauties.

She shook her head as if to dislodge a buzzing in her ears. Her beauties?

Behind her, the Challit had fallen into abandoned chaos. Sleih and Gryphon fled to the shelter of the caverns. Parents clutched babies to their chests. They hauled toddlers along so fast the little ones' legs barely touched the grass. Gryphons flew low, covering their friends' and neighbours' retreat, pressing them forward. Many had young Sleih clinging to their lion-like backs. Shouts and screams gave way to the panting of breaths, sobs of frightened children and panicked urgings.

Lord Tius, the king, queen and Varane had jumped from the dais to stare across the glacier beside Ilesse and Hestia. Ashta leaped after them, her rainbow wings raised.

The king shielded his eyes from the dazzle of the sun. 'What?' he murmured.

Sleih hunters lined themselves along the glacier's ragged edge, tearing off fancy ribbons to ready spears, bows and knives. Gryphon hunters flew low to meet the silent attack of the monstrous creatures.

Ilesse's eyes were fixed on the white horde. Her heart pounded.

Not from fear. A heady anticipation swept through her limbs like a welcoming blaze.

My beauties.

Hestia scraped a talon along the grass. 'Surely these are creatures of evil. We must retreat, with the others.'

Ilesse ignored her. She pressed her arms close to her sides, fighting a deep desire to extend them in welcome to the deformed white creatures. The icy band tightened in her chest.

'Ilesse, run!' Varane's eyes briefly begged her to follow the terrified crowd. He ran to the hunters.

Now her heart thudded with fear.

'Varane, no!'

Hestia's eagle head bumped her shoulder. 'Ride on me, Ilesse, hurry. They are nearly on us.'

Ride on Hestia?

'Varane? What about Varane?' Ilesse cried.

'Varane must fight.' Hestia's tone was taut with dread.

Both looked to the glacier. Varane sat astride Ashta, brandishing Celeste. King Iaton rode beside him, on Lord Tius. Both the prince and the king rode easily, as if gryphons had borne them their whole life, although this was not the case.

A confusion of emotions tumbled through Ilesse's mind. Part of her protested in horrified indignation. Who would dare attack the Sleih and Gryphon of the High Alps?

Part of her exulted to see these complacent people recoil in fear.

'You can save them, Ilesse,' a quiet voice whispered in her ear.

Olban had pushed his way through the frightened chaos to the pavilion. He laid a cool hand on Ilesse's arm.

Whispers filled her head: *Join with me, 'prentice seer. Together we can save them.*

She wanted to cry out with relief. Yes! Varane need not fight. Ashta's hunters need not be slain.

Olban's piercing eyes scalded her soul. She must surrender to his beckonings … she must join with him. To save the Sleih and Gryphon, to save Asfarlon …

Faintly she heard Hestia demanding, 'What are you doing, Olban?' She shoved at Olban's hand with her wing, failing to dislodge his tight grip. 'Let her be!'

Let her be? Didn't Hestia want Varane to be saved? The icy band tightened. It was hard to breathe.

She could save them. Olban's unspoken words assured her. They need not die.

You can save them all, 'prentice seer.

The whispers stroked her thudding heart.

My beauties.

A flash of understanding ripped through Ilesse's clouded mind.

Not the Sleih and Gryphon. Olban would save the monstrous white creatures … *my beauties* … She stared into the seer's dark eyes. Yes! Saving the wolves and bears made Ilesse's heart glad …

'Hold, Ilesse, resist him!' Hestia's anger tore at the tightness choking Ilesse's breath from her lungs. She beat at Olban's hand with her wing. 'Leave her!'

Olban flinched. He released Ilesse's gaze, but kept his grip on her arm. She swung back to the battle.

Gryphon hunters swooped low over the glacier, talons stretched to rip and tear. The invaders leaped, swerved, the first of the lines streaming onto the meadow. Sleih hunters shouted as they clashed with the horde. Wolves and bears bared long, yellow fangs, snarling, shrieking as they met the attack.

Varane bent low, swinging Celeste to hack at white fur jumping and writhing below. Ashta thrust out her strong eagle legs to tear at exposed necks and rip open bellies. Blood flowed from her lion sides.

The line of creatures crossing the glacier appeared endless.

Varane would die.

Olban's whispers beckoned: *Save them, Ilesse, save your beauties.*

Hestia cried out. 'Ilesse, be strong.'

Ilesse closed her ears and her heart to Olban's whispers. With a great shudder, she wrenched her arm from his grasp and hauled herself onto Hestia's back.

The gryphon lifted into the air. One great wing shoved against Olban, sending him staggering. Hestia flew, taking the path of the panicked crowd up the meadow to the caverns.

Ahead, a tiny girl stumbled. She lay on the grass, screaming, overlooked by fleeing people. Hestia dived. Ilesse bent down, grabbed the child by her embroidered belt and lifted her up. She crouched over her, holding her in place, soothing the girl with meaningless words.

Throw her down, useless brat.

Ilesse gasped as the sneering voice filled her head. No! She clasped the child harder and fought the band tightening around her pounding heart.

They reached the caverns, the last to enter. Behind them, the heavy iron gates, stiff with disuse, were forced shut with shuddering groans. Ilesse fell off Hestia, arms around the girl. She pivoted about to see through the closing gap, straining for a glimpse of what took place at the bottom of the meadow.

The white mass spilled off the ice onto the grass. Ashta's hunters hacked and sliced.

Ilesse searched for Varane. There! Beside the trampled pavilion, bending low from Ashta's back. The gryphon twisted, seeking out more prey. A circle had opened up around the two. Those maddened creatures which had escaped Celeste's lethal cuts and Ashta's talons raced away, tumbling over themselves to reach the glacier.

Ilesse lost sight of the battle as the gates clanged shut with a noise like an avalanche. She thrust the child at the nearest person, saying, 'Seek her mother.'

She pushed her way through the confused crowd to the stairs leading to higher levels, aware of Hestia behind her. In the lowest passages Sleih and Gryphon rushed here and there, purposeless, terror in their eyes.

Ilesse climbed higher. Others joined her, also seeking those caverns with views over the meadow and the glacier. She came to an eating room first. Its wide ledge held ancient Sleih and gryphons who had taken advantage of the view to watch the ceremony in comfort. They stood in silence, staring down.

'What's happening?' Ilesse panted.

'Ashtar and the prince will vanquish them.' A man with wrinkled arms and a deeply lined face spoke over his shoulder.

A jolt of anger shot through Ilesse's stomach. *My poor beauties*. She drew a sharp breath.

'What are they? Where did they come from?' She struggled against the anger, slowly replacing it with a reluctant triumph.

One of the old gryphons touched Ilesse's bare arm with a dulled, grey-streaked wing. 'Ancient evils, 'prentice seer,' she whispered. 'Who has woken them?'

'My fear also, Olwyn.' Hestia's melancholy murmur sounded behind Ilesse. 'Who indeed?'

'Are we beating them?' Ilesse stared at the chaos below. The cold band had loosened, gone leaving no trace of its presence. She loathed the writhing, silent mass of unnatural, deformed white fur. 'I can't see Varane. Hestia, where is he, can you see him?' Her stomach churned for a different reason.

'There!' someone cried. 'The prince and Ashta, the king and

Lord Tius have prevailed. See, the white beasts are overcome.'

Exhilarating relief flowed through Ilesse as the bloodied horde abandoned the meadow to flee across the ice. Many of their number lay dead or wounded on the grass and the glacier.

As did several of Ashta's hunters, both Sleih and Gryphon.

Chapter Fifteen

What power is this?

Hestia cast quick glances at Olban, seated on his stool at the Council table opposite her. Open contempt disfigured his shadowed face.

How did he dare to be here? Hestia raged. What she had glimpsed during his assault on Ilesse's mind filled her with horror.

'What did he say?' she had asked.

'He wanted the white beasts to win,' Ilesse told her.

'And what did he want from you?'

Ilesse turned her head away. 'I don't know.'

She couldn't, or wouldn't, say more. Hestia suspected it was all to do with the ancient book, and with diamonds. And with Ilesse's night wanderings. She squirmed on the thin rug, hearing Olwyn's muttered, 'Who has woken them?'

Her fault. She should have taken the book to the repository when she realised it spoke of great, and likely evil, powers. Best to resist curiosity, leave those powers undisturbed for centuries more, if not forever.

She dragged her mind back to the Council. Ashta sought permission to take a group of hunters into Arneithe, try once more to determine the source of the creatures.

'It is likely,' Iaton had said, 'these white creatures of evil are borne of those forest bears and wolves which have heeded a nameless call to drive them to the Alps.'

'If we can stop them from reaching the Alps,' Ashta said, 'we have a better chance of defeating those which appear to gather beneath us.'

'Wouldn't we be better scouring the glacier, destroying any creatures which try to attack?' a Sleih seer asked.

'Yes, we will do so,' Ashta assured her. 'However, I suspect'–she turned to Olban, who sat steepling his fingers in a bored manner–'we should also search out their haunts from below, try to seal them in.'

Olban's eyes slid sideways to the hunter. 'You would risk further deaths, such as Thrak and Rahin suffered?'

Although Hestia thought it a good point, his coolness grated. Rahin had been a good friend, a kind and diligent seer. The thought of what he had suffered, and Thrak too, weighed heavily on her.

Iaton intervened. 'Take your hunters east, Ashta, and send others to patrol the glacier. We will think about the wisdom of venturing underground a second time.'

Ashta rose from her place on the thin pelt and left the Chamber. A tense silence filled her absence. Hestia gazed out at low, dark clouds which obscured the far mountains like a dense, ash-laden fog. Her mind was as thick, as heavy. She sighed. Despite all her eagle vision and all her Gryphon senses, she found herself blind to what lay ahead.

Olban knew, she was certain. Knew more than he was telling. Hiding something.

The seer responded to her gaze. He lifted his top lip in a faint sneer and slowly moved his head to take in the gryphons ranged opposite him. Green eyes turned opaque as they stirred, discomfited.

The Sleih seers squirmed on their hard stools. No one spoke. The tension in the cool air of the Eternal Chamber hung as taut as a pending storm.

Hestia roused herself. 'Do you think, Olban, these attacks

might be to do with the book I gave you?'

The councillors peered at her, eyebrows raised or beaks parted.

'The book?' Olban purred. 'I told you, it was not worth the effort of translating. I returned it to the repository.'

Hestia knew he lied. Again, he seemed not to care.

'What book?' Iaton said.

'Do you remember, Sire?' Hestia lifted a wing. 'The text I told you about, talking of ancient powers, possibly evil, and, it appeared to say, able to be woken by a diamond's glow.'

'Yes, I remember.' Twin lines creased Iaton's forehead.

'Rubbish,' Olban said. 'You read too much into your feeble translation.' He grinned, the twitch of his lips so fleeting most would have missed it.

'Seer Olban.' Tius spoke. 'It gives me great pain to venture my thoughts here.' He held the seer's gaze with one emerald eye. 'Where does your contempt for us come from? Why do you lie to Hestia?'

Olban jumped to his feet. He kicked back his stool. Burning hatred flared from him like a glowstone lit with too intense a fire.

Hestia recoiled.

'Olban?' Her voice cracked.

He ignored her, his fever-bright eyes fixed on Tius.

A low moan of pain emerged from the gryphon. He swayed.

The councillors cried out. They stood, either to go to Tius' aid, or to flee. Hestia was already on her way to offer help.

Olban whipped his head towards her. She stopped with a breath-taking suddenness. She couldn't move. All around her, councillors froze. Heads slumped to chests. Half-lifted wings drooped to fold against bodies and tails curled between hind legs. All appeared to have fallen into instant sleep, whether sitting, standing or walking.

Iaton sprang from his stool.

'What are you doing?' he shouted.

Olban's gaze flashed to the king, who sank to his knees. He raised his arms to shield himself, but his head dropped, making it appear he bowed to Olban.

'No!' Hestia cried.

She alone remained wakeful, although motionless. She summoned all her magic, her mind darting this way and that, searching for a way to overcome Olban's penetrating gaze before it could cast her into this spell-like sleep.

Or death.

Olban waved a hand above Iaton's kneeling form and then at Tius, who fought to lift his head, failed, and slumped forward against the table.

Hestia tried to cry out. Nothing. Her mind reached to the opening into the Eternal Chamber, willing help to appear.

'Come!' Olban called, in a deep, commanding voice.

The quick patter of soft sandals on the stone stairs heralded the appearance of Hiasin, Zadir and Sheema. They moved swiftly across the space to Olban, their eyes fixed on the seer.

Hestia's breath came in short rasps. She could hear her heart's tumultuous beating.

The seers were transformed. Their honey-coloured skin had paled to a dull sheen like weathered white marble. Long white hair flowed loose and tangled about their shoulders, swept by a breeze Hestia could not feel. Each wore a formless white gown, with no adornment, no pattern, not even a belt about the waist.

Sheema shifted her gaze to Hestia. Her eyes were no longer green. They were black, dark pits of emptiness.

The three ranged themselves behind Olban, their backs to the high windows. They glared at Hestia. She tried, desperately, to move.

Olban gave a high-pitched giggle and lifted a hand. Hestia could no longer move her head.

He would kill her, as he had surely killed Iaton and Tius. She hunted frantically for ways to counteract the seer's commands. The pulse of her heart slowed. She waited for death.

'So terrified.' Olban mocked her in the harsh voice she did not recognise. 'No need to worry, not this time. Your usefulness is not past, gryphon.'

Hestia could not open her beak to retort. She could only blink, furiously.

Olban laughed. 'Such a shame the old Olban can no longer hear and therefore heed your cautious advice.' His voice grew serious. 'You were right, gryphon. The diamond's glow has done it, awakened me at last. How many aeons have I spent slumbering in the depths, waiting for one to brave the darkness and bring me to life?'

Hestia ceased her futile struggle. If not death, then what? Would he change her into the likes of Hiasin, Zadir and Sheema? She would wish for death first.

Olban brought his hands to his chest. 'Not a bad body to inhabit,' he murmured, 'until I can take the young one, the beautiful young one.'

Young one? Varane?

'No, not Varane. Pah, not enough imagination, not enough capacity for both good and evil. The girl. I shall be the girl.'

Ilesse? Hestia's pain forced out a silent, strangled cry.

'I tell you this, gryphon, so you drown in the depths of your anguished helplessness when the time comes.' The evil shaped like Olban sneered. 'She is already partly mine. It will not be long before she comes to me, of her own will.'

He held out his arms to take in the three seers behind him. 'Until then, we have things to do. Sleih and Gryphon to bring to our side, whether they wish it or not, lands to conquer, forests to plunder, seas to foul.'

He gestured sharply, and the three seers stepped silently to the opening. As they went, the colour returned to their skin, hair and clothes. Olban smiled after them, a father indulgent of his children. He followed, brushing close to Hestia's statue-like form. She shivered at the whisper of chilled air flowing between them.

Ilesse, she must reach Ilesse.

She concentrated with a fierce intensity on her talons and claws, willing herself to feel their familiar grip on the stones.

She was free. She could move. The Eternal Chamber spun slowly about her. She staggered. The spinning ceased. She could breathe.

She looked to the king. Iaton's hands trembled as he tried to right himself. Tius strained to lift his head. All around, councillors stirred, mumbling, their eyes unfocused or round with wonder, and fear.

Alive.

Hestia flew to the opening, down the stairway and along the halls, her stomach knotted in dread.

Chapter Sixteen

Where is Gweyr?

The last customer bought the last loaf. Allsop waved them out, locked the door and flipped the sign to Closed.

He deserved a drink at the Boar's Head. Since the morning before, when the master and Conall had left the village, he'd laboured long hours in the bakery keeping the shelves full and the customers happy. Flour encrusted his sticky, sweaty skin. His legs ached from dashing out of the kitchen to the shop–often with hands plastered in dough–whenever the bell jangled.

He had one last task before his drink, however. He must feed and water Chester.

The big black horse greeted him with a wicker and a nuzzle, hopeful of treats.

'No treats. As it is, with no exercise you'll be as fat as I'll be thin before all this is over.'

Chester pressed his nose against Allsop's arm, his deep dark eyes soulfully pleading. Allsop remained hard-hearted.

At home, he filled the tin tub and soaked his aching limbs in the tepid water. He wondered how Master Whittion and Conall were faring. He combed out his wet hair and dressed in clean, fresh trousers and shirt, assuring himself the two travellers couldn't have met with trouble this early.

At the Boar's Head, Barnaby placed Allsop's drink on the bar.

'Surprised to see you here,' he said, wiping an imagined spilled drop with a tea towel. 'Last night Gweyr begged today off because of Whittion and Conall being away on this journey of theirs. Said you needed help in the bakery, badly, and not to expect her until late tonight.'

Allsop's eyebrows went up. 'Gweyr said that?'

'She did.' Barnaby tossed the tea towel over his shoulder. 'Hope she's been useful, because I sorely miss her here, even with the new girl to help.'

Allsop rubbed his chin. 'I'm sorry, Mr Barnaby. I'm confused. I haven't seen Gweyr since before the master and Conall left.'

The innkeeper plumped his big arms on the bar and stared into Allsop's face. 'You mean she's not been with you today?'

'No sir, not one moment.' A fretting niggled at Allsop's mind.

'Where's she been then?'

'Have you seen her at all since yesterday, Mr Barnaby?'

'Since yesterday? No.' Barnaby put his hands together in front of his face and tapped his fingers against each other. 'Haven't seen her since she said about helping you out and then went to see to the mare.'

An awful thought rose in Allsop's mind. His niggling worry worsened. 'Have you seen the mare since yesterday?'

'Millie? Why of course … No, haven't had any need of her and Gweyr's supposed to be looking after her.' Barnaby tilted his head to the side. 'What are you getting at, Allsop? Why the frown?'

'Did she tell you anything about our talk with Master Whittion? Me and Conall and herself, about going off to this … to look for help, advice?'

'No.' Barnaby narrowed his eyes. 'So?'

Allsop's niggle blossomed into fear. 'She was keen to go too, desperate. Of course the master said No, and I thought she'd accepted it wasn't a clever idea. Now–'

'You think she's gone off after them? By herself? With Millie?' The big landlord's ruddy face paled to grey.

'I'm sorry Mr Barnaby. Yes, I do.'

Allsop jumped when the innkeeper slammed his ham fist onto the bar heavily enough for the untasted drink to bounce and spill. 'What's the silly girl gone and done?'

He stared into Allsop's face.

'I'll check on Millie.' Allsop pushed away from the bar and strode through the kitchen and gardens to the stable behind the inn. The mare was missing, together with her saddle and bridle. An empty hook told him the nosebag was gone as well.

***

'Come on, Millie, not much longer before we can rest.'

Gweyr wasn't sure whether she comforted the mare or herself, or both. In any case, it didn't work. Millie's head dropped lower and she snorted, a doleful sound that struck at Gweyr's heart. She swallowed a tired gulp which threatened to become tears.

She pulled Millie to a halt. Long shadows cast by the summer twilight made the quiet, lonely road more frightening. Directly ahead, a white line heralded the rising moon. Not full yet. She had a day or two to find Master Whittion and Conall. By then they should be far enough from Darnel to make it impossible for them to send her home. The thought of Master Whittion's round face and shrewd eyes, and of Conall's strong ruddiness, cheered her. She gently heeled Millie's sides and walked the mare on, peering into trees on either side of the road for somewhere to shelter for the night.

She should have stopped at the last farm they'd passed, sneaked into a barn or shed. She chewed her lip and urged Millie on.

They'd spent the previous night in a barn, after Gweyr's late evening escape from home. She'd counted on people not being about much and assuming, if they saw her, she was exercising Millie–as long as they didn't spot her rolled-up blanket of clothes and food. Or wonder why Da's dark, heavy cloak fell from her shoulders.

She'd ridden through the next village, Dorton, very late, the quiet road lit in patches by candlelight glowing through windows open to the night.

At the edge of the village, two labourers had lurched out of the inn, staggering into Millie's path. The mare shied. The labourers shouted their slurred abuse, threatening to haul Gweyr off her horse and teach her a lesson in manners. Trembling, she had spurred Millie to a canter and ridden into the darkness beyond. She'd been glad she had hidden her hair under Da's old cap. Glad also to be wearing trousers and a shirt, once left behind by a young guest and never reclaimed.

The barn, empty of animals at this time of year, had been a welcome refuge, warm and musty with the scent of hay. She and Millie had crept away in the pre-dawn darkness, following the road through two small villages and a scattering of farms, until, around midday, they had come to a fork.

A signpost pointing southeast said Banna, with no distance marked.

Banna? Gweyr thought she'd heard of it. Vaguely she recalled it was near the edge of the Deep Forest. The road must go more east than south. She hoped.

The northern road was signposted, Flaxburgh. Gweyr didn't want to go to Flaxburgh. Besides, that was the road where Master Whittion had fled the wolves.

She had set Mollie's head towards Banna.

***

'Well?' Barnaby wound the tea towel into a tight knot.

'Gone.' Allsop drew in a deep breath and exhaled. Gweyr, by herself, on the road. In the dark. With wolves about and who knew what else. Words rushed out before he could think about them. 'I'll go after her, Mr Barnaby, straightaway.'

'She's been gone a day and a night.' The innkeeper's fear showed in his widened eyes. 'And where has she gone?'

'A place called Ledrith, I suspect. At least, Ledrith's where Master Whittion's meeting those who might give us answers about what's going on.' A brighter thought came to him. 'Maybe she's already caught up with the master and Conall and they're bringing her home this moment.'

Barnaby's eyes flicked to the open door. Allsop hoped they would see Gweyr–no doubt angry at being thwarted but not eaten by wolves–being hustled through the door by Master Whittion.

The door swung open. A merry group of young people sauntered through.

'Do you know where this Ledrith is?' Barnaby's voice was tense with worry. 'I've never heard of it.'

'Not really–'

'Does anyone know where Ledrith is?' Barnaby appealed to the room at large, which denied all knowledge.

A small crowd of drinkers gathered around Allsop.

'Ledrith? What's Ledrith?'

'Why do you need to know?'

'I believe it's at the edge of the Deep Forest, north and east from here,' Allsop said. 'No more.'

He forgot his tiredness and the hot night. He must leave immediately, follow Gweyr as fast as he could before something happened to her. Millie wouldn't welcome having to move with any speed. Which meant Gweyr's chances of having already caught Master Whittion and Conall, on their younger and faster mounts, were slim, despite what he'd told Gweyr's anxious father.

Barnaby tossed down his tea towel. 'As it seems you're the only one has any idea at all, then you're the one has to go, Allsop.' He strode along the bar to its opening. 'And I'll come with you.'

The crowd watched, murmuring about silly girls and who was going to serve the ale?

It took Allsop a heartbeat to work out what was wrong with this plan. 'How will you come with me, Mr Barnaby?'

'On Millie … Oh.' Barnaby peered at Allsop. 'How will you go after her?'

Allsop gave a tight smile. 'Chester needs exercise.'

'Can't the farrier find us decent horses, like he did for Whittion?'

'I doubt it,' Allsop said. 'It took him two days to find those, and he told the master he was lucky to get them. No, it's Chester or walk.'

'Horses, anyone? Good, fast horses?' Barnaby appealed to the onlookers.

They shook their heads.

'Not many folks have riding horses hereabouts,' a farmer said with a shrug. 'You know that, Barnaby. And what they do have they want to keep for 'emselves.'

The innkeeper turned a weary grimace on Allsop. 'Seems there's no choice.' He grabbed Allsop by the arms and stared again into his face. 'It's you, Allsop, and Chester. Go and save my woolly-headed daughter, and when you bring her home you can watch me whip the hide off her.' The big man sniffed back tears. 'Silly, silly girl.'

Allsop didn't blame him. His heart contracted. Soon he and Chester would also be out there among the bears and wolves.

***

Gweyr slowly rode the darkening track, craving Da's comforting solidity. Had he missed her by now? After a night and a day?

Peering into the trees, her nerves stretched tight at the swift movement of a large animal which slipped between the trunks.

She gulped. One of Master Whittion's wolves? Mollie hadn't taken fright, so it couldn't be a wolf. A stray dog, a big fox?

Much more likely.

She clenched her jaw and rode on until she glimpsed a path, barely wide enough for a horse to walk along. She slid off Millie–which caused the mare to toss her head and quiver her hind quarters in relief–and led her off the road. The path took them to a thin brook which bubbled around a handful of rocks before sliding, more puddle than stream, further into the wood. A willow's long branches offered the perception of sanctuary from the wood's enveloping blackness. Gweyr unsaddled Millie. She let her drink her fill at the brook before attaching the nosebag and hobbling the mare close to the willow.

A crust of bread and cheese served for supper. A small fire gave comfort, although not enough to banish Gweyr's uneasiness at being alone in the dark. She pulled Da's cloak about her and lay down by the glowing ashes. Had this been a good idea? She chewed her lip. Good or not, she had to do it.

For Mam. The thought popped into her anxious head, as welcome and warm as one of Mam's cuddles. Her mother would have understood Gweyr's need. She scrunched her silver chain in her fist, pushing it against her throat, and let soft tears fall onto the cloak. Utter tiredness eventually eased her into an uneasy sleep.

***

Allsop left Barnaby to his fears and ran home. He stuffed a change of clothing into a bag, together with the wrapped remains of a loaf, a block of cheese and a handful of last year's apples. He emptied his money tin into a leather wallet and tied it around his waist with a frustrated sigh at its lightness. The tinderbox on the kitchen shelf went into the bag as well.

He paused in the doorway of his cottage, the bag at his feet, thinking of what else he would need. His eyes fell on his cloak, unused since the warm weather had arrived.

He'd need that, for sleeping in if nothing else.

He pulled on his strongest boots, took the cloak from its peg, clamped his wide-brimmed hat onto his head and hurried out into the quiet road.

Dusk had fallen and lantern light flowing from his neighbours' windows lit Allsop's way to the bakery stable. Later, there would be a waxing moon, not far from being full.

The wizards would meet at the full moon.

The thought made him quicken his steps.

Chapter Seventeen

The chase

Chester, comfortable in his fresh-smelling stall, turned sleepy eyes on Allsop's late arrival. And when his urgency made sausages of his clumsy fingers while he tightened cinches and ensured the saddle was secure, the horse twitched and side-stepped and nipped at his arm.

After an age and much muttering, Allsop brought Chester into the lane behind the bakery. He scrambled awkwardly onto his wide back. Chester froze.

'Come on, boy, please,' Allsop pleaded. 'Your friend Gweyr's in trouble and it's up to us to save her.'

The plea left Chester unmoved. Allsop kicked his heels firmly against the solid flanks. Chester jerked into an ambling gait which nearly unseated his rider, wandered to the end of the lane, and stopped. Allsop kicked a little harder. Chester walked a short way, and stopped.

They travelled this way through the village and into the countryside. Allsop grumbled angrily. Chester flicked his tail. At last the horse decided he might as well enjoy being outside, despite it being night. He lurched into a trot and kept on.

Allsop bounced along, his thoughts as uncomfortable as his rapidly bruising backside.

Where was he supposed to be going and how long would it be before–if–he caught Gweyr? She had a full day and much of two nights' start on him, and Chester was no race horse.

By the time they passed through sleeping Dorton, Chester's gait had steadied and he held his head high. He might possibly be enjoying himself. As long as Chester was willing, Allsop would keep riding, despite his growing misery at this night time ride among haunted shadows cast by looming trees. He had to catch Gweyr.

***

Gweyr shivered inside her cloak. She had woken to a dawn dampened by misty rain. She grimaced at the soggy ashes of her fire. No point trying to rekindle it. Bread and cold sausage borrowed from the Boar's Head pantry made do for breakfast, after which she joined Millie in drinking from the brook. She filled her water bottle, saddled the mare and made her way along the path to the road.

She peered both ways. The wet, glistening track was empty. Shivering harder, she mounted Millie and trotted on.

***

A thin dawn rain made Allsop grateful he'd remembered his cloak. He and Chester had rested for a short time in the darkest hours of the night, soon after passing a fork in the road signposted Flaxburgh or Banna.

He had not hesitated long before taking the Banna road. Both eventually reached the edge of the Deep Forest, but he trusted Gweyr wouldn't know this and would ignore the northward Flaxburgh road.

When he had dismounted, his leg muscles trembled like jelly. His thighs screamed like a knife had repeatedly plunged into them. He dozed, chilled and worried, for an hour before clambering once more onto stolid Chester. He couldn't help compare himself to the bags of flour Conall hefted with such ease.

The drizzling mist gathered strength from the new day. Rain fell in solid straight drops. Allsop tugged his hat lower and hunched into his cloak. He kicked gently at Chester's sides.

'Come on, old fella, let's speed things up, see if we can catch them today.'

Chester tossed his head and stretched into a canter. Allsop clutched the pommel. He groaned at the pain and the sharp sting of water against his face.

***

A chill wind buffeted heavy rain against Gweyr's face. She tucked as much of her hair as possible under her cap, wrapped Da's cloak more tightly about her and prayed she'd soon reach Banna. It wasn't all about the cold and wet. She would be glad to arrive somewhere where life and movement existed. The eerie quiet of the countryside she rode through unsettled her. Where were the sheep and cows? Here and there she spied a farmer ploughing, urging his great horses forward in the driving rain. They were few.

About mid-morning three wagons piled high with tables, bedding, chairs, baskets of pots and plates, and bulging sacks rumbled towards her. Cows and goats were tethered to the wagons.

Gweyr pulled Millie to a halt on the muddy verge. The first two wagons passed. Men, women and children trudged by their sides, heads down against the rain. They paid her no more attention than they did the dripping trees.

A man in a long coat and a big hat guided two oxen pulling the third wagon. A woman in a hooded cloak marched alongside.

'Hello!' Gweyr called through chattering teeth.

The man frowned at her through the wet. Water trickled from his hat and coat.

'Have you come from Banna?' Gweyr shouted into the blustering wind.

The man glanced at the woman, tipped his head towards Gweyr and urged the oxen on.

The woman hugged her cloak about her and stepped to Gweyr. When she looked Gweyr up and down from within her hood, Gweyr's chest tightened, sensing the woman's desperate fear and aching loss.

'What are you doing out on the road by yourself?' The woman threw out a hand. 'In this …'

'Travelling to Ledrith.' Gweyr squirmed under her frowning gaze. 'Which I hope is past Banna.'

'Banna? Ledrith?' The woman shook her head. 'We're leaving Banna, going west, as far from those packs of savage wolves as we can.'

'There are wolves in Banna too?' A chill tingled Gweyr's spine.

'Not when we left, but they came near in the night, ravaging farms 'round about. Our sheep …' Her lips trembled. 'Only evil ever comes out of Arneithe, that cursed place, and evil is what they brought.'

'I'm so sorry.' The woman's pain snaked around Gweyr's heart as sharp as if it was her own. 'There are wolves on the road to Flaxburgh too,' she said.

'Yes.' The woman scowled. 'It's worse in the north and rumour says more evil is to come from there. It's why we're leaving while we can. Others too.' She waved ahead to where the oxen plodded on before she turned back to Gweyr. 'I'd go straight back where you come from if I was you.'

'I can't.' Gweyr clutched her silver chain, reassured by her memory of seeing it around Mam's neck. She'd come this far. Her restless need to move on might be tempered by wind, rain and fright about wolves, yet it still drove her.

'Then good luck to you.' The woman tugged her hood further forward and walked to the wagon, head bent against the wind and rain.

Gweyr watched her for a while. Such terrible tragedy to force people from their homes. She recalled Master Whittion's description of the slaughter of the animals and gulped down bile rising in her throat.

Shivering harder, she urged Millie to a reluctant canter. She hoped she wouldn't have to rely on the mare to save her from wolves. It might be a good idea after all to hurry along, catch up with Master Whittion and Conall sooner than she planned.

'It'll be fine,' she said aloud. She ignored the prickling unease which chilled her far more than the water running down her neck.

***

Gweyr hunched astride Millie, gazing about. Empty stalls, as sparse as an old man's teeth, squatted under wooden awnings in Banna's market square. Shop doors were closed, no goods on display outside. Two men pushing a barrow hurried along a street leading from the square. A woman in a long cape and carrying a basket walked quickly along another street. She glanced over her shoulder from time to time as if expecting to be attacked in the middle of the day, in the centre of the village.

A gust of cold wind lifted Gweyr's hat. She grabbed it, tugged it down hard. Wet curls flew about her streaming face. She squinted through the rain. An inn, across the square. If it was open, she could ask directions to Ledrith, eat, and dry herself before moving on.

She tied Millie to a rail above a water trough. 'Won't be long,' she said to the mare and squelched to the closed inn door. It opened when she shoved against it, squeaking a protest. The wind banged it shut behind her. Inside, two men sat on stools by the bar staring into their drinks. Their coats dripped water to the floor's wooden boards.

'Ledrith?' The publican eyed Gweyr's trousers and man's shirt with a suspicious frown. 'Why?'

'Why what?' The question took her by surprise.

'Why do you want to go to Ledrith? Dangerous out there

for a young woman on her own. At any time and 'specially now with these wolves about.' The man folded his arms across his thick chest and frowned harder. He reminded Gweyr of Da. Her cheeks warmed.

'No, no, you misunderstand. I don't want to go there,' she lied. 'It's, it's … well … I've heard stories about wolves and I wondered how far it is and which direction, and am I safe here in Banna?' She crumpled her wet cap in her hands and prayed she wasn't flushing harder.

The publican uncrossed his arms and set both elbows on the bar, fists under his chin. He fixed his dark eyes on Gweyr. 'That right?'

'Yes.'

'Well,' the publican said slowly, 'I can tell you it's about half a day's ride north.' He leaned back, re-crossing his arms. 'As for being safe here … surprised you didn't meet some of our folk who've up and left, that's how safe they think it is.' He waved at his near-empty bar. 'Those of us still here hope they jumped too soon. We fervently hope the wolves kept going, past Ledrith, up to the high plains where someone else can deal with 'em.'

'Thank you.' Gweyr sensed more questions bubbling in the man's head, like who was she and where from and why was she in Banna? She backed away, mumbling, 'Must be on my way, goodbye. Thank you.'

The publican watched her leave, lips pursed.

Gweyr rested her hand on Millie's neck. The mare lowered her head, eyes closed against the gusting wind. The rain had eased, a little.

'Well,' Gweyr said. Millie bumped Gweyr's arm with her long nose. 'Let's hope it's like the man said and the wolves have gone elsewhere.' She hoisted herself into the wet saddle. 'And let's hope this rain stops and we can dry out.'

***

Thick black mud from the road coated Chester's legs. Allsop's trousers clung, cold and clammy as old dough, to his chilled legs. He wriggled in the saddle, trying to ease the pain in his backside. He and Chester had ridden hard all day and both needed drinks, food and rest. And to dry out.

He drew the horse to a halt outside an inn at the edge of Banna's market. The rain had stopped, although a wet wind suggested it hadn't entirely given up. He gazed around at the empty market square, the deserted streets. Seems the refugees he'd passed on the road weren't the only ones who'd sought safety further west.

He tied Chester to the railing and hobbled on stiff, sore legs into the inn, relieved it was open. A musty silence greeted him.

The sullen publican handed over a mug of brown beer in response to Allsop's request for a drink. He counted out coins and asked, 'I don't suppose you could tell me how far it is to Ledrith and how I get there?'

'Ledrith again?' The man crossed his arms. 'Why does everyone suddenly want to go to Ledrith which, by the way, is an untidy pile of ramshackle woodsmen cottages, if you could call 'em cottages. Hovels more like.'

Allsop's heartbeat quickened. Gweyr had been here.

'Was it a young girl, long curly dark hair, asking about Ledrith?'

'It was. 'bout dinner time. Dressed in boys' clothes, wet as a drowned kitten. Didn't stay to dry off.'

Boys' clothes. Sensible idea.

'Dinner time?' He wasn't long behind her. 'Where is this Ledrith, please?'

'She's bent on going there, hey?'

'She is,' Allsop said. 'And I need to catch her and take her home to her father before she gets herself into trouble.'

'Trouble like eaten by wolves.' The publican propped his elbows on the bar, fists to his chin. 'You know they've rampaged through the countryside round here these last couple of days?'

'No.' Allsop's urgency rose several notches.

'People terrified they'll be here in Banna itself next.' He scowled along the empty bar. 'Fleeing like mice from cats.'

Gweyr must have seen the refugees, she must know about the wolves. Yet she'd ridden on. Why would she do that?

The publican stroked his chin. 'I told your friend it was north of here, about a half day's ride. Which it is.'

Allsop pushed his coins across the bar, said, 'Thank you,' and strode to the door.

'Good luck,' the publican called. 'Let's hope those wolves kept going!'

Chapter Eighteen

Ancient Gryphon tales

Ilesse jumped up at the sight of Hestia hurtling, wings spread, through the cavern's curtain. She made an unsuccessful grab for *The Language of the Ancient Sleih* text–hunted down in the repository and studied hard–which fell from her lap.

'You're here!' Hestia cried.

'Yes, yes, I'm here, as you can see. What's happening? Are we being attacked?'

Her words were muffled against velvet feathers as Hestia wrapped her in her wings. The gryphon's body trembled. Ilesse let herself be held for a short time before pulling gently away.

'What's wrong? What's happened?'

'Olban.' Hestia's voice shook. 'A terrible evil has taken him over. He's transformed. A monster …'

Olban? Ilesse's spine tingled. Whispers filled her mind. The desires of her heart fulfilled if she heeded the seer's welcoming whispers … True wisdom, now, all knowledge granted her.

No. What were these awful whispers? They muddled her mind, upset her with their strangeness. Why did they come to her? Was she going mad?

'I thought he had killed the councillors, and Iaton and Tius too.' Strain showed in Hestia's shrill voice. 'And those three, Sheema and the others who went into the tunnels with him, they too are transformed. Slaves, unthinking slaves.' She stepped back, keeping the tips of her wings on Ilesse's shoulders.

'Yes.' Ilesse forced herself to return the gryphon's worried gaze. The whispers faded. 'Of course!' She moved away from Hestia's touch, struggling with her thoughts. 'The fall from the bridge, then to re-appear. How else could he have done that?' She clasped her hands in front of her mouth, mostly in horror at what Olban had become.

Partly because something deep inside her wanted to rejoice. No!

The curtain parted. Ilesse's mouth fell open. She bowed her head. 'Sire, Lord Tius, what …?'

'We needed to assure ourselves of your safety, Ilesse,' King Iaton said.

'The councillors?' Hestia tilted her head, her beak held open.

'They are recovered, at least in their bodies. I've sent them into the caverns to warn all not to approach Olban, or his followers.' Lord Tius bobbed his eagle head.

'And to gather the strongest in the ways of magic,' King Iaton said. 'I want the entrances to the caverns secure against anything which might come to us from underground by the end of this day. Doors and bolts will do us no good.'

'Olban and those he has enslaved?' Hestia said. 'They must be caught, imprisoned.'

'How?' Lord Tius said.

A spark of pleasure lit within Ilesse. She clamped her lips together to save them betraying her dreadful unwelcome emotions.

'Besides'–Lord Tius lifted his wings–'I suspect they are no longer in the caverns. They will have gone into the depths from where the evil which has possessed Olban–poor Olban–arose.'

A silence came over the room.

'But, if I may ask,' Ilesse said, 'why have you come here, my lords?'

Hestia looked from the king to Lord Tius and then to Ilesse.

'Olban,' she said, 'or rather what is now Olban, wants you. For the talent within you.'

All she wished for. Yes, Olban wanted her. Ilesse's heart fluttered between yearning and loathing.

'He will not have me.' She forced the words out, glad to hear them ring true.

'He will not.' The king smiled a tense smile.

Lord Tius peered into Ilesse's flushed face. 'Hmm.' He drew back, turned his gaze to Hestia. 'There are things the 'prentice seer should know. Don't you agree?'

Hestia shook out her wings, her calm restored.

'Come,' she said. 'Let's find somewhere we can talk.' Her talons tapped on the stone floor as she led them out of the cavern to a sitting room nearby.

Lord Tius settled himself on a thick rug near to the fire pit and beckoned with a wing for Ilesse to make herself comfortable on a cushion nearby.

King Iaton eased into a chair. He nodded at Lord Tius. 'My friend, will you tell us what you know, or believe, happened here today?'

'Is happening, Iaton. Is happening.' Lord Tius shifted on the pelt. 'Again.'

'How could we have forgotten,' Hestia whispered. Her eyes clouded.

Forgotten. Ha! Foolish Sleih, foolish Gryphon. Too late to remember now.

What disdainful thoughts were these? Where did they come from? Ilesse wriggled into the cushion. It may well have been made of stone for all the comfort it gave. Her legs ached, her arms leaden. Her mind, however, buzzed.

She concentrated on Lord Tius who said, 'The tale I tell is the most obscure of the stories of how the Sleih and Gryphon came to dwell in the High Alps of Asfarlon.'

'A tale known only to a few older Gryphon,' Hestia said,

'passed down by word of mouth.'

Lord Tius lifted a wing. 'My own belief is the truth was deliberately distorted so we could forget the horrors of those days and little Sleih and young gryphons could sleep easy.'

Sleepless little ones? Serves them right, the brats. What good are they?

Ilesse pressed a hand to her mouth, her eyes widening in shock. She recalled the voice urging her to throw down the young girl as they fled from the white attack. This wasn't her. She didn't think like this. Who was saying this to her?

'Do you suspect, Tius,' Hestia said, 'the tale is written down after all, in the missing pages of the ancient text I gave Olban?'

And fervently wished she hadn't.

Ilesse frantically fought the giggle which rose in her throat. She coughed.

'What horrors, Lord Tius?' she asked, battling the urge to rejoice in whatever horror the gryphon might be persuaded to tell. Her gut churned. She must talk to Hestia, try to make sense of these awful thoughts and feelings.

'Let me tell it from the beginning, as I know it.' Lord Tius closed his wings about his lion body and settled on his haunches. 'The common story is that the Gryphon tempted the Sleih to the High Alps to benefit from their artisan skills, offering them the learning of magic in return.'

Such a sweet tale.

The voice in Ilesse's head resonated with amused sarcasm. She took a deep breath, glanced sideways at Hestia, who remained intent on the storyteller.

'I wish it was that simple.' Lord Tius' sigh ruffled his throat feathers. 'The truth, however, starts well before then, with the flight of the Gryphon from their home in the Deep Forest of Arneithe.' He gazed through the south facing opening in the cavern wall. 'Our flight from a dread evil which maddened the Forest creatures who fought each other to the death. They destroyed the trees too, which revenged themselves.'

'The trees bent their boughs to the ground to snatch the creatures up and dash them down,' Hestia said bluntly. 'They threw nests and chicks from their branches to leave them dying.'

Useless birds. Who needs birds?

Ilesse's blood tingled. She tried to close her ears and mind to the dreadful voice. She fought with herself to not enjoy the images Hestia's words conjured. Her head whirled in horror. She swallowed and forced herself to follow Lord Tius' gaze.

Outside, a deep blue summer sky told of a bright, hot day. The Alps rose sharply, white tips shining in the clear air. Beautiful, so beautiful–Ilesse repeated the phrase to herself like a mantra, wanting the beauty to replace the visions of death and destruction.

Beautiful like you, my queen.

She rubbed at one ear, trying to dislodge the silken tones. Nausea roiled in her stomach. She must talk to Hestia. Not now, not in this company.

They will be afraid.

She clamped her bottom lip between her teeth and willed the voice to leave her. She stared at Hestia.

'What did the Gryphon do?' she asked. 'Did they defeat this madness?'

Not madness, my queen. Power through knowledge.

Lord Tius answered. 'We searched our spells and sorcery with deep diligence. Finally, it is said, we could force the evil to manifest itself as a towering cloud of stinking, oily ash.'

Stinking, oily ash. Ilesse drew in a breath. The night she followed Olban–

Yes, my beauty. Yes. You see, free once more.

The evil was here? In this room? Her heart pounded harder. She should warn the king, tell Hestia ...

They will not believe you. They will tell you it is more dreams.

Her pounding heart slowed. Dreams. Imaginings. She was

overwrought from the attack, from her fear for Varane, from the night of Olban's fall into the chasm. Her mind playing tricks. She shouldn't cry false alarms.

Hestia took up the tale. 'By then this evil had laid waste to Arneithe. The Gryphon had no choice. They were forced to flee.' She fell silent, her eyes half-lidded, her wings tight against her body. The tip of her tail twitched.

Ilesse sensed her hurt and grief at this mindless destruction. She wanted to share it, could not. The icy band wrapped itself around her chest. A shameful need to giggle rose. She sucked in a shallow breath, pressing a hand to her ribs as if she could physically force the chilling grip to loosen.

No, no. She was not glad of the desolation of Arneithe. Her eyes sought the beauty of the Alps beyond the window, her mind clinging to the pristine sight. The iciness melted in a rush of warmth. She took a deep, quivering breath.

'Are you well, Ilesse?' Hestia's question was sharp.

'I don't know.' Ilesse's mouth quivered. 'Such desolation. The pain of the gryphons must have been terrible.'

Lord Tius lifted his beak. 'Before the gryphons fled, they undertook one final act, desperately hoping it would serve as a protection into the future.'

'Which was?' King Iaton said.

'At the edge of the Forest, near the oceans, they created a grove in a secret valley shielded by the strongest enchantments.' He paused. 'This sacred place can be known only to our kind, or to those whom gryphons deem true friends. And then they flew west, to the High Alps.'

'And the evil? What happened to the evil?' King Iaton pressed his hands together.

Lord Tius ruffled his wings. 'We brought it with us, old friend,' he said.

Chapter Nineteen

Besieged

'Father, I've found you at last!'

Varane stumbled through the cavern opening, brandishing Celeste. His flushed face dripped with sweat.

A sudden revulsion roiled in Ilesse's gut at the sight of the sword. She pressed her hand to her mouth. The revulsion passed, leaving her wondering. Why? She had seen, had handled, Celeste many times in the past.

King Iaton jumped from his chair. He stared at his dishevelled son.

'The caverns are under siege!' Varane cried. 'Wolves, bears, all kinds of nameless monsters gather at every opening into the mountains! We are at war.'

My beauties.

Ilesse scrambled from the cushion, pushing down the unwanted voice. She ran with the others into the passageway.

***

Monstrous white creatures swarmed over the meadow and crushed against the gates into the caverns. Ilesse stared down from a high ledge, Hestia beside her. Bears with teeth to their chests paced beneath the cliff, mouths open in red snarls. Wolves with lumps on their backs which slid beneath their skin leaped in a mass of frenzied yellow-fanged howling. Other hideous creatures crowded among them. Grossly misshapen reptiles, glowing with shiny scales; giant cats with twisted tails and flexing massive taloned pads; and wizened beings on two legs with overgrown heads and bulbous eyes scrambling between the big beasts' legs and ducking from flicking tails.

Their white coats and skins and scales shone in the summer sun like polished pearls–or diamonds, the thought came to Ilesse. The roaring, snarling and howling pierced her brain. She wanted to clamp her hands to her ears and shut her eyes tight. The pulse in her neck throbbed.

Hestia spread her wings, shook them out and settled them against her body.

'We must find the text, Ilesse. The one I gave Olban. And, if we can, the missing pages. For there, I suspect, lies the means to their'–she snapped her eagle beak–'defeat. And whatever it is that has overtaken Olban.'

Defeat? My beautiful white creatures slain? Their blood staining the grass of the fields, reddening the ice of the glacier?

Ilesse's heart thumped in response to the melancholic appeal worming through her brain. She glared at Hestia, hating her, wanting to tear at her eyes, to rip her wings from her body. Her lips curled in a snarl …

'Ilesse?' Hestia stepped away. Her wings rose in alarm. 'What is it?'

Ilesse staggered as if she'd been punched. She reached out a hand to steady herself against the rocky wall. She wanted to vomit.

'Hestia, help me!'

Chapter Twenty

Meeting a myth

With Banna well behind him, Allsop hoped to overtake Gweyr before the day ended. He glanced at the sky. Black clouds broiled above the fields ahead, tossed by a wet wind. Drops of heavy rain fell, thickening to a steady, blown gush of water. His mind went briefly to his cottage, his chair and the book of fairytales he had not had a chance to re-read. He held the image in his mind–his gift to himself once he'd dragged Gweyr home for the whipping her father promised. Allsop might watch after all. He clenched his jaw and urged Chester into the storm.

Chester tossed his head and cantered forward. The big horse must have decided he enjoyed adventures after all, preferring to carry one rider, even in rain and wind, over the dreary drudgery of hauling wagonloads of flour. At times, he fair galloped along like he had wings.

Somewhere to the left of the muddy track, beyond blurred images of fenced and hedged fields and a sparse scattering of farmhouses, the sun neared the horizon. The darkness of twilight added to the grey of heavy rain. A cold wind roared across the empty fields. It whipped the hedges, sent Chester's mane flying. Allsop held tight to his hat with one hand, the other clinging to black-wet reins.

He squinted into the rain. A solitary horse and rider showed ahead. They rode north, like himself. Could it be Millie and

Gweyr? The rider travelled slowly, head bent. The horse's head drooped too, battling the squalling wetness. The sight screamed weariness. Allsop's heart softened. He forgot about whippings.

Chester whinnied and broke into a gallop, eager to catch the rider and horse.

'Gweyr!' He let Chester have his head. 'Gweyr! It's me, Allsop! Wait!'

***

Gweyr lifted her head at the shout behind her.

Allsop? The cowardly baker had come looking for her? Her frightened weariness fled at the thought of a friendly face.

She tugged at the reins to bring Millie about, wet curls tumbling from under her cap. Millie pulled up short, tossing her head and stepping sideways.

A pit opened in Gweyr's stomach.

She hauled Millie around, sank low in the saddle and kicked her into a gallop.

***

Allsop waved. 'No, Gweyr, it's me, Allsop. Stop!'

Gweyr rode faster, spurring Millie to a pace Allsop thought impossible for the exhausted mare in the churning mud, the howling wind and pouring rain.

Chaos fell on Allsop and Chester.

Four long brown shapes came from behind. They raced in the wet fields, two on each side of the glistening track.

Chester whinnied and reared. Unbalanced, Allsop swayed to the side. He clutched the slippery pommel, heaved himself upright.

Two long faces with red, panting tongues twisted to face him. The other wolves loped past their fellows, hunting Gweyr and Millie.

***

Gweyr risked a backward glance. Two wolves slowed, intent on Allsop and Chester. The others sped past them, racing towards her.

Adrenaline pulsed through her body. She crouched lower.

Millie kept her head straight, mane flying, galloping for her life. Mud showered the mare's legs, she stumbled, straightened, galloped on.

***

Allsop's thudding heart battered his ribcage. His arms and legs trembled, as watery as the air around him.

They would all die, left as a chewed pile of torn flesh, bloodied bones and scraps of flesh rotting in the mire of the track.

The chaos worsened.

A giant pair of twilight blue wings plummeted out of the storm. Massive taloned feet raked one wolf's side.

It shrieked and tore across the soggy fields.

The winged creature attacked a second time. It ripped the wolf's skull with its lethal beak, as if–Allsop had time to wonder as he clutched Chester's pommel–it was brittle as an egg. The wolf crumpled to the dirt, blood pooling from its wounds.

Allsop searched for its mate through the shrieking wind. Dead too, brought down by another of the winged creatures. This one–Allsop gaped–carried a gold-skinned person with flowing black hair.

***

Millie galloped on. Wolves loped either side, veering inwards to cut off her path. Gweyr's head lay on the mare's neck, desperately urging her forward, knowing the floundering Millie had no chance of outpacing wolves.

Wild shrieks of frustrated pain rang loud. Gweyr dared a glance to the side. She gasped. She glanced the other way.

Huge birdlike creatures swooped on the wolves.

Millie kept on, panic driving her, head tossing wildly.

The wolves leaped, snarled. Their teeth snapped at the strange birds. The birds swooped, talons outstretched. Howls of agony. Another swoop. The howls died.

Silence, except for the splashing of horses' hooves through churned up puddles.

***

Chester kept up his lunging gallop to Millie and Gweyr. Allsop peered up. The two strange creatures parted, flying over the fields. Their giant wings lifted and fell in a steady rhythm to disappear into the sheeting rain.

Millie slowed, stopped. Her head drooped to the ground, her sides heaved. As Allsop drew near he winced at the mare's wide, wild eyes. Gweyr had fallen from the horse, landing heavily in the mud. She struggled to her feet, hands on knees, gulping air. Her hair fell forward in stringy, wet strands.

'Gweyr, are you all right?' Allsop tumbled off Chester. The big horse trembled and snorted, stretching his neck to Millie. He breathed softly into her nostrils. Millie shied, stamped a hoof and grew quieter.

Gweyr screamed. 'Look out!'

More wolves? Allsop ducked and peered up to where Gweyr pointed.

Not wolves.

The giant birdlike creatures flew over them, descending rapidly to settle lightly on the track.

Gweyr clutched at the chain around her neck, eyes wide, mouth hanging open.

Hysterical laughter bubbled up Allsop's throat.

Chapter Twenty One

A conclave of wizards

Flickering light cast dancing shadows on the tunnel's walls. Gweyr, with Millie on a rein behind her, turned a corner and fell against Chester's rump. Allsop, leading the horse, had stopped behind the gryphon who had halted, a wing half-raised in a warning for silence. The gryphon! Ashta. She had told them her name was Ashta.

When the birdlike creatures landed on the track ahead of them, Chester and Millie had tossed their manes and whickered. Not a frightened whicker. To Gweyr's ears it sounded like a greeting, maybe a thank you. She had stared hard, mouth open.

Allsop also stared. '…rumours of great-winged beasts flying over the high plains,' he muttered, apparently repeating something he had heard. 'Bigger than horses, with tawny bodies and wings of many hues.'

'What?' Gweyr had pressed a hand to comfort the stitch in her side. She couldn't take her eyes off the creatures.

'Gryphons,' Allsop panted. 'They're gryphons.'

Gweyr's eyebrows shot up. She gulped in great breaths, the stitch forgotten. 'So the person riding one–'

'–must be a … Sleih.' Allsop's voice broke on the word Sleih. Then he was laughing, hysterically. A mad person.

Gweyr had joined in, her fright from the wolves cartwheeling to joy at meeting these mythical beings. All Mam's stories about magical flying beasts whirled in her head. It was like falling across an old, dear friend, someone whom you thought you would never see again and then, suddenly, they're there. Here in the shadowy tunnel, she sensed Mam beside her, could feel her warm breath on her hair, the soft touch of a hand on her shoulder, delighting in this … reunion?

'Come and see.' Allsop looked around to whisper past Chester, who pricked his ears.

Gweyr led Millie forward. A murmur of voices came to her. Warm yellow light glowed through a wide opening beyond the gryphon. This wondrous creature stood close against the wall, the colour of her feathers merging into the wavering shadows. Gweyr gazed past her, through the tunnel opening at a brightly lit scene which sent her already over-excited heart pumping harder.

Wizards. They had found the conclave. About half were dressed in normal clothes. Gweyr found this disappointing. Perhaps they didn't like to show the rest of the world they were wizards. Like Master Whittion had hidden his own wizardry.

The remainder wore dark capes embroidered with colourful designs, and tall hats over hair falling to their shoulders. Gweyr grinned. Proper wizards. Her grin widened at the sight of a small green dragon draped in a polished leather harness. It nestled against the rocky wall, eyes closed in sleep. Two horses nearby side-stepped and tossed their heads each time a smoky breath issued from the dragon's nostrils.

At the centre of the cave, a man on a low, flat rock held his arms out to silence the gathering. Gweyr's eyes brightened. A true wizard of her imaginings: straight silver hair flowing from beneath a tall hat, a short silver beard below a prominent nose and heavy-lidded eyes shaped like half moons which peered from under thick, black eyebrows. The light of the cavern shone on skin the colour of rich honey. In one wrinkled hand the wizard held a white staff.

'Wizards, welcome to our conclave,' he said. 'We are here

because danger threatens our communities. We have heard of or seen for ourselves the destruction of the wolves and bears pouring from Arneithe, devouring all in their path as they race northwards. They ravage our farms, forcing our people to flee south, or west, taking with them what remains.' He stared at someone in the crowd whom Gweyr thought might be Master Whittion from the familiar hat. 'We hear reports of curious scenes, like lightning which goes up instead of down. And'–he shifted his stare a fraction to someone by the master's side–'creatures whom many dismiss as myths are said to appear in our skies.'

Allsop grinned at Gweyr. She put a hand to her mouth to cover a giggle. A murmuring arose from the wizards, apparently in agreement at this summary of what was happening.

The tall wizard lightly banged his staff on the flat stone and silence fell.

'Once, long ago,' he said, 'a dread evil came to these lands. An evil against which no army could prevail. An evil which drove our Sleih cousins into the icy wilds of the mountains of Asfarlon, there to disappear forever from the sight of the Madach.'

Gweyr exchanged another look with Allsop. This wizard at least, considered the Sleih to be real–or real once upon a time. A voice from the gathering called out.

'Zoledore! Are you saying this is the same evil power come forth? The power of the ancient legends, for surely legends are what we are talking about?'

'Legends, Rebar?' Zoledore's great eyebrows came together. He lifted his white staff and struck it hard on the rock.

Gweyr jumped. This Rebar–she recalled he was Master Whittion's friend–had angered the old wizard.

'Yes, legends,' Rebar said calmly. 'Next you will be telling us the Sleih vanished into the High Alps of Asfarlon on the backs of winged lions with the heads of eagles.'

Soft laughter rose from the gathering, stifled when Zoledore raised the white staff once more.

Gweyr felt rather than saw Ashta pad lightly out of the tunnel and into the cavern.

'Yet that is precisely what happened,' she said, and stretched her wings to confirm their existence.

***

Allsop stepped into the cavern as the hush which followed the gryphon's entrance broke like a storm wave upon a cliff. A clamour of exclamations and the neighing of worried horses greeted him. The dragon briefly raised an eyelid, puffed a breath of white smoke and returned to sleep.

Master Whittion and Conall stood beside a tall man with short dark hair and a spiky beard, both threaded with silver. The deep lines which surrounded his eyes suggested he spent every day with worrisome thoughts. He must be Rebar, but the calm with which he had responded to Zoledore had deserted him. Along with the master and Conall, he stared, open-mouthed.

Gweyr giggled and waved. 'Conall, Master Whittion, come and meet our friend, Ashta.'

Conall rushed forward, eyes like saucers, hands fluttering at the end of waving arms. Zoledore brushed past him, shouldered aside Gweyr and Allsop and stood, straight and tall, before Ashta. Their eyes were on a level–two sets of the greenest eyes Allsop had seen.

'Lady Gryphon,' the wizard said solemnly. 'I am Zoledore, the senior of these wizards assembled here. I bid you welcome.' He bowed from the waist, straightening to continue staring into Ashta's feathered face. His long fingers twitched as if he wanted to stroke those feathers, to make sure the gryphon was real.

Allsop rubbed his eyes. Ashta's feathers had changed from their previous shadowy grey, invisible in the twilight outside and in the tunnel, to glow yellow in the warm light of the cave.

'Thank you for your welcome, Wizard Zoledore,' she said. 'I am not Lady Gryphon, however. I am Ashta the Hunter, leader of the Gryphon and Sleih hunters who serve Tius Lord Gryphon and Iaton King of the Sleih, rulers of the High Alps of Asfarlon.'

The exclamations had quieted to listen to the exchange of greetings. Now they rose in a mixture of surprise and disbelief.

'Gweyr, Allsop.' Conall's eyes flicked to Ashta. 'How come you're here and how come you're with a … with a …'

'A gryphon, Conall.' Allsop grinned.

'Ashta, and a Sleih hunter riding another gryphon, saved me and Allsop and Millie and Chester from wolves,' Gweyr said. 'Ashta wanted to know what we were doing on a lonely track too close to the Deep Forest with night coming on. We told her about the conclave and she brought us here.'

'Wolves?' Master Whittion shuddered.

'Simply brought you here?' Zoledore raised a dark eyebrow at Ashta. 'To our secret meeting place, in this well-hidden cavern?'

Ashta lifted her beak. 'It's no secret, Zoledore, where the wizards of the high plains meet,' she said politely. 'We came to Ledrith as these two Madach purposed. From there it was child's play to follow your footsteps and hoof prints to the cavern entrance.' She lifted a wing and gestured at the sleeping dragon. 'Dragon scent confirmed we were in the right place.'

Allsop wanted to tell Master Whittion to close his mouth. He did anyway, at least briefly, when he asked, 'Sleih? Did you say Sleih? Did'–he tilted his head at Ashta –'she, the gryphon, say Sleih?'

'It is true, even the wizards have forgotten us.' Ashta's neck feathers rose and fell.

'No, no, Lady Ashta.' Zoledore lifted his staff and set it down with a soft thud. 'Some of us'–he swept a narrow-eyed look at Whittion and Rebar–'have kept faith in the ancient stories. I welcome you with all my heart as we are in dire need of your help.'

'We are on the same mission, Wizard Zoledore.' Ashta lifted her tail. 'An alliance will bring strength.'

Chapter Twenty Two

'My beauties'

'I knew he lied.'

Hestia drew the crumbling text carefully from the shelf with her wingtips. She laid it on Olban's workbench. Her heart ached, knowing she would never again stand beside her friend studying Old Sleih texts, working out the translations, divining their hidden meanings and thinking through which jewels would best work in which cases. Carefree days, gone. All her own fault.

'Of course you knew,' Ilesse said softly. 'And he didn't care, because that … that thing … isn't Olban.' She threw her braid over her shoulder and reached out a finger to lightly touch the faded script, tracing the letters across the stained page. Her eyes lifted, vacantly roaming the gem-filled shelves.

'Ilesse?' Hestia stretched her wing to touch the 'prentice seer's shoulder.

Ilesse started, drew in a breath. 'Never leave this book with me. Promise?' She turned a pale face to Hestia, her eyes focused, and frightened. 'It speaks to me in ways it shouldn't.'

The ache in Hestia's heart deepened. All her fault. Olban, Ilesse, the hordes baying below the caverns. Meddling old fool, she should have known better.

'You couldn't know.' Ilesse–a normal Ilesse–lifted her arms to wrap them around Hestia's neck, burying her head in the feathers. 'You must not blame yourself.' Her muffled voice quivered. 'If there is any blame to be had, blame me for bringing the book to you. Or blame Varane for falling over it.'

'Thank you for your thoughts.' Hestia sighed. 'We should not waste time with blame. We must deliver this to the seers and concentrate on finding the missing pages.'

Hestia tucked the book under her wing, ushering Ilesse out of the chamber. They hurried along corridors to the cavern where Sleih and Gryphon seers pored over other manuscripts and books, seeking any mention of the ancient power which drove the Gryphon from Arneithe.

Hestia fretted as she hurried along. It was disappointing work. So far they had found only snatches, veiled references which made little sense even in this new light of understanding. Their vagueness could be interpreted all kinds of ways. Frustratingly, nothing had been found to give any clue how the Gryphon of old dealt with the evil before they fled Arneithe.

Hestia entered the cavern where a long table was piled with texts, Ilesse behind her. The seers weren't at work. They gathered, silent, at the opening which overlooked the once green meadow, now churned to a gelatinous mess by the grotesque white army.

Fear lodged in her throat. She placed the book with the others and kept walking. 'What is it?'

A wizened Sleih spoke without turning from the view. 'Prince Varane leads a charge against the invaders. Look how Celeste drives the evil monsters apart.'

Hestia peered down. Varane rode a young, green-feathered gryphon, soaring and diving above the howling creatures which milled below, pressing into each other in their bid to escape the sword. In the confusion, other gryphons, many with Sleih riders, swooped on the misshapen bears, the fanged wolves, the stunted gnome-like beings, thrusting talons and swords into chests and throats, strewing the field with dead and near-dead beasts.

The slaughter would have been more impressive if it hadn't been that for every creature slain, four more raced off the glacier onto the despoiled field.

'The sword! My poor beauties.'

Hestia twisted her head sharply at Ilesse's strained hiss. She drew the girl in close, covering her with her wing, whispering, 'No, 'prentice seer. Not your beauties, not yours.'

Olwyn scraped her talons on the floor, her tail twitching. 'What ails the girl? What is she muttering? Is she ill again?'

Hestia opened her beak, closed it. What to say? Telling half the truth might work. 'I believe, Olwyn,' she said, hoping the gryphon would not sense the missing half, 'she is in mortal fear for the prince. You know how close they are.' She lowered her voice, murmuring into Ilesse's hair. 'Be strong, my love. All will be well.'

'Why am I tangled in your wing? I can barely breathe.' Ilesse wriggled out from Hestia's wing. She gazed about at the staring seers. 'What have I …? I'm sorry, I don't know what–'

'Come, all.' Hestia released Ilesse and forced herself to move to the text on the table. 'We have found the manuscript I gave Olban. There is work to be done.'

She carried a deep reluctance to tell the seers what she believed ailed Ilesse, fearful of their reaction. This evil in their midst? Waiting to burst upon them like an avalanche? No, best to watch and guard, sustain the girl's strength and pray she held.

The seers closed around the fragile book, keener to examine this likely source of the horrors besieging the caverns than worry about a young girl's concern for her friend.

'We must find the missing pages, for there I believe lies the key to all.' Hestia peered around. 'So far, every gryphon and Sleih who owns a manuscript older than their own years has brought it to us. Yet nothing has come to light.' She tapped Ilesse's shoulder. 'Come, 'prentice seer, we have urgent work to do.' And hurried her from the cavern.

***

The slaughter of the white beasts haunted Ilesse's dreams. Their cries grieved her as if they were children, or true creatures of mountain and forest. Heat beyond the warm summer nights caused her to throw off her covers to lie sweat-slickened, tossing on her bed. She would wake to Hestia's wing around her shoulders, offering cool water flavoured with a draught of purple wolfsbane to send her into dreamless sleep. It also left her with a fogged mind the next day.

'I need my brain clear.' Ilesse sat on a stool, sipping a mug of ibex milk. A scarce drink these days, with the flocks in the lower caverns unable to graze and no meadow hay being harvested. If the siege did not lift, if the evil could not be vanquished, winter would be dire. 'Please don't bring me potions.'

Hestia's tail flicked. 'It hurts me to see you toss in your sleep, to hear you moan in pain, crying tears over these worthless beasts.' She flicked her tail. 'They are not real animals, Ilesse. They are the conjured spirits of an evil mind. They do not suffer.'

Ilesse bridled. 'How do you know? How can you say when you have no idea what they feel?' The ibex milk tasted sour in her mouth.

'They feel, 'prentice seer.' Olban's smooth voice came from somewhere within the room.

Ilesse pivoted towards the sound.

The thing that once was Olban smiled at her from the window opening. 'End their suffering. Come to me, let me come to you. Peace, there will be peace.'

Whispers filled her head. The white creatures suffer no longer. She herself is not torn by longing and loathing, but the desires of her heart are fulfilled. If she heeds the seer's beckoning.

'Ilesse, what is it? Come back to me.' Hestia's frightened

eyes stared into Ilesse's face.

'Tiresome gryphon.' Olban shook his white head–and Ilesse raised her hand to swat at Hestia.

With an effort, horrified, she stilled it.

'Can't you see? By the window.' She scrambled from her stool, brushing past Hestia who twisted to see whatever should be there. Nothing.

The desires of your heart, 'prentice seer.

The enticing murmur floated in the air, begging to be caught. Ilesse fell against Hestia, trembling. She must not succumb to the whispers, she must not join with this evil.

Hestia held her close, murmuring into her hair.

Chapter Twenty Three

Living the fairytale

Excitement at having a gryphon in their midst bubbled among the wizards. Gweyr sensed it with her whole body: awe, wonder, a glint of fear sparking here and there. She understood. She shared those feelings, only hers were heightened by a sense of rightness. The world should contain gryphons.

And Sleih.

Her glimpse of the Sleih rider who rescued them had been brief, and at dusk and in pouring rain. Gweyr had an impression of long, straight, dark hair and golden skin. And again, a sense of recognition. Surely she had seen such people before? Mam's tales, that was all.

'Lady Ashta, wizards and friends.' Zoledore had regained his stone stage. His eyes lingered on Gweyr. She stared back, puzzled. 'I have learned much from Lady Ashta these last few minutes,' he said. He gently pummelled the stone with his staff.

The wizards waited.

'Will you share it with us?' Rebar spoke with firm good humour.

'Of course, Rebar. Patience.' Zoledore spread his arms wide. 'There is much trouble in the High Alps of Asfarlon. In short, an old and evil power has awoken and–if it is the ancient evil I suspect it may be–will not be content until all there is destroyed.' He made a small bow to Ashta, who dipped her eagle head.

'I am Ashta,' the gryphon said, 'leader of the hunters among the Gryphon and Sleih who dwell in the High Alps of Asfarlon. Normally our hunting is for meat for our tables.' She moved her head to take in the gathering. 'At least, such was the case until the recent day when a mass of monstrous, deformed white creatures raced across the glacier to attack our young prince's Challit.'

Gweyr had no idea what a Challit might be. It must be very grand if it involved princes.

'Our people have been attacked too, and our livestock,' a young wizard said.

Gweyr's mood turned sombre, remembering the mother with the toddler in Darnel and the wagons outside Banna, feeling again the loss and desperation of the woman fleeing her home with her family, carrying away what she could. Or what was left.

'So I hear.' Ashta lifted her wings. 'I am sorry for these losses, which are assuredly connected with the creatures in the High Alps.'

Ashta told how the bears and wolves which raced across the Madach lands had continued up into the mountains, there to disappear–and re-emerge as the white monsters which attacked the Sleih.

Gweyr's heart ached at the likely slain and injured of the unforeseen assault, and in the middle of a celebration.

'Magic of the worst kind.' Zoledore struck the stone with his staff. 'It must be defeated. It can be defeated.'

A babble of 'how' and 'with what' and 'how do you know' filled the stuffy air. Zoledore waved his staff and the wizards quietened.

'If–I say if–this is the evil of the oldest of all the legends,' he said, 'it cannot be defeated by any army. Once, however, long ago, it was diminished, contained, by an enchanter of great power. The story is vague, the clearest bit being that the enchanter is said to have wielded a winged lion.' All eyes were on Ashta who stared ahead. 'Diamonds, among other gems, and fire and flame are involved, though whether for good or evil, is not clear.' Zoledore stopped and gazed over the wizards.

'Is that it?' Master Whittion rubbed his hand through his hair. 'It's not much to go on.'

'We will take what we can,' Ashta said. 'I will return to Asfarlon to add this to the knowledge of the seers.' She tipped her head towards Master Whittion. 'Nothing can be overlooked.'

Gweyr would have giggled at the master's blush, except she was too deeply enthralled by Zoledore's words. Diamonds were in many of Mam's tales, as were demons spreading fire and destruction. She opened her mouth to tell whoever was interested that she knew these tales too, given nothing should be overlooked, and started. Zoledore stood before her, staring into her face.

'Daughter of the Sleih,' he said, 'you feel, you see, you hear what others do not.'

'Me?' Gweyr took another step back. 'No, no, I don't, honest.'

Zoledore shrugged. 'Living with barbarians, never being trained to your birth right, will quell the magic.' He gently touched his white staff to Gweyr's shoulder. 'It's there, however.'

'What are you talking about, Zoledore?' Master Whittion frowned at the wizard. 'This girl is as Madach as these outsiders.' He swept a hand to take in Conall and Allsop who had joined in the frowning and staring.

'If you say it.' Zoledore spoke to Ashta. 'Lady Ashta, my old wizard bones tell me this young woman should be in Asfarlon.'

In Asfarlon? Gweyr's heart soared. Daughter of the Sleih or not, to go there, to where the adventures were real, where the fairytales lived and breathed. And then her heart fell. Master

Whittion would insist she go home immediately. Allsop would too, after all the trouble he went to, including being set upon by wolves. Not that she had to do what Allsop said.

'I agree.' Ashta gazed at Gweyr with her eagle eyes. 'I am unschooled in the magic of the seers. But as a hunter, I recognise the thrum and scent of blood.' She stretched out a wing to Gweyr. 'We will rest briefly, and then we will return to Asfarlon.'

'Return to …?' Gweyr's blood thrummed indeed, her pulse beating in her neck like a burrowing mole. 'How? I can't take Millie there.'

'You will ride on me.'

Gweyr's mouth fell open.

***

Too few hours later, Ashta's beak nudged Gweyr's tangled hair to wake her.

'Wake up, time to leave. We must carry this news to Asfarlon and then I will seek out my hunters, see what they have found in their search for the source of these wolves and bears.'

Gweyr woke slowly, her befuddled mind caught in a dream–the old dream which had played at the edge of her mind the last few weeks, which always faded before she could recall it. She lay on her crumpled cloak, staring into Ashta's green eyes. The gryphon's grey feathers blended with the dim light in the cave coming from low-burning lamps. The air was cold.

She must remember the details of the dream. It was important. It was about … She sighed and moved her head to see Allsop asleep, wrapped in his cloak, on the other side of her. He, Conall, and Master Whittion would ride to Darnel, warning villages along the way of the terror lurking in the High Alps, encouraging them to be vigilant.

'For this evil will not be content with destroying Asfarlon,' Zoledore said last night. 'Its appetite is voracious. If it is not destroyed by Gryphon magic …' He had gazed up at the high rocky ceiling, perhaps praying to greater powers than even Gryphon magic to save them all.

Conall complained about having to go home. Wasn't there something else he could do? Fight the wolves? Defend the Forest edges?

Zoledore humphed. 'Don't be a fool, young Madach. Your adventures are far from done.'

Which had cheered Conall somewhat, although he had cast envious glances at Gweyr for the rest of the evening.

Gweyr rubbed sleep from her eyes. 'I was dreaming, Ashta. An important dream.'

Ashta bobbed her head. 'Dreams are always important. Tell me this dream as we go. There will be time.'

'If I remember it.'

Gweyr unwrapped herself from her cloak and followed the gryphon to where loaves of bread, platters of cheese, bowls of fruit, and jugs of water sat on a long low table at the far end of the cavern. The remains of last night's meal, fresh enough in the coolness. She ate hurriedly, trying both to recall the dream and to quash her nerves at the idea of riding a gryphon. What if she couldn't hold on? Ashta bore no saddle or reins. Would she plummet to the earth, die in a screaming heap of broken bones? Da's anger would be well justified.

A sleepy Allsop strapped her rolled-up blanket with its spare few clothes to her back.

'This will be an adventure worthy of your ambitions, Gweyr. Good luck!'

She grinned. 'Thank you for chasing after me, Allsop. Go safe to Darnel, tell Da I'm well, please, and'–she kissed him lightly on the cheek–'enjoy your quiet life making bread.'

She said goodbye to Millie, who rubbed her cheek against Gweyr's hair.

'I'll see you soon, don't worry,' Gweyr whispered into her ear. 'You have Allsop and Chester to look after you, you'll be okay. And you wouldn't like it where I'm going, I'm sure.'

Mille tossed her head and whickered softly. Ashta approached.

'I had never seen a horse,' she said. 'Not close like this. A beautiful creature, with a strong heart.' She touched her beak gently to Millie's nose, held it there for a beat of two or three.

Gweyr held her breath. Millie showed no fear. Her eyelids closed briefly, she snorted, and Ashta moved to Chester. The big horse nodded as the gryphon approached. She laid her beak against Chester's nose too, before saying to Gweyr, 'We must go. The horses have strength for what is to come. Your friends will be grateful.'

A burst of happiness lit Gweyr's heart. A little Gryphon magic had passed to Chester and Millie, for all Ashta declared herself 'only' a hunter. She gave Millie a last pat on her shiny black neck and followed the gryphon down the tunnel and out of the cavern. The rain had blown away during the night and a summer pre-dawn stillness met them, the birds not yet awake.

Gweyr chewed her lip. 'Umm … how?'

Ashta crouched low. 'Climb up and hang on tightly. Don't be scared to hold on around my neck until you find your balance. It's tough.'

The glint of humour lightened Gweyr's worry. She clambered up, grateful for the borrowed trousers, and settled herself on the lion-like back, close to the neck.

'Ready?' Ashta peered around to gaze at her charge.

Gweyr's heart boomed. 'Yes,' she quavered.

She wrapped her arms about Ashta's neck and held fast as she was lifted above the black shadows between the trees, into the grey air. It wasn't too bad. Soon in tune with the steady motion of the gryphon's flight, her confidence grew. In fact, it was better than not too bad. The wind blew her hair from her face, fresh and strong. Gweyr imagined she was–

'Ashta! I've remembered my dream.'

Ashta lifted her head, and down again, giving Gweyr a dizzying view of the shadowed woods below them. 'Tell me,' she said.

'It's a dream I used to have when I was small, after the tales Mam told me about the Sleih.'

'Your mother told tales of the Sleih?'

'Oh yes, all the time. It seemed to make her sad to tell them but she did–magnificent tales about how the Sleih tended magical flying beasts–gryphons I suppose she meant–and rode them into battle against monstrous evils. And always won.'

'Let us hope the tales hold true.'

The reason Gweyr rode on Ashta stabbed at her. She hoped so too.

'And I would dream about being a beautiful Sleih princess riding my magical winged beast into battle.'

'And this is the dream you had last night?'

'No, no. This one's different. I've had it before, only it always slips away, leaving … well, a worry, a fretting about something needing to be done.'

She braved holding on with one arm so she could brush back a flurry of curls blinding her. The sun rose behind them. Far below, the wide grasslands of the high plains grew brighter with the new day. Ahead, the pink and gold tips of the High Alps beckoned her to their hidden world.

She was in one of Mam's old stories, and any moment Mam would wake her, tell her it was time to get up or she'd be late for school. Gweyr's excitement dimmed. She would happily give up the reality of all this for such an awakening.

'Worrying?'

Ashta's question brought Gweyr back to the dream.

'Yes. This dream is about a girl, a young woman. It might be me, it might not. It seems like I'm watching her. It can be like that in dreams, can't it? She's wearing a cloak with a hood, so I don't see her face.' Gweyr paused, squinting into the brighter light. 'She's carrying something in her hand which glows really brightly and she's using it to light her way. She's concentrating hard, and there's a bridge, a stone bridge … and …' The memory of the dream faded.

'Is there more?'

'I can't remember more.' There was more. Crucial more. For now, it lurked deep within her subconscious. 'Can you tell me what the dream means, Ashta?'

'I am a hunter, not an interpreter of dreams. But, Gweyr, Zoledore is right. You are needed in Asfarlon. This I can tell you without the training of seers.'

Chapter Twenty Four

Worse is to come

Allsop and his companions made good progress on their homeward journey, until a summer storm and the recent passing of heavy wagons softened the track from Dorton to the consistency of bread dough. He slowed Chester to a walk, secretly welcoming the delay and practising for the umpteenth time what he would say to Barnaby. The conversation would go like this:

'You didn't find her?'

'Yes, I found her.' He should leave the bit about the wolves out of it, at least to start with.

'Then where is she, Allsop Kaine?' Hands on hips, the constant tea towel slung over his shoulder. 'Where's my daughter?'

'She's flown on a gryphon to the High Alps of Asfarlon because a wizard believes she has Sleih blood.'

Allsop heaved a huge sigh. It wasn't the only thing weighing on his mind since leaving Ledrith. A wary nervousness lay over the land. In the villages and hamlets, tightly closed doors and windows rejected breezes which might mollify summer's heat. Farmers with scurrying dogs toiled in fields to clear dead stock and repair hedges and fences. Each time, the story was the same. Wolves, sometimes bears, raiding the farmlands.

'Brown or white wolves?' Master Whittion asked.

'Brown and black,' the farmers told him. 'Why?'

'Going north?'

'Yes, why?'

'Be vigilant. Worse may be coming.'

He would say no more to the farmers who put their fists against their waists and glowered.

'I don't want them to think I'm a mad man,' he said to Allsop and Conall, 'talking about wizards and gryphons and Sleih. I want them to worry.'

Master Whittion's urgency to be in Darnel showed itself in the fast pace he set and his deep frown. They sought brief rests twice, in barns where they could sleep by the horses and move quickly on. The howls of wolves, at a distance, disturbed Allsop's uneasy sleep. Which poor farmer suffered tonight?

The mud eased. When Allsop urged Chester to a canter he responded eagerly, scenting home and rest. Allsop patted the old horse's sweaty black neck. He'd proven to have far more in him than anyone believed. Allsop bent low and let Chester have his head.

Not for long. Carts, milling sheep and cows, and quiet, sombre people choked the road into Darnel. Allsop's heady pace came to a halt.

Conall pulled his horse and Millie, on a lead rein, to a stop beside Allsop. Millie whickered at Chester, who tossed his mane.

'More refugees,' Conall said.

'Yes.' Master Whittion joined them. 'The troubles in the north grow worse.'

They wound their way through the crowd. Weary, dull-eyed people took bare notice of them. At their head, a strong-shouldered man in a broad hat rode a great draught horse.

Master Whittion slowed further to keep pace with the man. 'Where have you come from?' he said.

Conall handed Millie's leading rein to Allsop and cantered on. He would let the villagers know there were more refugees to take care of.

The man turned anxious eyes on Whittion and Allsop. 'North, beyond Flaxburgh.'

'Brown and black wolves? Bears too?' Allsop asked.

'Not this time,' the man said. 'White wolves. Monsters, not like normal wolves.' He twisted to glance at the people following. 'We coped with the brown ones. Wolves, bears. Predators, after food. We get them from time to time, when winters are hard, though not in such numbers. And never in summer.' He gusted out a breath. 'The white monsters–they're something different. Evil is in the monstrous ones.'

'Many?' Allsop held in a breath.

'Enough to drive us away. A few of our folk stayed, with what remains of their stock. Locked themselves in their barns I hope.' He shuddered. 'And I pray it'll protect them.'

Allsop exchanged a frown with Master Whittion. The worse to come was on its way.

***

The meeting with Barnaby in the bar of the Boar's Head went as Allsop expected. Almost. The innkeeper's glare across his polished bar faded more quickly than Allsop had hoped for, replaced with a shining, tentative, pride.

'No whatsitcallit, Sleih, blood on the Barnaby side.' He stared at the wall opposite. 'Must be her mam. I knew her mam was special. From the first time I saw her. Gahain Day, in Flaxburgh, lasses from further north–well, we all know things are more wild further north, and not just the weather and the landscape. The way she danced …' He sighed and returned his gaze to Allsop. 'Still, young man, this is hardly news to ease a father's worry. If these Sleih are real, as you say, and the–what did you call them? Gryph …yes, gryphons–whose to say they'll make her welcome? What if this wizard –wizards!–chap is wrong and they don't take her in and she's up there in the snow and ice, left to perish–' He slapped the tea towel on the bar.

Allsop jumped.

'Have no concern.' Master Whittion set his tankard of ale on the bar to come to Allsop's rescue. 'The gryphon was certain too, scented her blood as a gryphon hunter can.' He said this with the air of one familiar with gryphon hunters all his life. 'And the stories tell us the Sleih might be strange, odd, but not cruel. Gweyr is likely safer there than here, exposed as we are to these marauding creatures of evil.'

Allsop agreed. A cavern way up a tall mountain sounded a good place to be. The refugees they met on the road were not the first to arrive since he and Chester had taken after Gweyr. Others had come and kept coming. He glanced through the open doorway into the summer evening, where another group made its way through the village. These didn't appear to be stopping.

'Look out there!' The discontented voice belonged to the miller, Beddle, seated at a table underneath the inn's window. He stared through it at the straggling group. 'Hope they keep going. Darnel is full to bursting as it is. No room for more.'

'Poor souls.' Master Whittion peered past Beddle at the dispirited group. 'What horrors drive them from their homes!'

'Horrors?' Beddle humphed. 'A few bears and wolves and they up stakes and head south, knowing it's safer here.' He tapped the side of his nose. 'And better farmland.'

Allsop and Master Whittion exchanged a raising of eyebrows.

'You know, Master Beddle,' Allsop said, his tone even, 'I've seen these wolves and they're terrifying, not natural. And worse is out there from what others have witnessed.'

'They say!' Beddle appeared as unconvinced of the threat as he had of Master Whittion's lightning which went up, not down.

Barnaby tossed his tea towel over his shoulder. 'There's nothing I can do for my wayward daughter, except pray she comes out of this alive.' He sighed heavily and sniffed.

For a moment, Allsop thought the innkeeper might cry.

Barnaby lifted a glass from the bar, held it to the light and replaced it, unpolished. 'Whatever the truth of these horrors, we here in Darnel should be thinking on what to do to protect ourselves.' He shook his head. 'Imagine the panic if those creatures rampaged through here.'

'Pah!' Beddle banged his mug on the table. 'Rumours and stories. Big fuss over a few stray wolves. No need to panic over stray wolves. These incomers, they're the ones we should worry about.'

Allsop pressed his lips together. 'You're right, Mr Barnaby –'

'Master Whittion, Allsop, come and see!' Conall's shout through the inn door cut off Allsop's response.

Chapter Twenty Five

Pure blood

Ashta glided to a graceful halt by a stony stream running across the high plains. Mid-morning and time for a short rest. Gweyr drank thirstily, deciding she had never tasted water this sweet and cold. She said so to Ashta, who waved a wing at the towering Alps ahead of them.

'You will taste the waters of the alpine lakes,' the gryphon said, 'and know this is a poor imitation of freshness.'

Gweyr believed her. She followed the gryphon's wing to gaze at the mountains. Soon she would be within them, flying through the valleys, across the glaciers, to meet the Sleih.

It couldn't be real.

Ashta stood very still, her wings upraised. She peered towards the Alps. 'What comes from the valleys?' she murmured.

Gweyr saw only foothills smudged by distance. She didn't have eagle sight, however.

'What can you see, Ashta?'

'It is too far to be certain, but a darkness seeps from the hills.' She crouched on the grass. 'Come, we must hurry.'

Gweyr clambered onto Ashta's back, holding her breath as the gryphon soared into the air.

As they grew nearer, Gweyr saw it too–a dark mist spilled from the valleys onto the edges of the high plains. She sensed Ashta's worry, felt the gryphon's urgency as she flew faster.

Soon the Alps filled Gweyr's whole view. The black mist

grew more distant the higher they rose between the soaring mountains. The chill air and the cold penetrated Gweyr's bones, despite tightening her cloak and snuggling close to Ashta's warm neck.

'Not long to go,' the gryphon said. 'There will be fires and hot food and drink when we reach Asfarlon.'

Had Gweyr heard a touch of doubt in her voice? Ashta's worry fed on Gweyr's cold discomfort.

'What is this?'

Ashta's cry and her sharp downward dip jolted Gweyr from her wonderings. She grabbed the gryphon's neck and peered at the ground.

'Oh.'

The valley below was clear of the black mist. Instead, it undulated like a white sea whipped by winds. Not a spot of green meadow or of shiny glacier could be seen. Wolves, bears and grossly misshapen creatures milled about in a snarling, growling mass at the base of a high cliff. Tall gates barred their entrance into the mountain.

'Asfarlon is under siege,' Ashta said. 'Hold tight.'

Gweyr clung on as the gryphon rose steeply, following the height of the cliff. As they rode higher, openings–most with ledges like balconies–appeared in the cliff face. The ledges were empty and what lay beyond them was in too deep shadow for Gweyr to see. It showed, however, that the mountain was a home of sorts. There were Gryphon and Sleih within, defending themselves against the white army at their door.

Her chest tightened. Soon. She would see them soon. The fairytales come to life.

***

'Who's riding Ashta?'

Varane's cry brought Hestia to the window, Ilesse on her heels. Too late. The gryphon and her rider had risen higher.

'A stranger?' A frisson shot through Hestia's body. Neither

good nor bad, only there. 'If this stranger is not pure, they will be unable to enter Asfarlon,' she said.

'I'm going to find out.' Varane ran from the cavern, calling, 'Ashta would never bring anything not pure here.'

'Pure?' Ilesse's high-pitched laugh grated on Hestia's hearing. 'Purity is in my beauties, and you will not allow them to enter Asfarlon.'

She turned to Hestia, her eyes dark, vacant pools. Her body shuddered as if filled with an icy cold.

'Ilesse, Ilesse.' Hestia enveloped the 'prentice seer in her wing. She probed the girl's mind as she had done a hundred times, trying to counter Olban's hidden whisperings. She blanched at what she found, sent comfort to soothe the tumult there.

'Come back,' she murmured, pushing harder against the resistance.

'Hestia?' Ilesse pressed against her. She was pale, damp with sweat, her eyes fever bright but focused, normal. 'Did I do it again?'

'Yes, my love.' Hestia pressed her beak gently to Ilesse's forehead. 'You are yourself now though. If you are strong enough, we should join Varane, find out whom Ashta has brought us, and why.'

'Yes.' Ilesse picked up a stone mug from a low table with shaking hands. She drank the contents down, sighed. 'These attacks tire me to my soul.'

Hestia's own soul cried out in shared pain. She touched her wingtip to Ilesse's arm. 'This torture cannot go on. We will find a way to overcome it, I promise.

'We will.' Ilesse's fingers, steady now, stroked Hestia's wing before she moved into the sloping passageways leading to the great hall from where the hunters took flight.

***

Ilesse glanced at Varane and Ashta, standing close together

in deep conversation, and away again to a girl a year or two older than herself.

The girl clutched a cloak tight around her shivering body with hands white with cold. Her long, dark hair waved about her lightly tanned face in a tangle of curls. She stared around with pale green eyes at the wooden spears, bows and arrows and other accoutrements of hunting which hung on hooks on the stony walls.

An enemy. But weak. She cannot harm us.

Ilesse shuddered, tried to force the murmur from her mind. It hung there, refusing to not be heard.

It needs to be heard.

Needs to be heard. Of course it does.

'Who is this stranger,' she found herself demanding, 'whom Ashta has brought into Asfarlon?' She peered at the girl through slitted eyes, her fists balled against her sides.

'Ilesse!' Hestia protested.

'This is Gweyr,' Ashta said to Hestia, ignoring Ilesse. 'She comes from the Madach village of Darnel, beyond the high plains and the grasslands.'

The Madach girl stared from Hestia to Varane to Ilesse. 'Hello.' She shivered harder.

'Here we have Varane, prince of the Sleih.' Ashta lifted a wing in Varane's direction. 'And here is Ilesse, a 'prentice seer, and Hestia, seer and councillor of Asfarlon.'

'Prince?' The girl bobbed an awkward curtsey.

Varane shook his head, denying the curtsey, smiling warmly.

Ilesse snorted. Hestia blinked at her and a prick of disappointment at her own behaviour stabbed Ilesse's heart.

An enemy.

An enemy.

The Madach flushed pink and looked to Ashta, who nodded her encouragement.

'Yes, I'm Gweyr, and it's amazing to be–'

'Why is she here?' Ilesse threw out a hand in a sharp gesture which matched her tone. Her glare fixed on Ashta.

The hunter lifted her head. 'That, 'prentice seer, is for others to know and to decide what should be done with the knowledge.' She lifted a protective wing over the Madach and again addressed Hestia. 'I should expect the 'prentice seer to have better manners.'

Hestia threw Ilesse a look of pity this time.

'This is not her normal manner,' she said softly. 'She has been unwell and we must forgive her.'

Ilesse didn't care whether she was forgiven or not. Here was an enemy. She kept her gaze on the Madach, surreptitiously seeking the answers in the girl's mind. She found only a confused wondering before being abruptly and roughly blocked.

Hestia stepped forward. 'Welcome to Asfarlon, Gweyr,' she said. 'You are cold and weary. Whatever reason you are here can wait until you are warmed.' She tilted her head at Varane. 'My prince, please take our visitor to my rooms, build up the fire and arrange warming food. Ilesse'–she faced Ilesse, bobbing her head to attract her attention–'you will come with me and Ashta to the Eternal Chamber. The king and Lord Tius meet there with our defenders. They will want to hear any news immediately.'

Ilesse ignored her. 'How did she get in?' she asked Ashta.

Hestia parted her beak in annoyance. The prick of disappointment touched Ilesse a second time. She shouldn't be behaving like this. She should be welcoming. There must be a reason Ashta had brought this Madach to Asfarlon.

The hunter has captured an enemy, my queen. Wariness is needed.

Ashta flicked her tail. 'It appears Zoledore was right,' she said, once more talking to Hestia. And to the Madach girl: 'I need to leave, Gweyr, and may not see you until after all this is over. It has been a pleasure, and I wish you well.'

'Come on.' Varane beckoned to the girl. 'Let's find you food and warmth.'

He led her from the hall. Ilesse stared after them, her fingers curling and uncurling from their clenched fists.

An enemy but easily vanquished.

***

Gweyr's brain whirled with the strangeness of it all. A prince? And a 'prentice seer, whatever one of those was, and a gryphon who was a councillor of something. She walked behind the prince, the 'prentice seer's accusing eyes dancing in her head. She had felt the girl probe her mind, poking around in there as if Gweyr was a larder and the girl needed a round of cheese. She had resisted, somehow, and the probing had stopped.

The Sleih girl didn't want her here. Why? She didn't know Gweyr. How could she hate her on first meeting?

She shook the uncomfortable thought off and gazed about, taking in the dwelling place of the Sleih and Gryphon. Late afternoon sun spilled through frequent wide openings on one side of the wide passage of smooth rock, lighting caverns furnished with rugs, wall hangings and heavy, carved furniture. Paintings adorned the rock walls and shelves held brightly jewelled ornaments and thick books. To the other side, where the daylight barely penetrated, similarly sumptuous caverns glowed with a steady yellow light.

Gweyr's companion, striding beside her, must be about fourteen, she decided. He might be the prince whose Challit was interrupted by the swarming attack on the meadow, or there might be other princes. He was of Gweyr's height, his golden skin glowing with health and his eyes with eagerness.

'One day, you must tell me everything about the Madach and their villages,' he said. 'I would love to see them. To live in houses and walk on roads, to ride horses.' He gazed at Gweyr, his dark hair swaying about his shoulders. 'It must be really exciting.'

'Exciting?' Gweyr giggled. 'No, Prince …?'

'Varane, call me Varane, everyone does.' He laughed. 'The prince bit is only for Hestia, who likes to remind me every chance she gets how one day, a long time hence I hope, I'll have to be king.'

'Don't you want to be king?'

Varane shrugged. 'I have no choice, so I guess I have to want it.' He blew out a breath. 'I'd rather fight.' He pointed to an opening where a wide ledge offered a view over the evening-shadowed Alps. 'Like those creatures down there. I want to take the fight properly to them, not just these brief forays we do, although I know Father's right when he says they'll not be defeated by pure physical strength.' He grinned. 'They fear my sword Celeste. They fled from it the day of my Challit. It's a shame I'm the only one with a Celeste.'

A magic sword? Of course there'd be a magic sword. Gweyr grinned too as they walked on.

Varane stopped at a cavern on the daylight side of the passage. 'This is Hestia's chamber. The fire is lit, it'll soon warm you up. I'll find someone to bring us food.'

Gweyr gazed around. A bed of meadow hay scattered on a thick pelt filled one corner. The rest of the cavern was furnished with carved chests and bookshelves. There were chairs for Sleih visitors and thick fur pelts and huge cushions which looked comfortable for gryphons.

She thought the fire burning too low to give out any real heat, yet its soft glow soon warmed her as it warmed the chill cavern air. She threw off her cloak and walked to the window, intending to go on to the ledge and look below at the besieging creatures. She reached the opening and came to a sudden halt. A tension in the air resisted her probing fingers, a protection against anything unwanted which might fly or climb to the ledge.

She recalled Zoledore's statement. Gryphon magic. Which was why the fire's low burn heated so intensely. Warmed, her hungry stomach made itself known, alongside a great tiredness. A shame Gryphon magic didn't extend to conjuring food on the spot. She curled up in a feather-filled leather cushion close to the fire. And fell fast asleep.

Chapter Twenty Six

Strange visitors

'Master Whittion, Allsop, come and see! We have visitors!' Conall poked his head into the inn, waving his arms about like a man drowning in air.

'More refugees?' Beddle frowned.

'No, not at all.' Conall grinned. 'They're looking for the master,' he said, and backed out into the street.

Allsop and Master Whittion followed, joining a gathering of gaping villagers. In their midst, the reasons for the gaping preened their wings with eagle beaks. One bore a Sleih rider.

'You seek me?' the master said.

'You are Whittion the Wizard?' the rider said.

'Umm, yes, although here I am better known as Whittion the baker.'

The rider smiled, briefly.

Allsop glanced at Conall, whose grin grew ever wider.

'I saw them descend,' he said, jiggling from foot to foot. 'The rider, the Sleih, asked me where Whittion from the wizards' conclave was. Lucky I knew you were both talking to Barnaby.'

'Yes, it was.' Allsop glanced back at the inn. Beddle hung in the doorway, his mouth opening and closing like a landed fish. Allsop's grin matched Conall's.

The rider jumped lightly from the gryphon, which shook out its wings and glanced around at the wondering villagers. They jostled each other, moving further from the beast. Mothers pushed their children behind them. Allsop relished his sense of knowing superiority.

'I carry messages from Ashta, our leader,' the rider said to Master Whittion.

Allsop's grin faded, taking in the sombre mood of the Sleih and the marks of hard wear, likely battle, which showed on his leather clothing. Dust dulled his skin as it did the feathers of the gryphons. Conall too had lost his grin, frowning at the state of the visitors.

'Asfarlon is under siege,' the rider said, 'from white monsters, abominations of an ancient evil which our seers cannot subdue. They ponder and discuss legends and tales'– his voice carried the faintest hint of dismissal–'but for us, the hunters, there is simply an enemy to be fought.' He set his lips firmly together.

'You've fought these creatures?' Conall's wide eyes and admiring tone caused Allsop to wonder if his fellow apprentice was more excited than fearful of the idea.

'What's happening?' Allsop asked.

'The white creatures mass in the foothills of the High Alps and onto the high plains, bringing a mist of darkness with them. From there they send out parties to harass the lands to the south, both west and east.'

'It appears they intend to encircle the land,' a gryphon said.

Barnaby, who had joined the group, stepped back in shock.

The gryphon's neck feathers lifted and fell. 'Yes, we speak. And think. And cast magic.'

The rider ignored this exchange. 'All living things will be trapped within their circle, prey to their evil hunger.'

Allsop's stomach lurched. Master Whittion's face paled.

Barnaby unslung his tea towel and crushed it in his hands. 'My apologies, Master Gryph…Gryphon,' he said. 'We're not used to visits from those many of us believed were fairytales.

Please excuse me.'

The Sleih rider barked a short humourless laugh. 'Be grateful for these fairytales, innkeeper. We keep death from your doors. So far. However'–he looked at Master Whittion–'we are few, we need to also defend Asfarlon. The Madach must take their part in this battle. All who can wield a sword.'

Allsop broke the wondering silence. 'None of us can wield a sword, or a knife, or any weapon.'

Conall punched his fist into the palm of his hand. 'Will you teach us?'

The rider gave another harsh laugh. 'Teach you? There's no time for teaching. You'–he addressed the master–'are a wizard. Magic will in the end prove a stronger weapon than swords and knives. You at least can help. We need you to join us, band with other wizards being gathered from across the Madach lands to protect your people.'

Master Whittion straightened his shoulders. 'Of course.'

Conall glared and Allsop could hear his thoughts as if he had shouted them into the summer afternoon. The fussy, wordy master had been called upon when he, Conall, a strong young man, was of no use. Allsop waited.

Conall stepped forward. 'I'll come with you, Master.' The words tumbled out. 'I'll be your guard, like last time.' He ignored the Sleih rider's swift raising of his eyebrows.

'Yes.' Master Whittion gave a small smile. 'Yes, that would be a comfort to me. You will tend to matters here, Allsop, you and Barnaby.'

The gryphon addressed Barnaby who listened with wide eyes. 'My strong advice is for you to prepare your village as best you can against attack.' The innkeeper nodded vigorously. 'Your blacksmith must labour in his forge to make weapons, however crude. Give them to those capable of handling them. Find refuges in hidden places, provision them and take shelter there with your stock until we can be assured of victory.'

'Yes, yes, of course.' Barnaby twisted the tea towel. 'Thank you Master Gryphon for your warnings.' He swallowed. 'Can you tell me if my daughter, Gweyr, is safely with your people? She–'

'The Madach girl? Your daughter?' He peered closely at Barnaby and blinked. 'I know only that Ashta brought her to Asfarlon and she remains in the caverns. She is as safe as any other there.'

The Sleih rider lifted himself onto the gryphon's back. 'We will move on to other villages where wizards dwell,' he said. 'On the western side, we gather near a hamlet, Atias. We trust there will be more, and better, news from Asfarlon very soon.'

'Atias?' Allsop's voice was sharp.

'Your home, isn't it?' Conall said.

'Yes.'

'Atias is where we take the battle to the creatures which rampage westward,' the rider said. 'If any power can stop them should the seers fail and Asfarlon fall.' He sat astride the gryphon, his cloak falling to the creature's lion-like back. 'We will see you in Atias, Wizard Whittion.' As the gryphon lifted its wings, the rider called, 'Ask for me when you arrive. I am Giliar.'

Conall gazed after the group as they rose over the inn. 'I would love to ride with them, whatever the dangers.'

Allsop patted his friend's arm, ignoring the nausea roiling in his gut.

'There will be danger enough, I'm sure,' he said, tracking the flight of the gryphons. 'This Giliar will see me as well in Atias.' He turned to the master. 'I go with you and Conall, Master. To defend my home.'

Chapter Twenty Seven

A deep-set evil

Ilesse's emotions churned like clouds on a stormy day. She stood before the lords of Asfarlon in the Eternal Chamber and listened to Ashta's tale of the rescue of the two Madachs from wolves.

The Madach girl. Why was she here? What was her purpose? Ilesse had not sought answers in the girl's mind a second time. The girl herself seemed not to know anything, and the blocking Ilesse received on their first meeting had been strongly, albeit amateurishly, delivered. How could she do that? The Madach had no magic in them, no powers of the mind. Was the girl more than she seemed?

Ashta's tale went on, about a meeting of wizards in a cave too close to the ground and how one of these proposed the evil which Olban had brought into Asfarlon–and the wider world–was the same ancient power which drove the Gryphon from their forest home aeons ago. And about a black mist which oozed through the lower valleys to run like a flooded river onto the high plains.

Ilesse wanted to grin at the wizard's cleverness. With an effort, she restrained the grin. But the unwelcome whisperings came, circling her mind.

Come, 'prentice seer, you are so close. You can save your beauties, have your heart's desire, all you wish for, if you come now.

'Ilesse?' Hestia's voice banished the whispers.

'I'm fine, thank you.' Ilesse forced a smile, knowing it would not fool the gryphon. 'Ashta–' She looked about. Ashta had gone. She turned to Hestia. 'How does this Madach girl come to be here, how could she be allowed in?'

King Iaton bent forward in his stone chair. 'I also would like to know.'

'And I.' Lord Tius fixed one eagle eye on Hestia, who sighed.

'It seems this wizard believes the girl has Sleih blood,' she said, 'and Ashta herself sensed as such.' She paused. 'There is something about her my lords. Like I have known her, long years past.'

'She should not be here.' It came out of Ilesse before she knew she was speaking, the high peremptory tone not at all appropriate to use before a king and a Lord Gryphon. Her hand flew to her mouth. Heat rose up her neck.

Hestia reached out a protective wing, wrapped Ilesse within it. 'My lords,' she said, 'you must excuse her, she is unaware of what she does, she–'

'Unaware?' King Iaton drummed his fingers on the arms of the stone chair. 'How is she unaware?'

Hestia's drawn-in breath sounded in Ilesse's ear. 'Our 'prentice seer,' the gryphon said, slow with reluctance, 'battles evil thoughts, hears whisperings, perceives things others do not.' She opened her beak, closed it. 'I … I fear a glimmer of the evil which overtook Olban may live within her.'

'A glimmer of evil?' Lord Tius raised a taloned foreleg.

'Why have you said nothing of this?' King Iaton's voice was stern.

An inane giggle rose in Ilesse's throat. She strangled it before it escaped, fighting for control over her confused emotions.

Hestia bobbed her head. 'I should have come to you, yes … Except, it is not proven, it may be the lingerings of her illness, nothing at all, and will ease in time–'

'You do not believe this, Hestia.'

Lord Tius' powers of the mind would read the gryphon like a book if he wished to.

Hestia's wing tightened around Ilesse, who squirmed in the embrace. She clenched her fingers, fighting the urge to free herself.

Foolish gryphon. To think you need, or desire, her pathetic protection.

Yes, she must escape the stifling wing. No! Hestia would save her. The icy band crushed her chest. She couldn't breathe.

'My apologies, Iaton, Tius.' Hestia's eagle heart beat hard against Ilesse's side. 'I worried, believing the council would be afraid, would want to lock her away … or worse.'

Imprisoned? Or worse?

Ah, you see! The gryphon threatens you. Join with me, my queen, fight no longer, let peace be yours.

Ilesse's blood ran frigid in her veins. An utter weariness fell heavily on her.

She craved peace, needed the whispers to stop.

Wanted, desperately, to say, 'Yes, I come to you. My heart's desire is simple: take this struggle from me, give me peace.'

She pushed hard against Hestia's wing, freeing herself from its stifling hold.

'I come,' she whispered, swaying before the two rulers, eyes closed. 'Let it be over.'

'Over?' Lord Tius rose from his pelt.

'No, Ilesse!' Hestia pulled her close again. 'It is not over. You are stronger than this.'

And powerful my queen. Too powerful to waste your dreams with these weak magicians. Come, join with me.

She was strong, she would be powerful, it was her fate.

The king and Lord Tius stepped forward. They laid hands and wingtips on Ilesse's head and shoulders.

No! They would not deny her. Rage welled in her chest. She writhed under their hot touch. She snarled, batted at their hands and wings.

Hestia held her tight, forcing her to hear the murmurings of the two gryphons and the king. Murmurings which promised to soothe, to bear the struggle on her behalf.

False promises, my queen. Come to me! I alone can give you peace.

Yes, peace!

No! She must not succumb. She must reach out, take the magic offered.

She fought against the evil to merge her mind with those of her would-be healers. Pain like shards of ice split her skull. She breathed deeply, raggedly.

Long moments passed. The whisperings of the king and gryphons became a steady hum against the scowling bitterness welling and subsiding, welling and subsiding inside her.

At long last, the bitterness retreated, the stabbing pain faded.

For now.

Hestia released her. Ilesse stood alone, tremulous, weary to her bones.

King Iaton passed a hand across his eyes. He sighed a long, slow breath as if he had taken Ilesse's struggle into himself.

'This is indeed a deep-set evil,' Lord Tius said. He touched his beak to Ilesse's damp head. 'Poor 'prentice seer,' he said softly. 'You are a fighter, strong. You will conquer this.'

Yes, she would conquer. The strength of three imbued with magic, with Gryphon magic, would help her triumph. Please.

A soft snigger chortled in her ear. Be gone, she told it.

'Yes, my lords.'

'It is late and you must rest, Ilesse.' King Iaton returned to his chair with a lingering frown. 'Tomorrow, early, we will meet this stranger who purports to have Sleih blood, to discover why she is here and if it is to our advantage.'

'Stranger, yet not a stranger.' Hestia gazed past the rulers to where a half moon shone on the distant softened remains of one of spring's avalanches.

Chapter Twenty Eight

Daughter of the Sleih

Ashta had flown to her hunters, having delivered her short message from Zoledore. Gweyr had no friendly presence to rely on as she presented herself to the rulers, although the prince, Varane, stuck close to her side as if urging her not to be overawed.

The evening before, while Gweyr ate a rich, warming stew her father would love to have on the Boar's Head menu and mopped the gravy with a flat, soft bread which would have had Allsop keen to know the recipe, Hestia gave her a short lesson on the sharing of power between Sleih and Gryphon.

Tius Lord Gryphon, and Iaton King of the Sleih.

Their stern faces didn't surprise Gweyr, although the matching green of their different eyes was startling. It occurred to Gweyr that all the Sleih, and all the gryphons, had the same emerald green eyes. Her own, of which she'd always been proud, were pale cousins in comparison.

She returned the rulers' penetrating gazes, heat flushing her face. The king's eyes softened. He looked to Lord Tius, whose beak parted slightly.

'Yes,' the gryphon murmured, and only then did Gweyr realise she had been holding her breath.

'Daughter of the Sleih,' King Iaton said, 'from whence is your pure blood?'

There it was again. Daughter of the Sleih. And what did he

mean by pure blood? Sleih blood?

'My lords.' Gweyr fiddled with her silver chain, gathering courage from it, sensing her mother's soft touch on her shoulder. 'I don't know why you think of me as a daughter of the Sleih. My father's a Madach innkeeper from a long line of Barnaby's, all from Darnel. And Mam came from a village beyond Flaxburgh, where her family has farmed for generations.'

The unfriendly 'prentice seer shrugged. 'The lords of Asfarlon cannot be wrong in this matter. Besides'–she flicked her wrist impatiently–'Ashta would not have been able to bring you here if it were otherwise. Not when the entrances are guarded by Gryphon magic and Sleih spells.'

'But she could and did.' Varane appraised Gweyr anew with welcoming eyes.

The king and Lord Tius exchanged looks. Hestia blinked rapidly at Ilesse.

Gweyr pressed her lips together, to save herself from a retort. Something must be wrong with the girl. Maybe she wasn't normally rude.

'Ilesse, please to remember Gweyr is a guest in our caverns. You will speak with respect,' King Iaton said, gently enough.

Ilesse flushed. 'Forgive me.' She held out her hands to Gweyr. 'I have had an illness, I am not myself. I am truly sorry.'

Gweyr took hold of the offered hands, which were cool and soft. 'It's okay,' she said. 'I'm not myself at this moment either. It's all too strange, like I'm in one of Mam's fairytales and any moment I'll wake up from my dreams and be home in bed in Darnel.' She laughed, nervously. 'And I don't want to wake up.'

'Dreams!' Varane humphed. The king glared. The prince dropped his shoulders and stared through one of the tall windows where the mountains sparkled like diamonds in the clear morning light.

'Dreams?' Lord Tius tilted his eagle head.

'My lord'–Hestia scowled at Varane–'Ashta strongly suggested I ask our guest about her dreams, and about her mother. Gweyr, would you tell us?'

The Sleih and gryphons looked at Gweyr, who twisted her fingers together. Why this fascination with dreams? Still, if it was important. Her lips twitched, remembering Zoledore reprimanding Master Whittion.

'The dream Ashta was interested in was one I hadn't had for years. It has come to me more than once recently, but I can never remember it properly. I dreamed it the night after the wizards' conclave.' She briefly told of the hooded young woman, the bright light she carried, the dark chasm and stone bridge. 'It's all I can remember, I'm sorry.'

'Stone bridge?' Ilesse spoke sharply. 'Where seer Olban fell,' she said to Hestia. 'We must find this bridge.'

Hestia nodded.

Gweyr frowned. Unsurprising there was a stone bridge in the caverns. There must be dozens of them.

'It is something,' Lord Tius said. 'The woman with the cloak …' His eagle gaze fell on Ilesse.

'And the stories your mother told?' Ilesse either ignored or did not notice Lord Tius' scrutiny.

'Lots of them. Fairytales and legends, or so I thought.'

Gweyr's eyes prickled, imagining the stroke of the brush through her messy curls, hearing Mam's soft voice tell of magical beasts and wise people doing battle against evil wherever they found it in the world.

'My mam died, not long ago, of a wasting illness,' she said. 'She was beautiful to look at, and in her soul. I knew her stories from before I could speak and every night she would tell them to me.'

'Can you tell us one?' The king clasped the arms of his stone chair.

The request didn't come with a smile, which suggested this was not a story for the sake of telling stories. Was Gweyr being tested? And for what reason? If a king asks for a story, she supposed she had better find one to tell. Which? Ah, yes, her and Mam's favourite.

'The one I love best,' she said, 'is about a Sleih princess who took herself on an adventure, leaving her castle in the high mountains to explore the world. I suspect it's where I got my own idea about leaving Darnel to see what else was in the big wide world.' Gweyr threw out her arms to take in the Chamber and her audience. 'I had no idea about any of this, of course. Anyway, the princess didn't go alone. She had her magical beast with her, for they were always together. The sun shone, too hot for early spring. The magical beast counselled the princess they should go home to the castle, for there were rumblings in the ground to herald avalanches. But the stubborn princess insisted on going on.'

'This story–'

The king cut short Ilesse's interruption with a raised hand and a frown.

Gweyr clasped her hands in front of her. What about this story?

'Carry on,' Lord Tius said.

'The princess,' Gweyr said, 'was bored with castle life. She wanted to live somewhere where no one knew she was a princess. The beast should go home if it was afraid.'

She paused, remembering how Mam's voice faltered at the next part of the story, though why, Gweyr never understood.

'Of course,' she went on, 'the beast stayed with the princess and when the avalanche came, both would have been buried in the snow except the brave magical beast dragged the princess out, setting her free. The chastened princess understood she had been selfish to put the beast in danger, and together they returned, wet and cold, to the castle.'

Gweyr looked up at the two leaders of Asfarlon. She opened her mouth in an Oh of surprise. King Iaton's eyes filled with tears. Lord Tius shuffled on his fur pelt. She turned to Hestia. The gryphon gazed at her the way you gaze at someone you have not seen for years, hardly recognise, but are sure you know who they are.

Ilesse stood, frozen. The scowl was back on her forehead.

Hestia spoke first. 'Gweyr, do you know where your mother learned this story?'

'From her own mother.' Gweyr smiled. 'I'm glad she passed her stories on to me.'

Ilesse came to life. 'Why do you ask?' she said to Hestia. 'Many of our stories must be known to the Madach, remnants of the time when Sleih and Madach knew each other.'

'Not this story, 'prentice seer.' King Iaton sighed. 'Varane, please take our guest and find rooms for her, and anything else she needs. Then both go to Hestia's chamber. She and Ilesse will meet you there.'

'That's it?' Varane said. 'Don't you want to hear more stories? They might be important.'

'Not as important as this one, my son. Please, go now.' King Iaton gestured to the stairs.

Varane blew out a breath and led a puzzled Gweyr out of the chamber.

***

'Could it be she survived?' Hestia bobbed her head. It was all so long ago, all of them barely old enough to understand. Hestia's memories were of a laughing face which teased her for her lack of interest in the world beyond the mountains. A laughing face which, caught unawares, showed impatience, pinched with discontent.

'Aseera, our princess.' Tius faced Iaton. 'Your sister, old friend.'

'A grandmother to this Gweyr?' Iaton slowly shook his

head. 'Time moves differently in the Madach lands.'

'It's not using the magic.' Hestia raised her wings. 'Not using the magic shortens Sleih lives. We know this.'

Tius faced Hestia. 'The gryphon perished, her body found in the debris after the avalanche. Aseera's body was never found.'

'Tius, Hestia.' Iaton held his hands out wide. 'If Gweyr is Aseera's direct descendant, through the women …'

Hestia's beak opened and closed. 'Yes, my king. Yes.'

Chapter Twenty Nine

What can destroy the evil?

'What is Yes, my king?' Ilesse had to stride to keep up with Hestia's fast walk down the passageways to her caverns. 'I thought the story was from long, long ago and now it seems it's not. Why does no-one know about this Aseera? What has it got to do with anything, and especially with the Madach girl? Why did they call her daughter of the Sleih?'

Hestia stopped so abruptly Ilesse stumbled. 'Ilesse, my precious Ilesse. The old ones remember Aseera, she is not forgotten. And her story has everything to do with Gweyr.' She brought her tail around to touch Ilesse's arm. 'As for Daughter of the Sleih … you must keep that to yourself. Until it is certain and until Tius and Iaton decide what should be done.'

Her chest feathers rose and fell and Ilesse was sorry to have upset her friend and teacher. It didn't stop her wondering what needed to be done, however. How did it change anything?

'Stories will wait until this evil is dealt with.' Hestia resumed her rapid walk, claws and talons tapping loudly. 'There will be time afterwards for sorting old histories and putting things back to where they should be.'

Where they should be. The whisper seeped into Ilesse's head as the icy band squeezed her chest.

'Oh!' she cried, and pressed her hand to the wall, bent double with pain.

Insignificant, all of it, 'prentice seer, Ilesse, my queen. Your heart's desires fulfilled. Queen of the caverns.

'Ilesse, Ilesse.' Hestia's beak pressed against Ilesse's forehead.

I grow tired of waiting, my queen. You will come to me soon. You know what you want.

The vision came to her, blurred. It was like she peered through a snowstorm, snatching glimpses of something real and pleasurable, desired. Herself a powerful, all-knowing queen, casting strong magic for the good of those around her. Ruling the High Alps alongside this powerful being which had once been Olban. More than the High Alps. The grasslands, the high plains, on to Arneithe, and beyond, over the endless oceans from whence the being came.

Was this the desire of her heart? Yes, no …

Yes, my queen. Always. We will draw on the magic of Arneithe to make us wise and strong, knowing all things, more even than now.

Hestia lifted her wings. 'Go from here, evil one. Leave her!'

The whispers mocked. *Do not listen to the old beast. It is an animal, knowing nothing.*

Knowing nothing? An animal? Hestia? Ilesse fought the horror of it. She could do this, she could and would win. She had no desire to rule the lands all around, whether for good or not. It was the power, pressing its own ambitions on her. Although … No!

Hestia's urgent mutterings slowly overcame the whisperings. 'Come back to me, Ilesse, by all the power of Gryphon magic, carry your heart and soul to me.'

'Hestia, I am here.' Ilesse's legs trembled. She leaned against the wall, bent over, eyes closed. Her heart hammered, her skin was slick with sweat. Hestia gathered her up and cradled her in her wing.

'Come, 'prentice seer. You need rest.'

They stumbled along the passage to Ilesse's cavern where she fell onto the bed, glad to lie down, to not hear the whisperings. She slept.

***

Friendly whispers woke her. Her mind clear, her body refreshed, Ilesse lay a while, listening. Hestia and the incomer, Gweyr. A short pain stabbed at her heart. Jealousy. She pushed it aside, sat upright, lifted the fur and swung her legs to the cold floor.

'Ilesse! You're awake.' Hestia flew to her side, laying her beak on Ilesse's forehead. 'Good, good, there is no fever. How do you feel?'

'Well, thank you. And starving.'

Hestia pointed to a low table where Gweyr sat, watching them both. Who was this person? Was it possible she belonged here?

'Food and drink,' Hestia said. 'Go and eat, and I will tell what I have already told the councillors and the seers searching for the missing pages.'

Ilesse pulled a shawl around her shoulders and walked to the table. Darkness had come to the High Alps and the chill in the air made her grateful for the fire pit.

'Hestia has told me what ails you.' Gweyr pushed a plate and a basket of flatbreads towards Ilesse. 'I'm sorry, and I so much admire the strength it must take to resist those whisperings. I can't imagine what it does to you.'

Ilesse tipped her head in acknowledgement. 'I can only do it with Hestia's help, and others if they are able.' She broke a piece of bread, cut a hunk of cheese and cold meat and placed them on the plate.

Gweyr poured a mug of ibex milk and offered it to her with a slight grimace. 'I have to say I much prefer cows' milk.'

'Cows? Ah yes, I know. It must be amazing to live among such creatures.'

'Cows?' Gweyr laughed. 'We take them as much for granted as you take living with gryphons, and I can assure you the cows are way, way less interesting.'

Hestia sat between the two, her forelegs drawn underneath her, wings folded. 'I am glad to hear I am of more interest than a cow, Gweyr.' She opened her beak in a smile which widened as Gweyr blushed and stuttered an apology.

'No need, no need,' Hestia said. 'Now, I must tell you the seers have not found the missing pages. What they have found are other references which remained obscure and without meaning–until we put them together with your dream, Gweyr, and with your experience of the night you followed poor Olban, Ilesse. It all means we believe we have made progress in understanding this evil.'

'Defeating it?' Ilesse asked through a mouthful of cheese.

'Not yet, although there are glimmers. The missing pages … we desperately need the missing pages.' Hestia fell silent for a moment. 'Tomorrow we will continue to search the repository, go over what has already been done. They must be there, somewhere. But now'–she turned her gaze on Ilesse–'you will remember Lord Tius telling us how the gryphons brought the evil which had destroyed Arneithe with them to the High Alps?'

Ilesse set down her empty mug. 'You have told Gweyr the story so far?'

'I have.' Hestia paused again. 'Before they reached the Alps, the gryphons had to cross the grasslands and the high plains. The common story merges with the truth here. The gryphons met with the Sleih, who were indeed living among the Madach, serving them as low wizards with weak magic.'

Ilesse watched Gweyr, who nodded as she listened, taking it all in.

'The Madach fled south,' Hestia said, 'away from the evil. Most of the Sleih followed the gryphons into the mountains. They hoped they could combine their magic with ours to at least protect themselves, if not outright defeat the power. The Gryphon, who had been forest dwellers, were glad to have the talents of the Sleih in metal and gems, and accepted the alliance. A few Sleih chose to remain with the Madach, offering what protection they could.' She fluffed out her throat feathers. 'It would have been very little. Fortunately for the Madach, the power swept past, pursuing the gryphons whom it seemed intent on destroying.'

Gweyr nibbled a corner of flatbread. 'The descendants of those who stayed are wizards like Master Whittion and Rebar and Zoledore?' she said. 'The ones at the conclave.'

'Yes.' Hestia bobbed her head. 'The same, and it seems some have been more diligent than others.' She shifted on the rug, settled. 'Here in the High Alps, we found the caverns and made them our home. And in an attempt to defeat the evil, the sword Celeste was forged by the Sleih, imbued with Gryphon magic and wielded in the battle against the evil. We have just learned this is the sword's original purpose, which explains why the creatures flee from it.'

Cold seeped through Ilesse's heart. The sword which hacked at her beauties, the hateful sword. She stilled the thought, concentrated on Hestia.

'Can it be used against the evil itself?' Gweyr stretched her hands over the fire.

Hestia half-lifted herself to shake out her wings. 'Sadly, no. Too many aeons have passed. Its magic is much weakened and it is never possible to restore lost magic.'

Nothing to hurt us now. The voice sneered, and left.

Ilesse breathed deeply. 'What happened?' she asked.

'The Sleih and Gryphon joined forces, flying from the mountain tops to drive the power into the deep chasms. What form this power took, legend does not say. It may have been the towering cloud of stinking, oily ash it manifested in Arneithe. Whatever, it resisted all attacks, until–'

'–diamonds tempted it into the depths, led it to the chasm in the cavern with the stone bridge.' Ilesse finished the sentence.

Her accusing eyes found Hestia. 'If you knew this legend, why did you give the book I found to Olban?'

Hestia humphed. 'I had forgotten it. And the book carried veiled hints, nothing outright and in obscure language.' She curled her tail, the bob at the end twitching. 'It was when Olwyn reminded me, the day of the Challit, I realised what a fool I'd been.'

'What happened?' Gweyr repeated Ilesse's question.

'We hoped the evil was vanquished. Gryphon spells sealed the chasm. Gryphon and Sleih stayed in the Alps to protect the high plains and grasslands. Arneithe was left to restore itself, which in time, it did. Although it is said remnants of evil lurk there to this day.' Hestia fell silent. Only the soft crackle of the firepit disturbed the air.

'And it worked,' Ilesse said. She fought the glee squirming in her bowels. 'Until now.'

Chapter Thirty

More flee

The hot sun which had beaten down all morning had hidden itself behind a gathering mountain of black clouds. The heavy, sultry air weighed on Allsop like the guilt which burdened him for his lack of visits home to Atias. The current circumstances would hardly make it a festive homecoming. His imagination failed him when trying to fit a gathering of wizards, Sleih hunters and gryphons into the quiet hamlet. His mam and dad would be upset at the strangeness, if not outright frightened. There could be fighting, on their doorstep. Literally.

The stone-like weight in his gut worsened at the idea of fighting. He had a weapon, of sorts. The blacksmith had laboured through the night to make two pikes, one for him and one for Conall. Allsop had tired of trying to hold the weapon upright. It hung awkwardly along Chester's side, forever threatening to send horse and rider into the road without ever meeting an enemy.

Master Whittion had planned to ride Chester. Until the horse ignored him, whinnying loudly at Allsop's approach when they went to prepare him for the journey.

'You must ride him,' Master Whittion said. 'After all, you might need to go into battle and I would rather you were on a horse you know.'

Allsop grimaced. Into battle? Soldiering was not for him. His childhood home was threatened and to defend it, he would fight. Or die fighting. He lifted his shoulders. Better to die a hero's death than cower in a locked cellar in the Boar's Head. Surely?

'More people fleeing.' Conall pointed to a dusty cloud travelling towards them. He rode beside Allsop, carrying his pike comfortably at an angle across Millie's saddle.

Millie pricked her ears and tossed her head.

Barnaby had offered Millie, saying to Allsop, 'The old mare's sprightly as a four-year-old. Whatever Gweyr did to her, it's perked the old girl up something lively. She needs exercise and I can't give it to her.' He rubbed his chin, the tea towel slung over his shoulder. 'Got enough to do persuading people to take all this seriously, what with Beddle telling everyone there's no need to panic, it's all happening elsewhere.' He stroked the mare's velvet neck. 'Make sure young Conall is careful with her, hey, and it'll be one less thing for me to worry about.'

Allsop could swear the mare knew what was going on. Same with Chester. He remembered seeing Ashta near the two horses at the time Gweyr left Ledrith. He leaned forward to pat Chester's neck. 'Did Ashta give you and Millie a bit of this Gryphon magic she says she doesn't have?'

Chester tossed his head and Allsop managed a smile for the first time in a while.

The dusty group slowly transformed into laden wagons with men, women and children walking stolidly beside them. Cows were tethered to the wagons. A small flock of sheep bleated along behind, herded by a grey and white dog.

Allsop, Conall and Master Whittion pulled to the side of the stony track.

'What news?' the master asked the first of the travellers.

This was a tall, handsome woman of middle years, with olive skin and long dark hair. She wore a deep red cape, a crimson hat and carried a staff. Allsop wondered if she might be a magician.

'None good,' the woman said. 'The white abomination heads our way, has harried too many of our farms and hamlets. So we flee.' She narrowed her eyes at the master. 'Will we be welcome in the south? You hail from there?'

'Yes, we travel from Darnel to Atias, to help as we can to defend our lands.' Master Whittion held himself taller.

The woman snorted. 'I hope there's more than the three of you, and'–she tossed a glance at Allsop's awkwardly held pike–'there are more experienced soldiers where you go.'

'There are many gathering, summoned by the Sleih and Gryphon hunters.' Conall brandished his upright pike and the woman rewarded him with a thin-lipped smile.

'You believe these fairytales?' she said. 'There's been talk of such on our way, though we've not seen sight nor sign of anything bar others fleeing as we do.'

'They exist, we have seen them.' Allsop held his pike firmly. 'Take courage. The Madach don't face this threat alone. The fairytales are true. We have met and spoken with them. They help us.'

'You've seen them?' The woman glanced at her people walking slowly by, showing no interest in her conversation with the strangers. 'I will tell them. It might cheer them. Thank you.' She nodded, and walked on, her step lighter.

The last of the complaining sheep passed them and Allsop urged Chester onto the track.

Hope. The promise of hope, however slight, had eased the woman's burden. Allsop tried to let it ease his.

Chapter Thirty One

The lost is found

Gweyr gazed about the repository in astonishment. Lit by giant glowstones, cavern after cavern of shelves, towering cupboards and wide tables overflowed with books of every age, size and thickness. Curious-looking instruments, multi-hued globes, statues, bowls and plates of metal and clay fashioned in a myriad shapes and patterns lay scattered between the books and on the smooth rock floor.

'Is there any order to this?' she asked Hestia.

Ilesse answered. 'There was. The searching has upset everything and no one has time to put it to rights.'

'It's vast.' An impossible task. 'Torn out pages, right?' A needle in a haystack.

'Yes,' Ilesse called, already on her way to a far shelf. 'This is as far as it's been searched the second time.'

Gweyr blew out a breath. 'I'll take'–she gazed around–'the room through there.'

Hestia raised her wings. 'Mainly statues in there. However, there may be papers in a drawer or a cupboard.' She waved a wing towards the opening. 'Yes, start there.' She moved off to search beside Ilesse, keeping the 'prentice seer close, as ever.

Gweyr had forgiven Ilesse's volatile moods, grieving for the girl's struggle. If this was how the evil showed itself in one person, what horrors were in store if it infected all? And the creatures of mountains, plains and grasslands. The trees too, Hestia had told her.

These missing pages needed to be found. More, they needed to tell the Sleih and Gryphon seers the secret of the evil's destruction. Gweyr marched to the cavern, praying her search would yield answers.

While not as big as the main repository, the number of statues, cupboards, and tables crammed into the space sent her mind into a whirl of indecision of where to begin. She walked between the tables, all bearing bowls, jugs and plates patterned with wildflowers. Movement caught her eye. The wildflowers, when gazed at long enough, swayed in an unfelt breeze. She ran a hand over an oval platter gritty with dust, her innkeeper eye admiring the utility as well as the artistry of what must be a dinner service for an infinite number of guests.

The pages! She was here to find torn out pages, not admire crockery.

She peered into jugs, ran her hand around the inside of pots and pulled out drawers. Cutlery with ornately worked and jewelled handles lived in them, with occasional carved mats and silvered rings, like serviette rings. What grand feasts these pieces would have seen.

She worked methodically around the room, table to table, cupboard to cupboard, squatting to push her hand between the statues and the rocky walls, hoping she would touch paper or parchment rather than stone.

The morning passed. Her throat became dry and hunger prodded at her belly, yet she had not found a scrap of paper anywhere, let alone torn out pages of ancient text.

Hestia appeared in the opening. Gweyr glanced at her.

'Nothing,' Hestia said. 'And noon meal calls.'

'Yes–' Gweyr broke off, her attention caught by a statue of a gryphon standing at the end of the table she had been exploring. The silver statue bore grey spots of tarnish. Jewels set into its wings glittered dully beneath dust, but it was the eyes which attracted Gweyr. They were white, either glass or diamonds. They shone, dust free. In every other statue Gweyr had seen, the eyes were green. The silver gryphon's beak was open wide, a brilliant red stone tucked into the opening. A ruby?

Gweyr reached a finger in to touch the stone. It fell away, inside the statue.

'Oh!' She waited for the clink of jewel against metal. A dull rustling sounded instead. Something, like paper, lay inside. She forgot her growling stomach.

'It's hollow,' she said to Hestia, who had come closer to see what Gweyr was doing. 'I think I should be able to get my hand–'

'What are you doing?' Ilesse crowded close to Gweyr, hissing. Her eyes were black pools, her mouth twisted in a snarl. The 'prentice seer raised her hand, ready to strike out.

Gweyr stepped back, heart thudding.

'No!' Hestia cried. She pushed Ilesse, sending her stumbling against a statue of a stag.

Ilesse scrambled up, screaming. 'Leave it, leave it, leave it! It's not for you, idiots, inept magicians. Not for you!'

She jumped between Gweyr and the gryphon statue, reached out her hand to push it down the open throat.

'No!' Hestia encircled Ilesse with her great wings. 'Go, demon, go from her, leave her.' She chanted into Ilesse's hair, nodding at Gweyr to do what she had to do, quickly.

Gweyr thrust her hand into the statue's mouth. She stretched as far as her arm would allow, the muscles pulling.

There, a crumpled ball of paper. She could, barely, wrap her fingers around it, hoist it out. Without stopping to see what she had, she fled the cavern, pausing at the entrance to briefly glance back.

Hestia held a sobbing Ilesse. 'Fetch Varane to Ilesse's room,' the gryphon called to Gweyr. 'With Celeste.'

Gweyr ran.

***

An exhausted Ilesse slept, watched over by Varane with Celeste at his side.

When Hestia had arrived with the shaking 'prentice seer, Ilesse had shied from the prince, her arm outstretched, palm up to shield herself. Gweyr watched, curious.

'Ah,' Hestia said. 'I should have understood earlier.'

'What?' Varane moved further from Ilesse.

'The sword. The evil hates the sword.'

Gweyr and the prince looked to Celeste.

'Like with the white monsters,' Varane said.

'Yes.' Ilesse had kept a good distance between herself and the sword, stumbling to her bed. 'It pains me, here'–she put a hand to her chest–'but it might help, like it helped in the fighting. I would rather suffer the pain than those whisperings.'

Gweyr and Hestia had left Varane to watch over the sleeping Ilesse, snatched a little food, and taken their crumpled find to the gryphon's chambers. They stood side by side at a workbench, peering at it.

'I have given Ilesse a draught to deepen her sleep,' Hestia said. 'I suspect it best for her to be unaware when we uncurl these pages, even if she is not present.'

Gweyr agreed. The fury and hatred on Ilesse's face in the repository frightened her.

'Your young fingers will be a better tool than these.' Hestia touched Gweyr's hand with a wing tip. 'We must preserve as much of the text as we can.'

The weight of responsibility lay heavy on Gweyr. 'Shouldn't we ask one of the Sleih seers to do this?'

'No. I worry what is written here and what power lies in the words, especially for one practised in strong magic.' She nudged Gweyr with her beak. 'You will do well, don't worry. I will guide you. Just go very slowly.'

The pages were of leather parchment, brittle and cracked

from centuries hidden in the dry dark. Gweyr prayed they didn't crumble to ashes the moment she peeled away one leaf. She drew a deep breath and bent to the task, aided by a bright glowstone, a palette knife and Hester's instructions.

It would be a long afternoon, and possibly night.

Chapter Thirty Two

What needs to be done

'We have found the missing pages of the text I gave to Olban and worked through the night to discover its obscure meanings.' Hestia let her gaze rest on the Alps, glowing pink with dawn through the Eternal Chamber's translucent windows. 'If our seers have translated well, if we have interpreted correctly, it holds the key to how we might defeat this evil.'

The councillors' paid keen attention. Hestia's gaze took them all in, resting at last on Tius and Iaton. 'My lords, the text confirms the fascination of diamonds for the power behind the evil. It desires them above all other gems. Hence its awakening by the diamond Seer Olban unwittingly carried to it.'

'I hope there is more than this, Hestia,' a tall, thin councillor growled.

She fluffed her feathers. 'Patience, my friend. There is more.' She closed her third eye, opened it. 'Legend tells us diamonds tempted the power to the chasms.'

'If only I could remember where.'

Ilesse's murmur to Gweyr–both standing at the top of the stairs into the Chamber–stole into Hestia's eagle hearing. Yes. To know that place would help immensely.

She pushed the thought aside. 'And when our ancient brothers and sisters sealed it within,' she said, 'they cast strong magic over other gems to make the bindings tight. Sapphires, emeralds and rubies.' She paused, looked around at the attentive faces. 'While never tested, these jewels might–might–subdue the evil, the text suggests.'

Ilesse barked a scornful laugh. 'Pretty tales indeed.'

Hestia swung about. The 'prentice seer stared from black, dull eyes. She clenched her fingers into tight balls. She sneered. 'Pretty tales to comfort the children.'

The councillors sat with mouths agape and eyes wide.

'You tell them, *No monsters here.*' Ilesse giggled, a high, grating sound. '*Pretty baubles will banish the darkness.*'

Hestia sickened at the scornful glee. She rushed to Ilesse, tried to enfold her in her wings. The girl shoved hard against her. She tried again and was repulsed with a strength beyond the 'prentice seer's own.

'Nothing,' Ilesse hissed, 'will stop me.' She spread her arms wide, grinning. 'Not your baubles, not your pathetic magic–'

Hestia wrapped her neck around Ilesse's head, muffling her rantings. She gripped the floor with claws and talons, holding solid against flailing arms and kicking feet.

'Begone, begone,' she cried.

Ilesse beat her arms against Hestia's neck, her soft sandals slithering on the shiny rock.

Gweyr pounced, trying to capture Ilesse's arms, to pin them to her side. And was sent sprawling by a wild punch.

Tius jumped from his pelt, tail flicking. He joined his power with Hestia's. Chanting rose across the chamber as councillors and Iaton added their own magic.

It went on for a long time.

Ilesse clawed at Hestia's neck, moaned and screamed. At last she slumped, eyes closed. Hestia blinked hard, heart thudding. She cradled the unconscious girl against her.

'She is nearly spent,' Tius said. 'She cannot resist much longer.'

'Resist what?' A gryphon councillor asked sharply.

'We believe,' Hestia said, attempting confidence, 'our 'prentice seer is attacked by this power from time to time. It wishes her to join with it.'

Iaton did not wait for questions. 'Pray she does not succumb.' He fell into his stone chair, brushing a shaking hand across his face. 'The horrors this evil unleashes will be magnified over and over if it captures the 'prentice seer.'

Tius touched his beak to Ilesse's head. 'You are right, Iaton.' He gazed around the chamber. 'We must find a way to defeat this wickedness. For the 'prentice seer has more innate power in her little finger than Olban had in a lifetime of learning. She is a rich prize.'

***

Gweyr pressed a hand against the wall, waiting for her head to cease its dizzying whirl. She had pulled herself up from Ilesse's blow, bent, hands on her knees, gasping. She had regained her breath, listening to the chanting grow, to seep into her mind.

A shiver had run through her, not unpleasant. It was as if a charge of lightning pulsed through her veins, awakening senses which had always lain deep within her and were now set free. The words were unintelligible, yet carried meaning. The chants had flowed through the air as tangible as streams of water across a plain.

When the chanting ceased, the pulsing of her blood steadied, leaving behind a fresh, tempered exhilaration.

Now Gweyr watched the councillors take in the implications of Lord Tius' words. Seated once more on stools and pelts, they bit their lips, opened their beaks and murmured to each other. Gweyr joined with their feelings of shock, their foreboding terror at what might come.

'Yes,' Hestia said. 'There is much at stake.' She looked at Gweyr. 'You must tell them the rest. It is fitting, as you were the one who found the clues.'

She allowed Ilesse to be taken from her by two Sleih healers summoned to help. They lifted the girl onto a leather stretcher and walked from the chamber. Hestia followed closely.

The rulers and councillors turned to Gweyr, who flushed hot to the roots of her black curls.

'Well, Gweyr?' King Iaton said kindly. 'The councillors know how you come to be here. I understand we are in your debt for finding what others could not. Will you finish what Hestia started to tell?'

He pointed to an empty stool and Gweyr sat, reluctantly. She would rather have stood despite the tremble in her legs.

'Yes, my lords … and councillors.' She let her hands rest on the table and forced herself not to look at them, instead lifting her head to address the king. 'There was a lot of argument over the translation.'

The councillors' soft laughter was strained.

'In the end,' Gweyr went on, 'everyone agreed the gist of it is that the evil can be destroyed, or at least defeated … they couldn't agree of course … by a silver winged lion … that bit was clear … of sapphires, emeralds and rubies, wielded, or maybe carried, by a woman–this was another big discussion, was it any woman or did it have to be one who carried magic within her?' She sighed. 'Anyway, to be on the safe side, someone with magic, maybe power, to resist.' She bit her lip.

'Ah.' Lord Tius bobbed his head. 'Thank you, Gweyr.'

'The silver winged lion, the jewels, all describe the decoration on Celeste,' a gryphon said.

'We cannot trust the sword's much faded magic to triumph,' another said. 'Good enough to scare abominable beasts. Not good enough to destroy them outright.'

'A new sword?' A Sleih councillor threw out his hands.

'Possibly.' King Iaton stroked his beard. 'I believe the evil will be prepared for a weapon, if it knows its own history. A silver gryphon with sapphires, emeralds and rubies is clear.

Whatever shape it takes needs to be subtle to fool the power into thinking it is in no danger. Maybe the wielder needs to offer diamonds first.'

'And it should weigh little,' Lord Tius said. 'The wielder should be unburdened, able to move swiftly out of danger.'

Gweyr pulled at her silver chain. Subtle, light. Yes, of course!

'A necklace.' She lifted the chain from her neck. 'A woman wearing a necklace is common. My mother gave it to me for my fourteenth birthday and it hasn't come off since.'

Lord Tius fixed Gweyr with an eagle eye. 'Your fourteenth birthday? May I see?' He padded around the side of the table to stand close to Gweyr. He glanced at the slim chain and then at King Iaton. Neither spoke. Lord Tius returned to his pelt.

Although desperate to know what that was all about, Gweyr understood she couldn't ask right then. She would find out eventually. She hoped.

'You are right, Gweyr,' the king said. 'And if you are willing, we do not need to forge a new necklace. I would use your chain and shape an ornament, a pendant, to be attached to it.'

'My chain?' It would mean lending–or giving–Mam's chain to someone else, likely a stranger. And if the stranger perished in her battle with this evil power, the chain would be gone. Forever.

'Yes, your chain. It is my belief your chain is our best hope of success. Especially'–the king leaned forward to look into Gweyr's eyes–'if you will consent to wear it.'

Chapter Thirty Three

Bitter struggles

'They want you to face this evil?' Ilesse stared at the Madach–Gweyr, her name was Gweyr–from her bed. 'They would send you to your death, with no thought?' Her tumbled emotions spun between mocking laughter and horror.

She lifted her head to speak to Hestia. 'Why send her? Who do they think she is? How can they think she won't be overtaken in the single beat of a heart? She has no magic, she knows nothing.'

Gweyr wriggled, clasping and unclasping her hands. Ilesse knew she agreed with her. Fear and uncertainty radiated from her as clearly as the orange flames of the fire pit flickered. Daughter of the Sleih? No, impossible.

Yet there was something else, something new. Ilesse hesitated, reached out and was met by a spark–of magic. Weak still, but there.

Yes, weak. An imposter, an enemy.

Ilesse drew on her fresh strength to squash the whisper. She frowned. 'Well?' she asked Hestia. 'Why do they choose her?'

'Hush.' Hestia blinked quickly. 'It is not my place to tell what is suspected.'

'What is suspected?' Varane wriggled on the cushion where he sat, hand hovering over the low table to choose what he might eat next.

'As I said, not my place to say,' Hestia said, with a curious glance at Varane. She ruffled her throat feathers. 'At this moment, Ilesse, we need your parents. We have to instruct them in the immediate making of this pendant.' She beckoned Varane with her wing. 'My prince, there is no time to be lost. Seek out Myar and Bakran and have them come here, please.'

Varane sprang up with a bounce which cried out his happiness to be doing something other than guarding Ilesse. She watched him go, struggling with the bitterness in her heart. Her parents would make this ornament. And a stranger would wield it. It made no sense.

'I am the one the power seeks,' she protested. 'I am the one who resists, overcoming it every time. It should be me!' She clapped a hand to her mouth, horrified at her demanding tone. The icy band tightened, squeezing her chest.

Yes, 'prentice seer, my queen, it should be you. The whispers filled her head, willing her to listen, to obey. *Your heart's desire, you and this jewel they make, both will be mine.*

Both? Yes, that was her heart's desire, to belong where her own power was valued. Not to have it ignored, to have her wearying struggles set aside as if they were nothing. Her pain grew.

They know not the power of the knowledge they bring us. Not to destroy. To strengthen. With this jewel, we will rule the caverns forever, and beyond, as far as the farthest reaches of Arneithe and all the Madach lands beyond.

To strengthen. Yes, it would make her stronger, grow in knowledge, know all things.

The whispers faded, the tightness loosened. Ilesse gazed up at Hestia who stared down at her, her third eye flickering. A cold stillness came over her.

'Is all well?' the gryphon asked.

'Yes, all is well.' Ilesse wearied of Hestia's fussing. Wearied too of fighting. They would give her place to a stranger and expect her to sit by and say, thank you. She would not. She would prove herself strong enough to bear the pendant, when it was made. She would surprise them all.

Soon, my queen.

Ilesse caught in her breath. 'Soon,' she murmured.

***

Being in one of Mam's fairytales wasn't quite as Gweyr had imagined. Not her fate, after all, to ride a magical beast into battle, waving a bright sword against evil yet tangible creatures. No, she would walk, her one weapon against a most intangible evil being a necklace with a pendant hanging from it.

A chilling doubt seeped into her, despite the heat in Myar and Bakran's workshop. The hot odour of molten metal hung in air which gleamed blue, green and red from the vibrant jewels being shaped to fit the silver gryphon's body.

Gweyr had gone with Ilesse to watch the silversmiths' handiwork and to see more of what went on in the unending maze of caverns. Varane would have been there if a more desperate than usual assault on the caverns' entrances hadn't called him away. Hestia too was absent, summoned to the Eternal Chamber. She had fussed and hesitated.

'I am well,' Ilesse assured her teacher. 'There has been no attack since the council meeting. Seer Olban must be distracted elsewhere, or has given up.'

Gweyr hoped so. She didn't believe it though. And neither did Hestia, who left with many a backward glance and pleas that she must be summoned if Ilesse showed any unease.

'There.' Bakran straightened from his workbench. He held the pendant out to Gweyr and Ilesse. 'Our gryphon is exquisite.' He smiled at Myar who had shaped the soft silver of the body and uplifted wings, shaping tiny talons and paws, drawing out a curling, tufted lion-like tail, and forming the open beak. Bakran had cut the jewels, covering the head and wings with feathered sapphires and inserting two brilliant emerald eyes and a minute ruby tongue.

'If you will give me your chain, Gweyr, I will put the two together,' Myar said. 'It will mean you can carry this in safety to the seers for the weaving of the spells.'

Ilesse's eyes narrowed briefly before she said, 'Yes, that would be wisest.'

Myar took the unclasped chain in her palm. She peered at it closely, ran a finger along the links, examined it every which way.

'Is something wrong?' Gweyr asked.

'Wrong?' Myar looked up. 'Not wrong, it's …' She lay the chain on the workbench and fetched an eyeglass. 'Ah.' She peered sideways at Gweyr. 'Has no one spoken to you about this chain?'

'No.' Gweyr recalled the king and Lord Tius exchanging looks over the chain, remembered their interest in how Mam gave it to her on her fourteenth birthday. 'Is it special?'

'Perhaps.' Bakran took the chain and threaded it through the ring on the gryphon pendant. 'However'–he gave Myar a warning glance–'it is up to others to know this and to pass the knowledge on.' He handed the chain and jewel to Gweyr. 'I will say this, however: I have not seen the likes of such a chain for many years.' He bent his head in a short bow. 'Go safe, Daughter of the Sleih.'

'Come.'

Gweyr, wondering again at the name, flinched at Ilesse's peremptory command.

'We cannot dawdle here. The seers wait for us.' The 'prentice seer turned to go, twisted back to her parents. 'Thank you. It is a wonderful gift you have made. One which will be remembered down the generations.'

Myar and Bakran frowned at the tone of their daughter's voice. Gweyr understood. It carried a hint of mockery. She followed Ilesse, the gryphon a strange weight nestling in the hollow of her neck.

A stranger weight settled in the hollow of her stomach.

Chapter Thirty Four

Green and silver fire

'Nearly there.'

Tension, worry, and riding all day through gusting wind and heavy, humid rain, bled into Allsop's weariness. A stream of refugees had slowed their way on this final day of their journey. It had also heightened his uneasiness as he searched for his parents among the wagonloads of families escaping the monstrous white threat. Hoping to make better time, he had left the road to the refugees once they were in familiar countryside, leading Conall and Master Whittion along stony paths sunk deep between drystone walls. The uneven, soaked and slippery ground forced the horses to a slow walk. Conall grumbled the roundabout ways didn't appear to save them much time.

They emerged from one such path onto a wider, smoother track. Allsop turned Chester left to where the dying sun reflected red against boiling, black clouds. The sultry air carried a faint smell, like molten metal, overlaid with the contrary smell of cold ashes. The rain had stopped, for now. He squinted into the meagre light and drew in a breath.

In the near distance, silhouettes of winged figures dived and rose.

'Sleih and gryphon hunters.' Anxiety beat at his chest. 'What are they doing?'

'Patrolling, I hope.' Conall's voice showed his own tiredness.

'Or fighting.'

'You think these creatures have reached here already?' Master Whittion halted his horse alongside Millie and Chester.

'Let's move on.' Fear overcame Allsop's fatigue. 'Atias is close, we'll be there before full dark.' He waved his hand and spurred Chester into a canter. His fear deepened when he rounded a tight bend between thick hedges.

Despite the blustering wind, tall flames leaped straight up into the sky. Their expected red and gold flickered oddly green, tinged with bright silver.

'The hamlet's on fire!' He reined Chester in, shouting over his shoulder.

'No.' Master Whittion stood in his stirrups to peer over the hedge. 'The flames come from fires in the fields.'

'In the fields? Are they burning crops?'

'Magic fire,' the master said, 'to keep the white horde at bay. See, the fires stretch either side of the hamlet.'

'There's fighting too.' Conall brandished his pike in the direction of a tall, wide-branched tree in a corner of the field. Two riderless Gryphon hunters attacked a swirling swarm which leaped at them before breaking apart and fleeing.

Allsop kicked gently at Chester's sides, urging him on. The need to know what was happening in his home clawed at him like a scrabbling rat.

With the heavy dusk settling, the strange fires cast a spectral light over the track through Atias. The molten metal smell grew stronger, diminishing the scent of ash. Nothing and no one moved. Had his parents chosen to stay, or were they trudging the churned up road south seeking safety? Allsop didn't know which he hoped for.

'Isn't that Zoledore?' Conall peered through the wavering light.

A torch hanging from an inn's sign lit a group of men and women standing in a tight circle. In the middle, tall, stately

Zoledore pounded his staff into the mud. Drawing near, Allsop recognised wizards from the conclave, including Rebar. Each had grown older than a few days should have allowed. Perhaps it was the greenish light, which didn't account for their tousled hair and wrinkled clothes. Their heavy eyes lit up at the sight of the newcomers.

'Whittion!' Rebar stepped forward and reached up to grasp the master's hand. 'You're a welcome sight. We can use all the wizardry we can muster.'

'The green and silver fire? Yours?' Master Whittion swung heavily off his horse to greet his fellow wizards.

'Gryphon hunters and Sleih riders woke the fire, which needs no timber or coal to keep it burning. It does, however, consume chants and incantations, which is a hot, wearisome task.'

'It's kept the creatures at bay, for the time being.' A woman in a purple cloak gestured at the blazing fields.

'We are fortunate they are few.' Zoledore stamped his staff into the road. 'So far. For every one which flees or is slain, three more appear from the high plains. Their numbers grow both day and night.'

Master Whittion handed his horse's reins to Conall. 'Find food, water and somewhere for the horses to shelter,' he said. 'I'll stay here and do what I need to do. You and Allsop search out the Sleih rider, let him know you've arrived.'

'Have all the people fled?' Allsop asked Rebar.

'Nearly all. But refugees take their place and more arrive every day, like the white creatures.' He gazed across to the green and silver fires. 'Most travel further south, where supposedly there is safety.'

***

Full darkness fell. Shadows passed across lighted windows as Allsop led Conall to his parents' home. They had not left, and were delighted and horrified to have their son appear out of the coloured darkness.

Allsop embraced his parents tightly.

'Your room is taken by a woman,' his mother said, 'and four tired, frightened little ones. She's the wife of one of those wizards who've come to help, wouldn't stay behind without him.' She lifted a ladle from a black pot simmering on the cooking range and sipped at it, frowning.

The aromatic steam stirred Allsop's hunger into a noisy clamour.

His mother set the ladle down. 'And a young man and his pregnant wife sleep on rugs by the fire.'

'We'll bed down in the barn with the horses.' Allsop twisted his lips in a half-smile. 'We're at home in barns these days.'

His father smiled softly at Allsop's feigned lightness.

Allsop ate sparingly, mindful of other hungry souls in the household and hamlet. Food ran low, his father told them. The folk who had joined the southward exodus took with them anything which could be carried away. The few cows left behind had been brought to the byres so they could be milked, with the milkers sleeping with the cattle and filling the pails of the villagers who ventured there. No bread was being baked, no cheese or butter made.

'Let's find this Sleih rider.' Conall swallowed the last of his meal and carried his plate to a wash bowl on a tidy bench under a window. 'What's his name?'

'Gilias, Giliar?' Allsop added his plate to Conall's and turned to his parents, sitting at the table. 'Mam, Dad, you'll stay inside no matter what happens, won't you? Keep the others here. Bolt this door once we leave.' He gave a firm nod. 'Conall and me'll be home by morning, I promise.'

Pulling open the door, he hoped the promise could be kept. The fires' green and silver flames glittered brighter as the night darkened, reflected against the louring clouds. The wind whipped shouts and cries across the roofs and along the track, whether in anger, triumph, fear or pain, he could not tell. The molten metal smell gave more weight to the already heavy air. Allsop found it hard to breathe.

Conall shut the door with a firm click. 'Let's see where this Gilias, Giliar, is and get our orders.' He marched towards the inn. Allsop hurried behind, his heart thumping at the thought he would soon be in the thick of whatever was happening out there.

The inn stood on a rise, giving a view over the fields. Gryphons with and without riders harried those creatures which tried to slink between the green and silver blazes. Two to three wizards gathered at each fire, staffs held upright, their heads bent to the flames. Some fires blazed fiercely, others sank low. Two figures, possibly Rebar and Whittion, moved swiftly among the wizards, sending some to different fires, urging others across the black grass to the inn, and rest. The failing fires flared with stronger magic. At the same time more, further away, faltered. There were not enough wizards, there was not enough power, to keep the defences strong.

'Wizard Whittion's apprentices?' The Sleih rider, Giliar (Allsop remembered) strode out of the inn into their path.

'Yes, we came, both of us,' Conall said.

Giliar's tired eyes settled on Allsop. 'Yes, your home. Of course you came. Though what you can do …'

'What of your home? Of Asfarlon?' Allsop said.

'Asfarlon holds against the siege, for now.' Giliar shrugged. 'I have come from there today, with new rumours of an ancient wizardry being finally discovered which might help. Who knows what is true.' He pressed his lips together and peered into the green light. 'When I left the caverns, I rode above more of this horde. They swarm east and west like a plague of white rats, accompanied by a creeping black fog roiling from the valleys onto the high plains. A great mass of them will be here by morning.'

Allsop's stomach lurched. 'Can we hold them?'

'Possibly. If the wizards have the strength to keep the fires going, we may keep the creatures from Atias itself.'

'They will go around, won't they?' Conall said into the short silence. He shifted from foot to foot like a child trying to contain his eagerness.

Giliar nodded.

'What can we do?' While not sharing Conall's excitement, Allsop hoped a clear task might distract his fretting fear.

Giliar eyed the two of them, his appraising eyes suggesting he saw them as Allsop knew they were: sadly unprepared to face the dangers outside the hamlet.

The Sleih rider pulled in his lips. 'There is something.' He bent his gaze on Conall. 'Before the white creatures arrived,' he said, 'we set two signal beacons on the hill to the west. I need someone to light those beacons when the time comes. One beacon warns others we are defeated and the creatures' ravages go on. Two signal victory.' He moved his scrutiny to Allsop. 'Sending a Sleih rider means one who can no longer fight. You are no use to me here. Your usefulness is in watching what happens and choosing when, and how many, of those beacons to light.'

Go out there, beyond the defensive fires, into the jaws and claws of those creatures? Alone, the two of them. Allsop had an urge to curl into a ball and tuck himself under a rock.

'We can do that.' Conall bounced on the balls of his feet, grinning.

Giliar shrugged and spoke to Allsop. 'You are a native of this hamlet, well placed to fulfil this role. Should you take it.' He stretched back his shoulders and waited.

Allsop lifted his head high. He didn't glance at Conall, too taken with returning the Sleih rider's challenging stare and quieting the thump of his heart.

'It's an honourable role. We will do it,' he said.

Chapter Thirty Five

Gryphon magic

Forty seers, Gryphon and Sleih, clustered around a long stone table centred in a vast shadowy cavern. A large diamond sat at one end of the table, glinting in the dim light. At the other end lay the chain and pendant, the silver blending into the smooth, grey surface. Ilesse eyed it, her face solemn as expected, hearing whispers fall as soft as night snow inside her head.

Soon my queen. Bring it to me. All your desires ….

She clasped her hands together, gripping her fingers hard to stop from reaching out to grab the jewel.

Not yet, my sweet. Too soon. Let the ignorant magicians do what they must do. We have waited so long. Minutes more do not matter.

Ilesse's eyes followed old Olwyn as she reached out a wing to touch the chain.

'My eyes fail me. My magic does not.' Olywn ran her feather tips over the chain, her eagle eyes half closed.

What was special about the chain?

'Hestia?' The old gryphon peered into the crowd.

'She's been summoned to the council,' the imposter girl said. 'She'll come when she can. She said you should start.'

Olywn, balancing the chain on her wing, limped to the girl.

'The chain is yours?'

'Yes.'

'Where did you get it?' Olwyn fixed her with an eagle stare. The gryphon's tail lifted, fell.

Ilesse wanted to shout: 'Can you do what you must do, not ask these inane questions?' She fought to silence herself. The whispering voice urged, *Patience, my queen, patience.*

'Mam gave it to me for my fourteenth birthday.'

Olywn stared into the imposter's eyes. Ilesse simmered with irritation. After an age, the gryphon hobbled to the table, set the chain and pendant down and began to mutter incantations over it.

Other seers joined her. The cavern filled with a lilting chanting which soothed Ilesse's temper.

Yes, my queen, it has begun.

Magic flowed in coloured ribbons from the mouths of the seers, wafting to the chain and its pendant. The silver gryphon swelled and shone, bigger and brighter until it glowed like a winter moon to light the deepest corners of the cavern. The chain also grew, lifting and coiling, snaking about the gryphon pendant, claiming it for its own.

As the chain grew, shallow etchings in the links appeared. Ilesse strained to read them–Old Sleih lettering.

Queen. The Old Sleih word for queen.

My queen, you see? This belongs with you. It is meant.

Ilesse's lips tugged at their corners in a stifled gleeful grin. She pressed them together and looked to the girl. The imposter stared at the magic unfolding in front of her pale green Madach eyes, as large and round as a watching owl's. She lifted her chin, breathing deeply as if sucking the magic into the depths of her soul. Her eyes grew darker. She clasped her hands against her chest, which rose and fell in time to the chanting.

Ilesse drew a deep breath of her own, savouring the power which rose from the chanting of the seers. Opaque silvery streams, soft as clouds and glittering with light from the pendant, swirled in the air. Slowly at first, then more quickly, the streams whirled above the heads of the seers, gathering into a shape which spun in on itself, faster, faster, meeting the swelling light from the pendant until they melded, feasting on each other to form a whole.

The chanting slowed, stopped. The gryphon pendant and its chain shrunk slowly to their normal size. They glowed with a white, bright light. The gryphon rested on its side, one wing raised, beak closed, hiding the tiny ruby tongue.

The faces of the Sleih seers bore new lines. The gryphons' wings fell loosely at their sides.

'It is done,' Olwyn said, running a wing tip above the pendant, not touching it. 'Powerful magic lies within this trinket.' She looked from Ilesse to Gweyr. 'Magic to enhance both good and evil. Which one it is, depends on the wielder.'

She nodded to a young Sleih seer by her side. The seer picked up chain and pendant and offered them to Gweyr who stretched out her hand to receive them. Her face glowed but her darkened eyes were troubled.

'No!' Ilesse's cry sprang from her, harsh, demanding. 'I am the one who should have them. Who can deny me? I am strong, I have magic, I have resisted. It is my right.'

She reached out to grab the jewel. The seer clamped his fingers tight around it, glancing at Olwyn. The old gryphon glared into Ilesse's eyes.

'What goes on here?' Hestia's breathless voice broke the silence of the cavern. 'Is it done?' She raised her wings, fluffed out her feathers. 'The siege is broken, monsters swarm in the lower caverns. We must destroy this evil before it destroys us.'

Ilesse held herself tall, her palm held out. 'Give me the pendant and I will show you how.'

'How?' Olwyn shielded the young seer whose fingers remained wrapped around the jewel.

'I remember.' Ilesse spoke calmly. 'The bridge over the chasm, where I followed Olban, where he fell, taking his diamond too close. I know where it is.' A snigger rose through her throat at the memory. She gulped it down.

Hestia tilted her head to one side, fixed Ilesse with an emerald eye. She could feel the gryphon probing, searching for any taint of what should not be there.

Ilesse closed her mind to the gryphon and Hestia blinked. She sighed and Ilesse knew, not that she had fooled her, but that Hestia understood. Ilesse must bear this task. It was her right.

'Then lead us there,' Hestia said. 'Olwyn, let Ilesse have the gryphon. She is our one hope.'

'It does not belong to her.' With a quickness which did not match her years, Olwyn pecked at the seer's palm. It opened. The old gryphon used her beak to lift the chain and thrust the jewel into the imposter's hands.

Hot hatred flared in Ilesse's heart.

'It belongs to the Daughter,' Olwyn said. 'She must carry it, as Iaton and Tius know.'

The imposter's troubled eyes widened. 'Yes,' she said. 'You're right. Although I have no idea why.'

Ilesse sought Hestia's eyes. Would she argue?

'I do not know the rights of this,' Hestia said, without returning Ilesse's gaze. 'But we waste time. We must go, now.'

Yes, this squabbling wasted time. Ilesse must have the jewel, she must carry its magic to where it would be most powerful.

Come, my queen. Bring them with you, foolish amateurs.

She drew a breath. So be it. She whirled about.

"'Let the Daughter,' she said, softening her sneer, 'carry it then. I will carry the diamond, to tempt the power forth.' She paced to the far end of the table, snatched the diamond up. Its sharp, smooth edges pressed into her palm. She squeezed it greedily. A further gift.

'Come then,' she called. 'Hestia, Gweyr, I will lead you.'

To their deaths.

Chapter Thirty Six

White cats

'We might get to use our fancy javelins after all.' Conall's mouth twitched in a sickly grin.

Allsop didn't return the grin. No amount of false cheeriness would soothe his roiling nerves. He led his fellow apprentice along a stone-walled meandering path towards the hill where the beacons waited to be tended. More black clouds broiled above them, storm-heavy. The walls shielded them from the worst of the wind, but the air again carried the stink of cold, greasy ash.

Would they light one beacon? Or two? Would they reach the beacons at all?

Despite the sticky warmth of the night he tucked his cloak more closely about him. The garment felt no different against his body than it had an hour before. Had the shielding spell Zoledore cast on him and Conall worked at all?

Giliar had bade them search out the wizard.

'He is the strongest of them, has studied his craft over many years,' he had said. 'He may be able to offer you protection.' As he spoke, he folded the rough map of Atias and the near countryside Allsop had drawn for him.

The map showed landmarks like the mill on the river, farmhouses, brooks and–Giliar offered a brief nod at this–the openings to disused mines, built into the hillsides ages ago to tunnel out iron, long exhausted.

He had tapped a long finger on the markings. 'We can't get the villagers to safety further south,' he said, 'but we can bring them to these tunnels tonight, before the horde surrounds us. And pray Asfarlon prevails.'

Allsop's own prayer too.

'The animals in the barns and byres?' The thought of Millie and Chester left to the horde's cruel ravaging sickened his soul. He and Conall would take them if necessary, although it meant they would be more easily seen.

'They will come. The horses will carry the elderly, the young, food and blankets.'

With these assurances, Allsop and Conall sought out Zoledore. They found him near the edge of the hamlet, supporting an ashen-faced wizard. While Conall helped the exhausted man to where rest and food would be found, Allsop explained their mission and their need. He had tried to keep his voice calm, to sound brave, pretending to himself he stole through evil, not-of-this-world creatures every day.

The wizard gave a sardonic smile. 'I see your fear, Allsop Kaine, and it leads me to greatly respect your willingness to do this task.' He tapped his staff into the mud, thoughtful. 'Even your friend who thinks he wants adventure understands this is no game.'

'Can you help us?'

'A little. I can offer shielding which should make it hard for these monsters to sense you, by smell or hearing. They appear not to have much sight, rampaging through anything in their path.' His piercing eyes met Allsop's. 'Anything.'

Allsop squirmed. 'It's something at least,' he had murmured by way of thanks.

Something. He tugged at the cloak, wanting to sense magic there, however magic could be sensed. Heavy wool, as normal. He must trust Zoledore's abilities.

'Is this a good idea?' Conall waved his javelin at the steep, crumbling stone walls hemming them in. 'Bit of a trap if we come across one of those things.'

'It is.' Allsop stopped. 'The alternative is to cross open fields. Zoledore thinks the creatures have poor eyesight, but our movements would be sensed much more easily in the open.'

Conall puffed out a heavy breath and marched up the slippery, stony gully, using the javelin to guide his way in the moonless darkness.

They climbed in a silence unbroken by calls of night hunting birds. Neither were there furtive movements in the grasses and wildflowers at the base of the walls. Allsop shivered within the warm stuffiness of his cloak. The wild creatures of the fields sought sanctuary in their nests and burrows. He hoped it would save them.

A waning moon rose, glimpsed as a faded orb behind the clouds. The steep gully ended at a track where Allsop paused, catching his breath. To the east, the flames of the green fires resisted the gusts of wind, lengths of sparkling emerald jewels on a velvet cloth. They would be beautiful if they had a less dire purpose.

'Do you think Giliar got the villagers out?' Conall panted up beside him. Sweat sheened on his brow.

'I hope–watch out!' Allsop swung his pike awkwardly, sending Conall staggering sideways. He hauled the weapon back, swiping at a cat-like creature the size of a big dog. It hissed and spat, clawing at the iron, not touching it.

Conall lurched, twisted his pike about. He stabbed it into the cat's side. Greyish liquid burst from the wound, splashing Conall's cloak. The creature convulsed, emitted a scream like a ghoul, and vanished.

Allsop bent over, gagging. His heart thundered.

'Got you, evil spirit.' Conall stared about him. 'Where did it go?'

'Who cares?' Allsop straightened, steadied himself. 'I'm not going searching for it.'

Conall waved his pike. 'No. We need to move on. It might have relatives come looking for it.'

Chapter Thirty Seven

A silver gryphon

A tide of Sleih and Gryphon filled the passageway, rushing to higher safety in their flight from the beasts which had breached the gates in the cliff. Gweyr wrapped her palm tightly around the silver gryphon, pushing against the flow in Ilesse's hurrying wake. Children cried, adults wore taut, anxious faces, and gryphons harried their neighbours, muttering hurry, hurry. Their fear brought home the stakes Gweyr faced.

When, earlier, she had made to clasp the chain around her neck, Olwyn had growled, 'No, Daughter. Carry it, for who knows how it is to be used.'

'Wielded,' Hestia had said. 'Olywn is right.'

The terrified part of Gweyr would have given the jewel up willingly to Ilesse. The greater part of her wanted to clasp the pendant to her chest and let its magic seep into her veins to bolster much-needed courage.

A fairytale? She snorted softly. Harsh reality weighed as heavily on her as a cart horse's harness.

'Ashta has returned,' Hestia said, watching Ilesse push her way through the throng.

'What news?' Gweyr hoped it might matter, hoped it would diminish the death or victory nature of her own mission.

Hestia's throat feathers rippled. 'Not good,' she said. 'The white hordes have ravaged their way across the Madach lands, west and east. It appears they intend to encircle the land.'

Gweyr's stomach churned. Da. He would be caught up in this. She should have stayed at home to help in Darnel, not run off to play at fairytales.

'Ashta left warriors behind to meet the onslaught.' Hestia blinked.

The flow of those seeking safety thinned. The gryphon quickened her pace to match Ilesse, a short distance ahead. Gweyr lengthened her own stride, trying to quell her self-reproach, and her terror.

'The old wizards have gathered, helping as much as their weak powers allow.' Hestia bobbed her head. 'It will not be enough, not unless we destroy the evil here, at its source.'

Gweyr imagined home, the old and the children, and how few were able to fight. Did the blacksmith labour into the night forging swords? Did the wood whittlers shape bows and arrows? And what good would these makeshift weapons be against wolves such as those which had attacked her and Allsop? Worse, against the horde she and Ashta flew over? Her heart beat harder, her throat constricted. She tightened her grasp on the pendant, willing its warmth to give her bravery.

The gryphon squirmed, tickling her palm.

Courage, my daughter.

The thought slid into Gweyr's head, quietly reassuring. Mam was with her on this quest. Her thudding heart slowed. Courage battled her fear, winning, slowly, slowly.

'Where is she going?' Hestia rounded a corner after Ilesse.

The 'prentice seer led them down, further down. A heavy, oily stench hung in the air, growing stronger the lower they went. Shouts and screams trailed their descent. Gweyr sensed heat, smelled burning.

She glanced at Hestia.

'The monsters prevail,' the gryphon said. 'Iaton and Tius took the battle beyond the caverns, to the meadow. Varane and Ashta led the hunters, but the force beyond the gates proved too much.'

A failed plan. And what of Varane and Ashta? Did they live? Gweyr's heart ached.

Ahead of them, Ilesse stopped.

'Down here.' She waved at a dark, steep opening with a rusting, broken iron gate leaning crookedly across it. Strange runes were carved into the rock above.

Hestia lifted her wings. 'Of course,' she murmured. 'How could I not remember? The treasure beneath. It seems'–she blinked–'we had it wrong all these years.' She again glanced at Gweyr, opened her beak, shut it.

A cacophony of howls, grunts and shrieks rose behind them. The oily stench thickened. Ilesse hesitated at the iron gate before swerving past it, as far from its pitted bars as the entrance allowed. She disappeared down the staircase.

Gweyr followed, clutching the pendant. Blackness soon engulfed her. It wasn't only the lack of light. A stinking dampness pressed against her face. She squinted into it, gagging. She took short, shallow breaths, touched her palm to the cold stones of the wall and inched her way down, step by step. Was the 'prentice seer struggling too? How was Hestia managing? Surely the tight space could not contain her?

A silver glow seeped between Gweyr's fingers. She uncurled them, letting light break through the darkness. The bright light of her dream. It was enough for her to see she had reached the end of the stairs.

She peered through a churning smokiness like massing thunderclouds.

Ilesse stood on a slender stone bridge a short way ahead, chin lifted, seemingly immune to the smoke and stink rising from the chasm below. She stretched both arms forward.

Thin ribbons of white light shone through one clasped hand. The diamond. The evil's temptation.

Ilesse dropped the diamond into the chasm with the

casualness of one dropping a stone in a river.

Her other hand opened and shut, summoning.

'Give me the pendant,' she said.

'No.'

The silver gryphon fluttered in Gweyr's hand. *Courage.*

'Give it to me!' Ilesse screamed. She lunged.

Gweyr clasped the pendant to her chest. She stepped back, into Hestia. The gryphon nudged her to one side and placed her taloned forelegs on the end of the bridge.

'No.' Her voice was taut with anguish. 'Ilesse, my Ilesse. Has it won? Has it taken you?'

Ilesse's eyes narrowed. 'Give me the pendant.'

'No.' Hestia lifted her wings. 'Let Gweyr do what she must do.'

In Gweyr's palm, the glowing light pulsated like a breathing animal. What must she do? No one had told her how it should work. Should she throw the pendant, and Mam's chain, into the maw of blackness? She remembered the ancient text, the woman wielding the winged lion. She held the chain high, the glowing pendant hanging down. She kept a careful distance from Ilesse's grasping reach.

'Do I say something, Hestia–?'

'It is mine, give it to me.' Ilesse grabbed for the chain.

It swung aside with no help from Gweyr.

Screams, howls, the clang of weapons against stone echoed down the staircase. The smell of burning mixed with the heavy oiliness of the air. Shadows flickered on the walls and stairs.

'The caverns are on fire.' Hestia briefly pressed her beak against Gweyr's head.

Ilesse snatched at the pendant. 'I am the queen, it is mine,' she shrieked.

The acrid smoke from the chasm curled higher, thicker, spiralling and shaping itself. Gweyr watched, her free hand across her mouth and nose, eyes wide. The smoke formed into the semblance of a man. Alabaster-skinned and white-robed, he appeared on the bridge behind Ilesse. His black eyes looked past her to fix greedily on the pendant before shifting to meet Gweyr's staring gaze.

Her heart boomed, sweat slicked her skin. Her hands trembled.

'Olban!' Hestia cried.

The man stretched his white lips wide. 'Olban is long gone, stupid gryphon. Now is the time I gain my new form.' His grin fell on Ilesse.

The 'prentice seer had lost interest in the pendant. She waited beside the man on the bridge, arms at her sides. Her eyes were black. And filled with pain, and grief.

Chapter Thirty Eight

Iron

Whipped purple clouds rumbled thunder. The ashy, greasy stink grew stronger. It tasted bitter on Allsop's tongue. He sweated in his cloak, unhappy about casting it aside despite his certainty Zoledore's shielding had long worn off.

With his back pressed into a stone midway between the beacons, he stared into the shadowy distance. Jagged lightning streaks caught the hamlet in their harsh, brief glow. The green fires flickered in the fields. One would die and shortly afterwards another would rise more strongly, for a time, before guttering out like a candle. As the night passed, the fires grew further apart, their brightness dimmed.

Allsop grieved for whatever horror might have befallen the wizards tending them. Would the same horror come to him and Conall?

Beside him, Conall leaned on his pike to peer down the slope. 'What's happening down there?' he muttered.

Three times the white cats had come at them. They showed first as pale shapes against the dark, bare hillside, coming singly, racing upwards, heads lifted, scenting the air for vulnerable flesh.

The iron pikes had saved them. The sight of them sent the cats into a spitting, howling frenzy, swirling in mad circles before bolting down the hill. Once, Conall's stab had found its mark and, like the creature on the track, the cat screamed, and vanished.

'Must be the iron,' Conall said after the third attack. He gulped deep breaths. 'If the Sleih riders knew–'

'And if there were enough iron weapons lying about …' Allsop's voice quivered.

'There aren't. But they can be made, and maybe give hope while whoever it is in this Asfarlon place works out their spells.'

Allsop pointed his pike down the slope. A writhing mass of pale fur and skin stole towards them. 'And if we survive to tell anyone.' He was grateful his voice sounded steadier.

Conall gripped his pike, waved it high. 'Come on then. Let's see what you can do!'

Chapter Thirty Nine

Ilesse's battle

Ilesse fought to move, every muscle straining. Her body refused her. Only her eyes obeyed. They sought the figure which was not Olban. They sought the pendant.

The pendant. She vibrated with greedy desire for the pendant.

She must not have it … she must not … for if she possessed it …

A tangle of emotions boiled within her.

Your heart's desires, my queen.

The whispers fell on her ears, warm and comforting. Her heart's desires. All she ever wanted. All she would ever want.

Forever.

The susurrations echoed in her head.

You are strong my queen. Take the pendant.

'The gryphon, Ilesse, look at the gryphon.' Hestia's steady voice pierced her mind. 'Its magic will heal, if you truly desire healing. Hold firm.'

Yes. She must not possess the jewel. She must draw from it magic imbued by the weaving of Gryphon and Sleih spells. Fresh, shining, powerful magic. To quell the evil, raise up the good.

Yes. She cherished the energy, let it caress her exhausted mind.

Pitiful magic. Amateurs. In our hands, together, we will create true power from these base roots.

True power. Of course. What she desired was true power.

'See how the gryphon shines for you, my love.' Hestia's voice came strongly, bracing Ilesse's pitiful strength.

The imposter–Gweyr, her name was Gweyr–held the pendant high, murmuring words which Ilesse heard without understanding.

Bring me the pendant, my queen. It is yours. You have earned it.

'Resist this evil, Ilesse, my precious Ilesse.' Hestia's voice lost its steadiness. She pleaded, her wings held high like arms open to embrace.

Or to shelter against temptation.

The pendant, my queen. You desire the pendant. Take it!

The power on the bridge clawed at Ilesse's mind, demanding to be obeyed.

Bring it to me!

Her fingers twitched. She lifted her arms. No. Only with her eyes should she reach for the pendant.

As she stared at it, the little shining gryphon unfurled with the slow deliberateness of a spring flower. It lifted its wings in imitation of Hestia, opened its beak to show its ruby tongue.

'Let the magic heal, Ilesse.' Hester's voice, soothing, calm now. 'Open your heart to the magic.'

Ilesse's whole being concentrated on the ruby. She wanted the ruby. She desired power.

Forever.

No, she wanted the jewel to destroy the evil, silence the whispers, banish the voice. Plunge them into the abyss.

She lifted her eyes, caught Gweyr's.

'Strength,' Gweyr shouted, above the noise of battle. Shadows of fire fell down the staircase. 'You are strong.'

Courage suffused Ilesse's body. She drew from its well, breathed it in.

She dare not take her eyes off the gryphon. Words swelled inside her. Brave words. She whipped about, screamed into the white figure's face.

'I will never be yours! You will not have it!'

The figure snarled. *Coward.*

It pitched forward, hands reaching for the jewel.

A frozen wind forced Ilesse aside. Her legs faltered, her arms flailed. She stumbled, swaying at the brink. Through the swirling black smoke, she strove to hold her newly won courage. She tore at the figure's white gown, caught it, pulled.

The figure staggered, recovered. It dived at Gweyr.

Hestia cried out. 'Be gone, demon!'

Gweyr raised the pendant high. Her hands shook. As the white figure lunged, she forced the shining gryphon against its face.

It shrieked as if the pendant spat fiery flames, waved its hands to ward off the touch, snarling.

'Curse you, gryphon!' it spat at Hestia. 'Your meddling tongue be silenced forever!'

Ilesse hurled herself against the screeching whiteness. It whirled around. She heaved a second time–and sent it spinning off the bridge into the chasm.

Glittering green and red light rained from the silver gryphon's eyes and tongue, chasing after the falling, shrieking evil to devour it.

Unbalanced, Ilesse wavered, arms flailing.

Hestia let out a raucous cry. Gweyr screamed.

Chapter Forty

Escape

The cat's scratch burned like hot coals. Allsop peered at the clotting line of deep red on his arm. Poisonous. Had to be. Would it kill him?

Hunger and weariness dulled his need to care. Too weary even to hold onto his fear. He hunched against the rock, eyes straining into the thunderous, windy dawn. Sharp cracks of light streaked across black clouds.

Below the hill, the outline of Atias struggled to show itself, the roofs a darker grey against the murky sky. Beyond the hamlet, Sleih riders and gryphons–far too few–harassed a swarming mass of white monsters. Sparse dots of stuttering green fire spelled the wizards' weakening hold. Allsop set his lips in a straight line and swung his gaze to the track out of Atias.

'No! Conall, look!' He jumped up, his good arm pointing to a group hurrying along the track. 'Not everyone's reached the tunnels. See, there?' He gasped. One of the figures wore a bright pink shawl around their shoulders.

Two black horses–somehow he was certain they were Millie and Chester–trotted ahead of the group, laden with hunched small riders–children–gripping their manes.

'It's my parents.' Allsop let out a low groan. 'I know the pink shawl, it's Mam's favourite.'

Conall gripped his arm. 'There!' He thumped his pike on

the hard earth. 'White bears, heading for those people.'

Allsop's chest tightened. 'Why aren't they in the tunnels already? How could Giliar have let them stay all night?'

Conall searched the brooding sky. 'Where are the riders? Why aren't they attacking?'

The bear-like animals lumbered, fast, over the trodden crops, drawn to the exposed prey on the track.

'Mam, Dad, the children–they'll be slaughtered.' Allsop hefted his pike, grown heavier with his own exhaustion. 'Run, run!' he screamed. His panicked heart beat louder.

From a corner of his eye he glimpsed cats racing to him and Conall. He couldn't think of them, couldn't deal with them. The bears were close, closer. He took in a breath, held it.

The lead bear hurled its bulk at the black horses. And …

Millie and Chester rose into the air.

Allsop let out the breath. His mouth fell open.

The children swayed, clung on. The horses flew higher, above their attackers, towards the tunnels.

A Sleih rider swooped to the bear. And pulled up sharply. The gryphon's talons clawed at air.

The rider swung about as a second bear reared to strike the trailing, faltering figure in the pink shawl.

The gryphon stretched its talons …

The bear vanished.

Beside a stunned Allsop, Conall yelled at the sprinting cats. He swung his pike at–

Nothing.

Chapter Forty One

A curse

Hestia's wings yanked Ilesse off the bridge to the ledge. She huddled, shaking, within their warm curve. Black smoke thickened around them. Ilesse gagged on the stink.

The stone bridge cracked with a tearing rip. The edges of the chasm trembled, threw off parts of itself. Rifts opened along its length.

'Come on,' Gweyr shouted. 'It's all falling down. Hurry.'

She ran up the quaking stairs, pausing halfway to look down.

Ilesse shuddered a breath. Her head swam, her thoughts confused, dreamlike. A deep, troubled weariness filled her.

She could not, must not, succumb. She had more strength yet. She reached deep inside herself.

Hestia's wing encouraged her forward. Coughing, with shaking legs, she scrambled after Gweyr, hearing Hestia clawing her way behind her.

***

Flames and smoke filled the passageway. Gweyr held the shining gryphon before her. It cleared the caustic smoke from her path, held the fires at bay. It didn't stop their searing heat reddening her skin, scorching her eyes.

She squinted, looked over her shoulder. Ilesse and Hestia followed on her heels, within the sheltering circle of magic. Gweyr raced forward, desperately seeking a way up and out of the burning halls.

She stumbled against a staircase, ran up, and lurched against a body sprawled over the steps. A young Sleih hunter, judging by his broken spear, his chest ripped by jagged claws.

Ilesse spluttered a ragged breath. 'No! This is my doing.'

Gweyr stepped over the hunter, murmuring apologies. No more dead barred her way to the next level. The smoke thinned, the fires burned less fiercely. Wounded Sleih and Gryphon leaned against the walls, tended by their fellows. The dead lay where they had fallen.

Gweyr frowned. No dead and dying wolves, bears or other misshapen monsters littered the hall. Had they escaped, leaving this slaughter? All of them? Nausea rose in her throat.

Were they attacking those who had fled to the highest caverns? Had their efforts, Ilesse's near death, her own terror, been for nothing?

Hestia peered around. She opened her beak. Bobbed her head.

'Where are their dead and injured?' Gweyr's voice trembled.

A Sleih woman dabbed a salve smelling of pine and sage into a bloodied gash. She glanced up at Gweyr. 'Disappeared. Vanished. Just like that.'

Hestia bobbed her head again. Faintly, Gweyr heard her cry out, although her beak didn't open.

My voice, my voice. Gone!

The gryphon's shocked despair pierced Gweyr's heart. She heard again the thing that wasn't Olban's dying words.

Curse you, gryphon. Your meddling tongue be silenced forever!

Forever? Her heart contracted.

Hestia flicked her tail. She turned her head to Gweyr. *You have triumphed, Daughter of the Sleih.*

The thought came clearly to Gweyr. She glanced at Ilesse who stared into Hestia's eyes as the gryphon's beak opened and closed, opened and closed, soundlessly.

'I hear you, Hestia,' Gweyr said. 'You too, Ilesse?'

Ilesse nodded, as voiceless at this moment as her gryphon teacher. Tears flooded her eyes.

Hestia pressed her beak gently to Ilesse's white, perspiring face. *My precious 'prentice seer. You too have triumphed.*

Ilesse gave a trembling smile, and crumpled to the blackened floor.

Chapter Forty Two

An heir

The Eternal Chamber bore no sign of the battle. Its translucent windows offered clear views across the High Alps, its walls unscorched. The king's stone chair and Lord Tius' pelt remained, almost, as they were before.

Despite the victory over evil, Hestia's heart lamented the loss and ruin of so much. Some things–blackened walls and charred rugs, burned pelts and cabinets, broken sculptures–could be put to rights over time, even perhaps the loss of the repository to fire and claws. She feared the loss of her voice was not one of them.

Hestia wasn't alone in being struck dumb by the evil figure's last curse. All the gryphons had lost their voices. That they could be understood was small compensation.

Tius sat on his haunches on the thick fur, his black wings shredded by the tearing bites of white wolves. The feathers would re-grow. The deep distress in his eyes affected Hestia more.

The stone chair beside Tius was empty. Iaton lay with his ancestors in the deep crypts of the caverns, slain defending a fleeing family from a pack of long-toothed, snarling bears moments before the dreadful monsters vanished.

When Gweyr struck the figure of evil with the silver gryphon, when Ilesse had sent it plunging into the chasm, that had been the moment the distorted creations of its imaginings were destroyed. Hestia prayed the evil was also destroyed.

The day after the attack, when the fires had damped, she led the most senior seers down the blackened stairs to the cracked bridge and the wider rift. Small stones slithered from its crumbling edges.

They brought with them sapphires, emeralds and rubies and worked weavings of magic over the chasm and up the stairs. Blacksmiths from the grassland villages would forge a great door of iron to be placed across the staircase opening. There would be no handle, no lock.

Today, Hestia and the councillors formed a circle before Tius. Varane stood to Tius' left, the scabbard holding Celeste at his waist. He held his head high. From time to time he glanced at his father's stone chair and away. Often he looked to Gweyr.

She was to Tius' right, shifting uncomfortably, her eyes flicking across the councillors. They eyed her in return, some with wonder at her part in what had happened, others perplexed as to her presence in the Eternal Chamber.

Ilesse would have been there too, if she could have walked the distance. She recovered slowly, subject to slumps of misery. Hestia's long conversations with her about how, in the end, she had broken evil's sway on her mind–a testament to her inner strength and innate goodness–could not stop the 'prentice seer reproaching herself for the deaths of so many.

'I am tired to my soul, Hestia,' she said. 'A stained soul.' She had wept. 'I will never feel clean, ever ever again.'

One more reason for Hestia's despair, this loss of innocence.

Hestia. Tius lifted his beak and Hestia moved out of the circle to stand before him. *Your fellow councillors have been summoned to hear what happens now our beloved Iaton has passed. I wish for you to be the one to tell this strange tale.*

The words 'strange tale' set up a murmuring from the councillors. Hestia sighed.

My fellow councillors. She paused. *It is indeed a strange tale.*

***

The councillors listened with the same fascination with which Gweyr had listened the previous day. She let her mind wander to the scene.

Ilesse lay on a pile of furs on the floor. Gweyr, Varane and Hestia sat on rugs around the 'prentice seer. Pelts, chairs, tables, and clothes bundled in neat piles showed how the vast cavern near the top of the mountain had become a temporary home for displaced Sleih and Gryphon.

'My grandmother was a Sleih princess?' Gweyr had swallowed. 'Did Mam know?' she asked herself softly.

It's the chain. It belonged to Aseera, Iaton's older sister, and is the only one of its kind. Hestia's words came clearly to Gweyr.

'But the old Sleih letters on the links spell Queen,' Ilesse said. She shuddered, and lifted herself higher against the pillow which softened the rock wall.

Yes. Hestia paused. *Aseera would have been queen if she had lived.*

Gweyr had nodded absently, and jumped when Varane punched the air with a whoop.

'I don't have to be king,' he said. 'You're queen, Gweyr. I can be a hunter, join Ashta and search out what remains of these monsters, protect the Madach lands, fly all over the country–'

'What?' Gweyr's stomach revolted. 'What nonsense is he talking?' she asked Hestia.

No nonsense. Hestia reached out a wing to touch Gweyr's shoulder. *It is how lineage works here. You are the granddaughter of the rightful queen. You must have your inheritance.*

'But … but … if King Iaton had lived? Surely I wouldn't be queen then?'

No. Hestia's beak had opened and shut. She had blinked rapidly.

Gweyr wanted to throw her arms about the gryphon and comfort her.

You would, however, be the heir before Varane.

In the Eternal Chamber, the councillors listened in astonished silence. When Hestia finished her story they turned as one to Gweyr.

Gweyr pressed her lips together and suffered their judgement with heat rising in her cheeks. After what seemed an age, first one councillor, then another and another, knelt in their different Sleih and Gryphon fashions until all had welcomed her as their new queen.

The heat in Gweyr's cheeks spread throughout her body.

Welcome home, Gweyr. Lord Tius bent his eagle head. *There will be a coronation and celebrations at the proper time. Before then there is much to decide about the future of the Sleih and Gryphon who dwell in the caverns of the High Alps of Asfarlon.*

'Yes.' Gweyr straightened. 'I've an awful lot to learn and there is, as you say, a lot to talk about. But first, if I may, I would like to visit my father, let him know I'm okay.' She fingered the silver chain around her neck, stroked the silver gryphon pendant and frowned. 'He must be extremely worried by now.'

Epilogue

After all that happened, it came as only a mild surprise to Barnaby his daughter had inherited a kingdom. Her mam not being there to learn this made him sad, although he suspected she knew.

Gweyr didn't want to live such a long way from her father. And he had no wish to give up the Boar's Head (which had grown famous, with people travelling long distances to boast to their friends they had been served ale by the queen's father) to live in a cave in the wilds of the Alps (as he put it).

She suggested the Sleih might return to the grasslands. After a discussion which lasted three days, the Council agreed. Given how much had been lost, they were happy to leave the scorched caverns behind, together with the memories of the horrific day of death with its stench of burning feathers and scorched skin. Besides, despite the iron door and weaving of deep Gryphon magic at all entrances to tunnels and mines, a dread remained the evil was not destroyed, simply vanquished. For now.

Atias, as the site of the last defence against the white horde, became the new capital. Gweyr renamed it Il-atias, in honour of her friend who resisted the evil, joined her strength to Gweyr's own new magic, and made their triumph possible. The Sleih built a tall, elegant citadel with high strong walls on the hill where Conall and Allsop had protected the beacons

(which they had finally remembered to light, once Giliar came to them on the silent gryphon to remind them.)

Gweyr had the throne room built in such a manner that people would enjoy the sense of finding themselves in a beautiful forest. She also took the name 'House of Wood' as her family name. Both were in honour of the Gryphon's first home, the Deep Forest of Arneithe.

The Gryphon did not join the Sleih. Conversation was difficult when it had to be by thought and they were truly comfortable only with each other. They sought out unspoiled caverns nearer to the high plains, called them Asfarlon, and continued to study the magic of jewels. They sought always to ensure the knowledge gained from the rising of the evil power stayed learned. It did, for centuries anyway.

Allsop Kaine returned to Darnel and became a master baker. He and his descendants were especially famous for their pies which they sold throughout the Madach villages from a big, lumbering wagon.

Conall Godwin joined the Sleih riders, seeking out and destroying those brown bears and wolves which still sought the icy crevasses of the High Alps. He married a Sleih woman and became one of the early fathers to the Danae, which is a different story.

Millie and Chester revelled in their new ability to fly. It became apparent one needed to have Sleih blood to fly them (which the children of the wizard had, of course). Allsop wasn't disappointed. He never rode again. Gweyr did, living her dreams of flying on her magical beast with the wind whipping her curls about her face. She nurtured the bloodline, always with black horses which the Sleih hunters–now turned soldiers–rode instead of gryphons.

Ilesse became a councillor, the youngest ever. She was given the title Lady Ilesse of the House of Alder for her courage overcoming the whispers of evil which would have dominated the land, and for casting its embodiment into the chasm.

Although she did not want to be separated from Hestia, the gryphon insisted Ilesse go to Ilatias and study there. She gave the young councillor much of her own library and visited regularly, until, many, many years later, her old wings would no longer carry her. Ilesse journeyed to the new caverns of Asfarlon to be with her teacher when she closed her eagle eyes for the last time.

When she returned to Ilatias, Ilesse determined the alliance of Sleih and Gryphon should not be forgotten. In her high tower which looked across the shiny new red roofs, she set about writing a long text. She called it *The Ancient History of the Old Sleih, and How They Came by Their Magic through Ponderous Schemes and Long Collusions with the Fabled Gryphon of the High Alps of Asfarlon.*

In the book she wrote of the Legend of the Winged Lion, to explain the origin and magic of the gryphon pendant.

She bound the book in blue leather and used silver lettering for the title; blue and silver being her favourite colours.

Gweyr wore the gryphon pendant her whole long life, for she studied magic under Queen Ceantha and became a skilled Healer as well as wise ruler. Her descendants also wore the pendant although knowledge of its origins and use faded over time. One day a young Sleih prince found it on his mother's dressing table, thought it a pretty piece and gifted it to a Sleih girl with whom he was deeply in love. She accepted the gift then chose to marry a Madach and become another of those who gave rise to the birth of the Danae.

There's that name again, Danae.

Many, many, many years later, four children of the Danae (whose surname happened to be Godwin) found themselves in a new story. Gweyr's gryphon pendant, Ilesse's book, pie-makers, and horses which may or may not be able to fly, played special roles in the story. As did a powerful seer whose favourite colours were blue and silver.

The End

What next?

If you have enjoyed this story please take a few minutes to leave a review on Amazon or Goodreads. These reviews are extremely important to independent authors who don't have the might of publishing companies to help them get their books known. You could also recommend it to a friend whom you know would enjoy it.

To satisfy your curiosity about the Danae, read *Guardians of the Forest.* The trilogy is available on Amazon or you can read how the story came about and find the links on my website cherylburman.com

Book One The Wild Army

Callie's forest rings to the thwack of enemy axes. Her people are trapped. Their leaders scoff at her warnings of the Danae's fate at the hands of the invaders. The wild creatures will fight, but will Tristan, the destroyer's son, fight with them?

'The twists and turns of the story keep you reading, wondering who to trust, what might happen next and what it all means for the Danae.' Amazon review

Book Two Quests

Gwen and Mark battle wolves, robbers and the dangers of the Deep Forest in their quest for the Sleih. And where is their lost sister, Lucy? Did she fall foul of the Madach robbers too? But all will be for nothing if the ambitious Seer, Lady Melda finds Gwen and Mark first.

'I couldn't put it down and read the whole book in one sitting. I highly recommend this book and series.' Amazon review

Book Three Gryphon Magic

Callie's wild army harasses the invading Madach. Lady Melda plots to steal Gwen's powerful gryphon pendant. Gwen, Mark & Lucy hurry home with the Sleih rescuers–only to find desolation. Can gryphon magic save the Danae, and the Forest?

'My granddaughter and I have read all three books because we just had to know how the story was going to end. We were not disappointed.' Amazon review

Acknowledgements

There are always many people who contribute to a book. My list of thank yous is in no particular order and each one is heartfelt.

Jodi, Paula, Lily, Dreena, Victoria – my brilliant critique partners and/or beta/proof readers. Some undertook all three roles. Plus moral support.

My brother Justin for his exceptional sculpting talent which gave me our exquisite gryphon.

My good friend Rue for their patience with me over covers.

The same thanks for patience for my husband David who turns all this stuff into an actual book with endless revisions.

Dean Writers Circle and Twitter friends for beating my back blurb into shape.

The grandchildren of friends, and my own grandkids, for their timely feedback on all kinds of things. The honesty of kids is brilliant.

Which leads me to a very special thanks to the teachers and children of St John's school, Coleford, who love *Guardians of the Forest* and are eager for this new story. I hope you love it as much. Sharing it with you will be a real pleasure.

Having said all that, any spelling, grammatical or design errors or flaws are entirely my own.

About the Author

Cheryl Burman lives in the Forest of Dean, UK with her husband and border collie. She is the author of the fantasy trilogy, *Guardians of the Forest* and of *Keepers*, her first novel for grownups. Her flash fiction, short stories and bits of her novels have won various prizes, including being longlisted for the Historical Writers Association Short Story competition 2020, shortlisted for the Flash500 Opening Novel Chapter competition 2020, finalist Stroud Short Stories 2021, and winner of the Retreat West Fourth Quarter 2021 flash fiction competition. Some of these stories appear in her collection, *Dragon Gift.* To find out more and what she is currently working on, visit her at -

Website and newsletter sign up https://cherylburman.com/

Twitter @cr_burman

www.facebook.com/cheryl.burman.56

Printed in Great Britain
by Amazon

76735385R00139